Go Back to Sleep

Robert Scott-Norton

Copyright © 2020 Robert Scott-Norton

All rights reserved. This book or any portion thereof
may not be reproduced or used in any manner whatsoever
without the express written permission of the publisher
except for the use of brief quotations in a book review.

Contact the author at:
www.robertscottnorton.net

ISBN: **9798614262365**
(20200224)

1

La Gustosa was alive with the murmurs from a crowded dining room. Laughter erupted on a nearby table and cutlery clinked against dishes filled with steaming pasta. None of it was able to mask the pain in Adrian's voice as he looked at his daughter, fork adrift from his mouth, linguine hanging like greasy string.

"I don't understand," Adrian said, his eyes blazing.

Judy couldn't take her gaze from Lisa. Her sister-in-law's face had turned ghostly white. Judy wanted to reach across the breadbasket and take her hand and tell her she was doing the right thing, but she held back, mesmerised by the scene unfolding in front of her.

"I want to find my birth parents," Lisa repeated.

Lisa's mum, Faith was sitting across the table from her and her eyes glistened as her hand grasped Adrian's.

"But why?" Faith asked, "I mean, why now? It's been so long."

What she wanted to say, Judy reckoned, but wouldn't say, because no middle-class mother who loved her children would ever really say what came to mind in situations like this, was "What's wrong with us? We're your parents."

Those words wouldn't ever leave Faith's lips, but they were there all right, balanced on the tip of her tongue. But maybe Faith didn't need to say anything at all. Adrian's response was proving to be just as effective at causing a scene.

Lisa glanced at Judy, a flash of disappointment in those hazel eyes. Eyes that would forever remind Judy of Phil, Judy's husband and Lisa's twin. A brother that had died less than twelve months ago. A man that was missed by four of the people around this table. Jemma squeezed her mum's arm, gently so the others wouldn't notice, and without thinking or looking, Judy handed over her daughter's phone. A distraction would be a good thing for her daughter right about now.

"It's been on my mind a lot recently. Ever since Phil died." Another look at Judy. Was there something else left unsaid? Perhaps. "I know he had said he had no interest, but I think he did, really. I mean it's hard to explain but unless you're in our situation, it's impossible to know what it's like, not knowing where you came from."

Adrian placed his fork on the rim of the bowl where the pasta slipped off. Adrian took his wife's hands in his own and clasped them. A solid unified front.

"We love you. You know that."

"I do. You're my mum and dad. That will never change. You will always be Mum and Dad. I don't want that to change. It won't." And she wiped the edge of her finger under her eye and flashed a sad smile. "But that shouldn't mean that I don't want to find out the rest of my story. It's like there are some pages missing, and as much as I love who I am and who you are, and everything we've done, it doesn't stop me wondering, what was at the beginning? Why was someone willing to give us up, and so young?"

The waiter chose the wrong moment to return to the table and ask whether he could get anyone more drinks. Adrian dismissed him with a wave of a hand like he was a fly bothering them. Lisa picked up her empty glass of diet coke and swirled the almost melted ice cubes around the bottom. Judy wondered whether now would be an appropriate time to put some money on the table and slip out with Jemma. It was a school night after all, and Jemma was looking exhausted.

Adrian let go of his wife's hands and reached across for his daughter's. He clasped them and bounced them gently on the table like one might with a distracted toddler. "We love you."

"I know."

"And I fully support what you choose to do."

"Good."

"But."

The temperature dropped.

"But what, Dad?"

"There's nothing left to know. The adoption agency has long since gone. There's no one to get in contact with. And even if it was still there, you're talking over forty years ago. Record keeping wasn't what it is now. I don't want you to be disappointed."

Lisa laughed a sort of half laugh, an escape of tension, that could so easily have turned into a cry.

"Mum," Jemma whispered beside her. The phone had not been a great distraction. She knew what was going on and it was uncomfortable. For a twelve-year-old, she was remarkably astute about other people's feelings and motivations.

"OK," Judy murmured. "One minute."

"Listen to your dad, love. He just doesn't want you to get upset. It was so long ago; you're not going to find out what you need."

"There's this thing called the internet now, it's good for more than online shopping." Lisa shot her mum a look across the table and Judy stood up.

"Thanks for having us," Judy said, "but I think now might be a good time to be going. You've clearly got a lot of stuff to sort out."

Adrian looked up but didn't say a word. Yes, Judy thought, you may not have been Phil's biological father, but I know where he got his tantrums from. Tonight is not going your way but you're nothing to me and I don't have to be here any longer.

She'd wanted to say that and more to him for months, but her life had not been a quiet one over the last year. First there was losing Phil, then there was the nightmare of Ravenmeols and her brushes with near-death experiences.

No one seemed to care that Judy had stood and was about to leave. The restaurant was busy, La Gustosa's always was, but that didn't stop Judy noticing the shadow at the rear of the dining area, a woman possibly, difficult to tell in the low lighting. She didn't think it was one of the waiting staff, so it had to be a customer. But why were they staring in their direction?

Judy took her purse from her bag.

"Put that away," Faith commanded. "You're our guests."

"I can't. Don't be silly."

"Put it away," Adrian said. A flash of irritation crossed his eyes, and he shifted in his chair, before pushing the rest of his dish away and dabbing at the edge of his mouth with his napkin.

Judy complied, not wanting the focus to shift to her. She glanced at her watch, then smiled at Jemma.

"Aren't we going?" Jemma asked.

Judy nodded, then dived in. "I think it's very brave of you to want to do this," she said to Lisa. "And I know Phil would have supported you."

Lisa's smile was unsteady, but her gratitude was clear. "Thanks, Judy. I'm doing it for him as well. And of course, I'll share everything I find out."

"There will not be anything to find out. I've told you." Adrian's voice was firm. The kind of controlling tone that Phil had used all too well. He wore that authority like a policeman wore his uniform. "You can look on the internet all you like, but those papers weren't digitised. They'll be lost, buried in some filing cabinet somewhere, if they even exist at all."

"Why are you taking this so badly? I've told you it doesn't change how I feel about you. But you've got to respect that I need to know."

"Why now? What's changed?"

"You don't get it. Why are you being so bloody obtuse?" Lisa banged her fist on the table and the wine glasses shook. At the table next to theirs, two middle-aged couples made a concerted effort not to notice but the surreptitious glances and their pause in conversation indicated they were revelling in every moment.

"Don't speak to your father like that. There's no need, Lisa." But Faith's support was too late as Adrian got up, knocking the table with his thighs as he moved.

"I'm going for a vape."

The silence in the aftermath could have drowned them all.

"I'm sure he doesn't mean it," Judy said.

"He means it," Lisa said.

"He just needs some time to get his head around the idea. I'm sure he's wrong, there's bound to be paperwork. And there are organisations that can help reunite families."

She could feel Faith's eyes burning through the thinned atmosphere. "Our family is united," she said simply.

"I know it is. Of course it is. That's not what I'm saying."

"It was a stressful time for all of us. That's why Adrian's upset."

Judy didn't have an answer that she felt wouldn't pour fuel on the fire, so took her purse out and dropped two twenties on the table. Faith didn't protest, instead she picked up her wine glass and took a sip, then another, before picking up the bottle and pouring herself another half-glass.

"I'll be in touch. Thanks for dinner." Judy leant down and gave Lisa a kiss on the cheek.

"Thank you," Lisa whispered in her ear.

"Never a problem."

As Judy walked out with Jemma, a light breeze caught the back of her neck and she pivoted. That same figure was standing by the pass at the back of the restaurant, watching them leave. A waiter crossed in front of her view and when she tried to spot her again, she couldn't. The figure was gone.

2

Judy felt the cool February air outside the restaurant and shivered as she led Jemma to their car in the small car park. She unlocked, let Jemma in then noticed Adrian four cars over, sitting inside his car. Sparks lit his face as he held a lighter to a cigarette in an attempt to get a light.

"I'll be one minute. I'm just going to say bye to your granddad."

Jemma groaned, but complied and sat back in her chair, her phone already open on YouTube.

Judy knocked on the window of Adrian's car and he glanced up, a guilty look as he saw who it was. He got out from the car then managed to get a light from his lighter. He lit the cigarette tip and inhaled before flipping the lighter closed and extinguishing the flame.

"Stupid lighter. Would do better with a cheap one from the petrol station."

"So, what's stopping you?"

"My dad bought it me when I left school," he said, holding the silver lighter up and turning it. Judy caught sight of initials on the side and a message she couldn't make out. "It's the only present he ever got me." He pocketed it, then took another drag of the cigarette. "Don't tell Faith. She thinks I'm only vaping now."

"Yeah, well, unless she's noseblind I think she probably knows."

"That bad?"

Judy shrugged.

"I'm sorry about back there. Is Jemma all right?"

"Jemma's in her own world. I don't think she knows what all the fuss was about to be honest."

"I'm sorry. I'll make it up to her. We don't get a chance to go out for meals very often. I thought tonight would be fun."

He was not a bad man. Yes, there were those moments when his mannerisms smacked of Phil's, and truth be told, even his expressions reminded her of her dead husband. But it hadn't even been a year since Phil had died, and it was too easy for Judy to forget that his parents were grieving too. Coming up to the anniversary was as difficult for them as it was for her.

"Lisa loves you both very much."

He nodded. But there was that haunted look behind the eyes and a shine to his forehead that could have been sweat despite the chill air.

"This isn't a rejection," Judy continued. "This is just her finding her own place now that she doesn't have Phil around."

"They were close. I understand that."

"And no matter how much she loves you, remember that she's grieving just as much as you and Faith. I think this is just another outlet for her. It sounds like it might help her come to terms with what happened to Phil. Help her move on. Maybe help you all move on."

"And what about you?"

"What about me?" she replied, confused.

"What if she finds something she doesn't want to find?"

"What like?"

"What if her parents want to stay in touch? What if they want to be a part of Jemma's life? Are you ready for that?"

No, of course she wasn't ready for that. Christ, Lisa had sprung this surprise on all of them at once, she'd not yet considered what this meant for her and Jemma.

"Adrian, I will support Lisa. And I suppose if the answers she's looking for aren't what she's hoping for, I guess we'll deal with that as well."

He nodded. "I'm sure you're right," he said, and leaned in to give her a hug. His jacket smelt of the discarded cigarette, and she recoiled.

When they separated, Lisa was approaching with Faith. There was a moment of awkward silence, then Lisa froze before heading towards Lisa's car. "Would you mind dropping me off home?"

"Don't be silly," Faith said, frowning. "We brought you, we'll take you home."

Judy caught a glance from Lisa and nodded. "Sure, not a problem."

Faith shrugged then shook her head but didn't bother fighting. She got into the driver's seat of Adrian's car and started adjusting the mirrors. Judy offered a feeble wave then got in her own car, Lisa jumping in the back. As Judy drove from the car park, Lisa burst into tears on the back seat. Without skipping a beat, Judy passed her the packet of tissues she kept in the side pocket of the door. "Don't worry."

Jemma looked nervously around, unsure what she was meant to do in this situation.

"I'm sorry," Lisa said. "I didn't think it would go like that."

"I know you didn't. I'm sure it will all work out OK."

"Thanks for the lift. I didn't fancy getting back in the car with Dad. I don't know why he reacted so oddly."

"He's just going to take a while to get used to the idea."

They drove the rest of the way in silence. Exhaustion had beset them all and even Jemma was slouching in her seat, the phone forgotten on her lap. By the time they'd navigated the town's endless series of traffic lights and pulled to a stop outside Lisa's house, it was almost ten.

"Do you want to come in for a drink?"

Judy glanced at her daughter. "We'd best not, school night."

"Wait," Jemma said, more alert than she'd been for most of the evening. "Is Ellis in?"

Ellis was Lisa's housemate. The pair shared the rent on a semi-detached house and had always been friendly enough when Judy had dropped in. Despite the age difference, Judy had often wondered whether Lisa and Ellis would have made a good couple. Judy looked up at the windows. They were black, the curtains hadn't yet been closed and she could make out nothing but dark shadows and unfamiliar edges.

"I don't think so. He said he was going out."

Movement from a front bedroom window caught Judy's attention, and she glanced across, certain that she'd seen…

"Why are you interested in Ellis?" Judy asked. Then she remembered that Ellis had the latest Xbox and had invested in a 60-inch TV for the shared lounge. "You're hoping for a game of Fortnite on his big telly?"

A smirk appeared on Jemma's face.

"Come in," Lisa said, smiling for the first time in what must have been over an hour. "If he's not in, you can still play, just use your own account."

The house was empty. Ellis had left a note saying he'd gone out to the pub to watch the game. Whilst Judy switched the kettle on, Lisa helped Jemma get settled with the Xbox.

"Just one game," Judy shouted from the kitchen.

"I'll pretend I didn't hear that."

"You can pretend all you like, but it's one game and then we're done."

Lisa pulled out a stool from the breakfast bar and sat down. "I shouldn't have said anything to Dad. I could still have done this without him."

"Has it been on your mind a lot?"

She shrugged. "Off and on. I spoke about it a few times with Phil but he was never that interested. I think he thought it would upset Dad too much. I guess he was right."

"He should have respected your right to find your birth parents."

"Well, we both know that's not how it was with Phil."

Lisa knew Phil as well as Judy did, probably more so, but then there was that side of him that she doubted anyone but Judy had got to witness. The angry side that would be let out as simply as the wrong word said at the dinner table, or the wrong type of beer being in the fridge on football night. Tarnishing his memory with his wider family was never on Judy's agenda. What would be the point in destroying their image of him just so she could score a few points? It would only be them she would be hurting. Phil had been dead almost a year and the time for getting even with him had long passed.

"Do you miss him?"

A strange thing to say. "Sometimes. Do you?"

"When we were kids, we were pretty much inseparable." Lisa's voice trailed off.

"I'm sorry that you miss him." Judy poured the boiled water into their cups, stirred, then added the milk.

She passed Lisa's cup across. "Is that why it's important to you now to find your birth parents, because Phil's gone?"

Lisa cradled the cup in her fingers and let the steam drift up over her face. "Maybe. I don't know. Is that wrong?"

An expletive came from the lounge and Judy shouted at Jemma to mind her language. There was no reply, only the continued sound of guns blasting. Another curse and then Jemma called out, "I've been disconnected. Has the internet gone off?"

Lisa checked her phone. "Yeah, looks like it." And then to Judy. "I'll check the router. Won't be a minute."

She hurried from the room, her footsteps patting on the hall floorboards.

And Judy was not alone.

She shivered, then glanced around looking for the open window that must be causing the draft she could feel across her neck and back. The windows were all closed behind her. Instinctively, she began counting doors. A habit she'd gotten into after the paranormal night of hell at Ravenmeols. Her life had gotten very complicated, very quickly after Phil died. She'd been exposed to the paranormal and found that she herself was attuned to the unnatural. Counting doors was her way of protecting herself against the portals that would sometimes appear in paranormal hotspots—doorways to another realm that housed the worst of the worst.

But, there were no more doors here than there should be. They were safe.

Lisa came back into the kitchen. "The ethernet cable had come unplugged." She shrugged. "Jasper must have knocked it."

Judy stood and tipped the rest of her drink into the sink then placed her cup on the draining board. "So sorry, but I'm really tired. Can we catch up later in the week?"

Lisa grinned. "Yeah, of course. I didn't mean to keep you out all night."

"It's not a problem. What will be a problem is trying to get Jemma out of bed in the morning. She might not yet be thirteen, but to all intents and purposes, she's acting like a total teenager pretty much most of the time. Just listen to this."

Judy poked her head into the lounge. "Time to go, sweetie."

But, Judy had been wrong. Jemma was fast asleep on the sofa, the Xbox playing loudly on the screen, the controller ignored in Jemma's lap.

3

Something woke her.

Lisa had been dreaming. Deep dangerous dreams where her imagination and her anxiety came together into a furious melting pot. She was in the middle of an argument with her dad over who should get to pay the bill for the meal. As it was her announcement, she demanded that she should pay, but he was being as stubborn as ever and countered that as he was her legal owner, she was technically a pet who couldn't have her own money. She was about to throw the table aside and enjoy the sight of linguine hitting his smug features, when the floorboards creaked and she was thrown out of her dreamworld and into reality.

The reality of her bedroom at night.

Her fingers stumbled at the bedside table as she reached for the lamp, but she only succeeded in knocking her phone onto the carpet and almost tipping over her glass of water.

"Jasper," she whispered, reaching a hand over the top of her duvet, looking for the comforting touch of her tabby's fur. In the middle of winter, he'd normally be found either curled up in his radiator hammock, or lain beside her. But he wasn't beside her, and her eyes hadn't yet adjusted to the dark edges and corners of her room to say for certain whether he was in there.

She blinked, readying her eyes for the light.

Another noise that could have been the floorboards at the end of her bed.

Someone was in her room.

She sat upright, and scrambled for the light switch a second time, this time finding it, not caring what she knocked over. The light came on, the initial burst of pain that came with it subsided, just in time for her to see her bedroom door swing wider open.

She must have startled Jasper, he heard her struggling in her dreams and came to see if she was OK, then got scared by the noise of her messing with the light and bolted from the room instead.

Her heart began to slow down to its regular pace. Jesus, why did her imagination do this to her? Was it trying to put her into an early grave?

Lisa almost convinced herself that she was being the most irrational person on the planet, when she noticed the black shadow stretching out from the cat bed on the radiator. Jasper hadn't been as flighty as she'd thought. She took another look at the bedroom door and noted it was still swinging ever so gently.

4

Judy woke with a headache and a surprising amount of guilt. She wasn't sure what she had to be guilty about so racked her memories of the conversation she'd had with Lisa the previous night. What had she said about Phil? Anything that would get back to Adrian and Faith and cause upset?

She took her time making breakfast. There was no rush this morning. Despite the late night, Jemma was already in the bathroom getting ready for school. She needed to leave the house in a little under an hour to meet her friends at the bus stop. Jemma hadn't spoken much about her dad recently. It can't have escaped her memory that it was coming up to the anniversary of his death. Should she bring Phil up in conversation? Would that be the right thing to do to give her daughter a chance to talk about him?

A notification sounded on her phone. An email from the bank. A tremble in her stomach as she tried to recall the balance of the account.

Seconds later, another notification popped up. This time a jobs website with three positions that fitted her experience. In a prior life, Judy had taught primary school kids. Eight-year-olds mainly. Everything she'd wanted in a job. Apart from the money—that could never hope to compete with Phil's. He'd suggested she move to part time status when Jemma was born and after a year of that, had recommended she should give it up completely. After all, there was no need for both to be working and then having to waste money on childcare when they didn't need to. Regretfully now, Judy had agreed and thrown away a ten-year career at the school. She'd told herself that it was for the best and that when one door closed, another surely opened. But life had gotten complicated, and she'd never sought to go back, not even when Jemma moved to high school and Phil had become ill.

What about now? She'd filled in the forms on the job site and here she was, looking at three positions for teaching jobs, none of them local. The nearest was an hour away in a part of Liverpool she didn't much care for. But they were jobs. It would be a foot back on the ladder and who knew where it might lead?

Upstairs, the toilet flushed. Judy checked her watch and then flicked the kettle back on. A flash of memory of the previous evening came to her, making tea in Lisa's kitchen, feeling not quite alone after Lisa had gone to check on the router. A sensation that had made her think of the Almost Doors and her time at Ravenmeols. She glanced at her phone again. It would only take a minute to send Seth a text and see how he was doing. She almost did it too, had the phone in her hand, unlocked and scrolling through her contacts. Seth's number wasn't in the most recently contacted list. Seth was busy working for the Vigilance Society, or Vigilance, or whatever they called themselves.

Vigilance had been hovering around the periphery of their lives for the last few months, monitoring the aftermath from Ravenmeols, and then later when Adam Cowl had targeted Seth's uncle. Since then, Seth had been quiet with her. He owed her nothing, she'd realised, after that first week of no contact. Together, they'd defeated the Adherents' plans twice, and she considered him a friend, but that didn't mean that they needed to live in each other's pockets. Seth had a whole new life ahead of him with his uncle's occult collection, a new house, and mysterious job with Vigilance.

And Judy had nothing going on in her life that would help her move forward. It wasn't exactly jealousy she was feeling. Seth had been through a load more pain than Judy ever had and deserved to have some direction to his life.

"You OK?" Jemma asked, startling her from her thoughts. Her daughter, so smart in her uniform with immaculately braided hair and bright eyes. She had no right to look this energetic after their late night.

"I'm a little tired. How are you this morning?"

"What's for breakfast?"

"Whatever's in the cupboard."

"Pancakes?"

"If there are some in there, knock yourself out."

Judy fetched a plate and cutlery and pulled a tub of ice cream from the freezer. For herself, she settled on a single piece of buttered toast and that second cup of tea. Whilst Jemma scooped a huge portion of ice cream, she glanced up. "You were talking in your sleep." A teasing smile flashed on her face.

"Really?" Judy thought she'd slept well, free from the many interruptions she'd normally experience. "What was I saying?"

"Nothing much, I guess."

"You guess?"

A pause. Then Jemma snapped the lid back on the ice-cream tub. "It sounded like you were talking to Dad."

Judy's stomach fluttered. She circled the rim of her teacup with her finger, enjoying the heat from the china. "Just a dream."

"You were angry at him." Jemma avoided her mother's gaze, concentrating a little too much on chopping up pancakes with the side of her spoon. "It was a little spooky to be honest."

"I'm sorry. I didn't mean to scare you. Really, just a bad dream."

"I thought it might be something to do with…"

"What?"

"The other stuff. The stuff from a few months ago when you were still talking to Seth. The hospital and everything."

"No. Don't think about that. It's all in the past."

"But is it? You're different, aren't you?"

"Not the last time I checked."

"You see things. The doors. And the rest."

"Not for a long time." Judy took her daughter's hand and squeezed it. "Sometimes it can be just a dream. It doesn't mean anything."

Jemma smiled in relief and Judy went back to sipping her tea. She wanted to believe everything she'd just told her daughter, but the hairs standing up on the back of her neck were making it difficult to.

5

The Costa was crowded, and it had taken Judy a few minutes to find a decent table in the corner. A discarded tray from the previous customers had been left on the table along with a napkin soaked in hot chocolate and a teaspoon sitting in a puddle of coffee. She grabbed a handful of napkins from the counter and did a quick tidy, trying to focus out the noise from the other tables. A middle-aged professional couple were heatedly talking about a client who'd tried to mess them about with missed appointments and deadlines. A young mum was futilely entertaining her three children that were running around her table, playing with plastic toys from a half-eaten McDonald's box.

Lisa appeared at the entrance and spotted Judy. She hurried over.

"What can I get you?" she asked.

"No, sit down, I'll get them," Judy said. From the table behind her, wafted the tempting smells of toasted panini and her stomach grumbled. "Did you want something to eat?"

Five minutes later, Judy was sitting opposite her sister-in-law, two paninis and coffees in front of them.

"Busy day?" Judy asked.

"No more than usual. Feel like I've gotten a rotten hangover though."

"You weren't drinking last night."

"I know, totally not fair."

Judy frowned. There was something else going on here. Lisa wasn't hungover, she was upset. There were shadows under her eyes that she'd done her best to cover with makeup.

"Have you spoken to your parents yet?"

"Mum's sent a message asking if I'm OK. I've sent a message to Dad but no reply. I really didn't think he'd react like that. I thought he would be happy for me."

"I don't know how I'd feel if I was in the same situation with Jemma. It'll just take him a little while to get used to the idea. Once he sees you're serious—."

"I am serious."

"Yes, I know. But once he sees that, I'm sure he'll do all he can to help."

Lisa shrugged. "Perhaps it doesn't matter. Just me being stupid again. Phil told me enough times to let it go. Maybe I should listen to that advice."

"Phil gave out plenty of advice over the years. I'm not sure how much notice you should take of it."

Lisa's eyes narrowed. "You rarely talk about Phil."

"What do you mean?"

"Were things really that bad between you?"

Judy hesitated. "It was complicated. I guess I'm still trying to process that." She picked up her plate and took a tentative nibble from the edge of her panini. The cheese had cooled enough to not melt the roof of her mouth off, so she took another bite.

"If you ever want to talk about it, you know where I am."

Judy nodded, swallowing. "Thanks. One day, perhaps. But, we're here because you wanted to talk. You said there was something else on the phone."

Lisa hadn't touched her coffee or her food, but now that she was asked a direct question, her hands took her cup and she cradled it in her hands.

"I think there's someone else in my house."

Judy's heart stumbled. "What do you mean? You mean Ellis has been bringing someone home?"

Lisa shook her head. "I mean there's someone uninvited getting into the house. I see them. And the thing is, I don't think they're even bothered about being seen."

Judy thought back to the shape she saw last night in the front bedroom window. The shape she'd first thought was Ellis, only Ellis was out when they'd arrived at Lisa's house.

"I don't understand. You're saying that someone else has a key, or someone has broken into your house?"

"I don't know. I only know what I see, or rather what I think I see. It's usually at night. Take last night for example. I woke up at, must have been gone two AM, and I could have sworn the cat had been pawing at my covers. I battered it aside, as you do when you're half-asleep, and then I heard the floorboards at the end of my bed. That was enough to wake me up because Jasper isn't heavy enough to make the floorboards creak, and besides, it sounded like someone was standing there."

Judy had picked up her sandwich whilst Lisa had been talking but her stomach was no longer rumbling. Her mouth was dry, and she swallowed as she put the plate down. Her appetite was the last thing on her mind.

"You must have been dreaming."

Lisa nodded, but then shrugged. "I don't blame you for thinking that. My dreams are not what you'd call normal by any means, but it wasn't a dream. I'm sure of it. I turned the light on and just as the room lit up, I saw—" She broke off as a boy from the next table bumped into theirs spilling Judy's coffee.

"Oh God, I'm sorry about that," the tired mother said, grabbing the boy and dragging him back to his chair.

With the interruption, Lisa's face had gone pale. Her eyes had glazed over and her head had tilted a little. She wasn't paying attention to Judy or the troublesome kids, but was staring beyond, at some place over by the serving counter, against the far wall. Judy tried to get a look at what had caught her attention, but a large group of office workers chose that moment to crowd in, searching for tables.

"You OK?" Judy asked.

"Oh, yeah, sorry."

"What did you see in your room?"

A little colour had returned to Lisa's cheeks and her eyes locked with Judy's.

"A woman. I know it sounds ridiculous, but there was a woman in my room last night."

"Not Ellis?"

"No, it wasn't tall enough to be Ellis."

"Have you asked him?"

"No, I didn't want to scare him."

"Who do you think it is?"

Lisa shook her head. "Literally, no idea."

"Have you called the police?"

"I always lock the front and back doors. The police will think I'm mad."

"You've got to do something though. You can't let this continue."

"I am doing something. I'm talking to you." Lisa's expression lifted a little. "Jemma told me about some of the things that have happened to you."

"She always was one for a story."

"About the doors appearing in your friend's house. About the things he kept in his basement. She says you can see things."

"Lisa, if I could help, I would. But Jemma's exaggerating. There's plenty of stuff Jemma doesn't know."

Lisa picked up her plate. "So, there is some truth in it? You sense things. You're perceptive. In a spiritual sense I mean. Last night, you felt something in my house. When I came back into the kitchen, you were acting weird, something had spooked you. And then I saw the woman in my room. You sensed her, didn't you?"

Judy's mind was a tumble of ideas and fears. This was the world she was trying to escape from, and Lisa was encouraging her to embrace it.

"I don't know what I felt. A draft most likely."

"Don't give me that. Why are you denying it? If I could do what you can do, I'd be totally owning it. Look at those idiots on TV. Most of them are frauds, you can just tell. You'd make a mint if you put yourself out there."

Judy shook her head. "It's not like that."

"Well, maybe I'm getting carried away with it, but forgetting that, won't you help me out? I can't go on like this. What does she want with me?"

"I don't know how I can help."

"Come around again. Spend some time in the house. Tell me if you sense anything unusual. All I want is reassuring that I'm not going mad."

"Right. I'll think about it."

"You promise?"

"I promise. I'll think about it."

And as she took another bite of her panini, Judy realised that she wasn't ever going to escape this terrifying life, this curse of hers that lay waiting, just beneath the surface.

6

Judy had met Jemma at the bus stop, much to Jemma's annoyance. Judy was determined to keep Jemma close after Adam Cowl's people had threatened her last year. She'd drop her off at school every day if she could, but Jemma wanted that time with her friends on the bus before the day began. Perhaps it was just her way of showing her independence, and that her mum really didn't need to mollycoddle her.

Once the bus had pulled away, leaving the pair of them alone, Jemma seemed to relax, and let her mum take her school bag.

"Good day?" Judy asked.

"Same old."

Jemma proceeded to tell Judy about the substitute teacher they'd had in PE who'd made them run over the sand dunes for an hour in an attempt to tire them out.

Adrian's BMW was parked outside the house by the time they arrived home.

Judy frowned. Why would Adrian be here?

As they approached the car, Adrian got out and closed the door behind him.

Jemma gave him a quick hug then went inside leaving the two adults alone to talk.

"Is everything OK?" Judy asked.

"I wanted to see you after what happened at the restaurant."

"Do you want to come in?"

Adrian shook his head. "I suppose I can't really stay. There are some things I need to finish at work. Those flats don't let themselves and if I let the pedal up, there's a few in the office that will coast through the rest of the day instead of filling up appointment slots."

Judy was back to being worried. "If it's about Lisa, she's fine. The adoption is on her mind, but it doesn't mean that she's thinking any differently about you."

"But that's just it isn't it? I mean, she must be thinking differently about us. Up until Sunday, we were the only parents she would talk about. Now, we're the second-class citizen parents. She's thinking of her birth parents instead." His voice was full of frustration and until now Judy hadn't really considered what it must feel like being on the other end. How would she feel if Jemma started to consider someone else as their mother? Even the passing thought was enough to cause a shiver.

"I don't think it's as black and white as you think."

He nodded. "But how can you know?" There was a steely glint in his eyes that she didn't much care for. "You know she's ill don't you?"

"No. No I didn't. What's wrong with her? She seemed fine when I saw her earlier."

Adrian tapped the side of his head. "Ever since she was in primary school, we've had concerns about her behaviour. It started when she tried to stab a boy in her class with a pair of scissors she was using to cut out farmyard animals for a collage. The psychiatrists said it was likely to be a phase that she would grow out of. Something to do with testing boundaries. But she kept on pushing those boundaries. By the time she was in high school they were prescribing her Valium."

"Wait, I'm not sure you should be sharing this with me. I don't want to hear any more." But that was a lie because Judy desperately wanted to hear more. All of it. A new light had been cast on part of Phil's family and as much as she found hearing the news from her father-in-law slightly horrific, she couldn't not think that as Phil's twin, was there a tendency towards that blip in mental health? It might explain a lot.

"I'm guessing she's told you about the dreams." Adrian raised an eyebrow. "She has, hasn't she?"

"She's told me she has some trouble sleeping. She thinks there's someone coming into her room at night."

Adrian nodded, like a man who knew the answer before he heard it. "A woman perhaps? Only, she can never quite see her?"

Judy nodded, embarrassed by talking about her friend behind her back.

"She's been telling her psychiatrists the same stories since she was a little girl. None of this is new."

"I had no idea."

"No reason why you should. For the past twenty years, she's been making excellent progress with her doctors and the medication she's on has really helped her focus. I'm only telling you because I'm worried that her behaviour at the restaurant was the start of a new deterioration in her mental health."

"She was fine at the dinner. I didn't see anything different about her."

Hadn't she? It was an unusual meal. Lisa hadn't broached the subject of the search for her birth parents until after they had served dessert. Now that she reconsidered the evening, there was an undeniable tension in the air. Conversation had seemed stilted, driven by Faith and Judy and throughout it all, Lisa had been eating her food and giving one-word answers, often not speaking unless prompted by her dad. And there was that lack of presence, like she was thinking about other places. Judy had put it down to her having a bad day because she was never like this in her company or was it the awkwardness of a meal with Lisa and her parents when that was usually reserved for Christmases? And of course, Phil was no longer here to bring both parts of the family together.

"She was distracted, no doubt, by what she wanted to talk about," Adrian continued, "but I've seen her in that place before and it's generally only a few steps away from when she needs to see a doctor again."

Adrian wasn't just upset about the thought of Lisa searching for her birth parents, he was concerned about her mental health and what this search might do to her. And he was right to be concerned. Was Lisa ready for this? What if her birth parents didn't want to see her? There were reasons Lisa and Phil had been put up for adoption, so many reasons, and Judy could only think of bad ones. There would be surprises ahead and Lisa was unlikely to find any happy news waiting for her.

Adrian stepped forward and Judy thought for a terrifying moment that this usually stoic figure was moving in for a hug. Instead, Adrian reached for her hand and took it gently. He gave a gentle squeeze, then let it drop. "You don't have to respond. I just thought it was the right thing to do. For her wellbeing and your own. I know that she's important to you, perhaps more so now that our Phillip is no longer with us."

Judy nodded. "She is important. I don't want to see her get hurt."

"No one does. So, I'd appreciate it if you could do me a favour."

"Of course."

"Let me know how she is. She's not returning my calls. If you think she's deteriorating again, and you don't get the impression she's getting any help for it, I'd like you to let me know."

Judy frowned. "I'm not sure I can do that."

"I'm not asking you to spy on her," he said, "I just want to know if the rest of the family need to step into help. You would want the same if this was Jemma we were talking about, wouldn't you?"

"Yes, I suppose so." Judy sighed. "Yes, I'll let you know. But, don't give up on trying to get through to her yourself."

He nodded. "I'll never give up on her. She's foremost on my mind. Always will be. But I've got to get back. Like I say, those lazy arses in the office will run my business into the ground if I let them."

Adrian opened his door, then paused. "One more thing," he said, "Faith thought it would be a nice idea to take Jemma up to the lakes for the weekend. Give you a couple of days break and a chance for us to spend some time with Jemma. We've already got a cottage booked. The wifi's not meant to be work and live with none of the problems she'd had with previous tenants.

"Oh sorry, didn't know you had a guest," Lisa said.

"Hi," Nina said, then smiled and picked up a plate with two rounds of toast on it. Lisa tried to ignore the fact it had been made with the granary loaf she'd bought yesterday. It didn't matter. Both her and Ellis put into a shared grocery budget. None of this food was hers or his.

"Hey, do you want some breakfast?" Ellis asked. He was already dressed in his favourite pink shirt and was halfway through his own toast. Nina leant across and brushed aside a crumb hanging from the edge of his mouth. Lisa tried not to roll her eyes.

"I'm good thanks. I'll get my own. You two get back to it."

"Kettle's just boiled. We're running low on milk though. I'll pick some up on the way home."

"Right."

Nina smiled. "It's a great house."

"Thanks. My dad helped me find it." Lisa didn't point out that the house belonged to her dad's property business.

"That's nice," Nina continued. "Don't know what I'd do without the bank of Mum and Dad."

"Yeah, well, I wouldn't know. I've always had to pay rent. He's not that generous."

Nina laughed nervously. "If only they were, eh?"

Lisa smiled but directed her next question at Ellis. "Don't suppose I can cadge a lift?"

He glanced at his watch. "Afraid not. I promised Nina we'd stop off at her's before we went in."

Classy lady. Obviously, she hadn't meant to spend the night then. Judging by the three bottles of wine on the countertop, they'd be working with delicate heads all day.

"OK. Well, best not keep you then." Lisa opened the cupboard looking for a plate. Empty. A glance at the sink told her where they were. Ellis may well be fair when it came to contributing to groceries, but he sucked big time with the housework. She was always having to do the dishes, along with most of the vacuuming. A rota existed but Ellis treated it as more of a guideline than a firm commitment.

Wonder how much of a commitment he's making to you, Lisa thought, taking another look at Nina. Her hair was pulled back in a ponytail, and she hadn't taken off yesterday's makeup.

"There's some cleansing wipes in my room if you want to borrow some before you head out," Lisa offered.

Nina's eyes widened. "Really. Oh, that's great. I meant to ask last night, but you were already asleep."

"Wait, you didn't come into my room, did you?" Lisa's chest tightened. She left the bedroom door open for Jasper to wander out and get to the cat flap, not so a stranger could spy on her.

"Oh no. I just heard a noise when I came back from the loo. I thought you called for help. But when I looked in on you, you were asleep."

"Right," Lisa said, her tone betraying it was definitely not all right.

"Have I done something wrong?" Nina was genuinely confused, looking from Lisa to Ellis then back again.

"Ellis, this isn't OK."

Ellis looked like he'd just been batted on the back of his head. "What just happened? What's the problem?"

"Your girlfriend's been in my room."

"No, I haven't. Honestly. I just opened the door a bit and made sure you were OK."

"Were you here the other night?" Lisa remembered the figure she'd seen leaving her room in a hurry. "That was you wasn't it? This isn't the first time you've been in my room. I can't believe this." Lisa face burned. She felt like a child again. How dare they put her in this position.

Nina looked at Ellis for support. "I didn't. I don't know what she's talking about."

Ellis nodded. "I know. She's just a little—"

"A little what?"

"You're over-reacting. Nothing happened."

"Someone was in my room last night. They've been in my room before. Your girlfriend—"

"I'm not his girlfriend."

"—admitted checking up on me."

"You were crying in your sleep," she said with a condescending tone that Lisa did not care for in the slightest.

"I was not crying."

Ellis raised his arm, gesturing that Lisa should calm down. "To be fair, Lisa, it's not that uncommon for you to be talking in your sleep. I've heard you before now. I just don't like to say anything. I know how much you like your privacy."

"So, you should have told Nina not to come into my room."

Nina dropped her plate on the counter. "I'm going. I didn't come here for a row."

"Then what did you come for? Fast track to a promotion?"

Ellis's eyes became piercing dots of coal in a face of stone. "That is way out of order. You're being ridiculous, acting like a child. Who I choose to bring back home is none of your business. I've always respected your privacy and I expect the same thing in return. If that's too much to ask, then I'll have to start looking for somewhere else to live."

No. That would not be acceptable. Lisa forced herself to breathe, then she lowered her head and closed her eyes. "I'm sorry. I didn't mean to say that."

"Jeez, we've all got to work in the same office together. Why did you need to kick up a stink?"

Lisa looked up and brushed her hair away from her face. If only it was as easy to brush away the shame she was feeling. "Ellis, I'm sorry. I'll apologise when I see her at the office. It's just—"

"Just what?"

"I've not been sleeping that well. I'm having bad dreams. She probably did hear me talking in my sleep."

"Maybe you should go the doctor."

"I don't need to see the doctor. I just need to ease up on the caffeine."

"You need to do something. I don't want to fall out with you." And Ellis turned to leave but something caught his eye. He gestured to her neck. "That looks nasty. Did the cat do that to you?"

She reached a hand to her neck and rubbed. It did feel like there was something there. "I don't think so."

"It looks sore. There's some anti-septic cream in the bathroom cabinet." And then he left. She heard him hurry to the front door and speak to Nina before running back up the stairs. A minute later he was gone, and she was alone in the house. Well, alone apart from Jasper.

She made her coffee and checked the time on the clock above the fire in the lounge. It said it was two fifteen. Batteries had died.

Great. In her bedroom she pulled off the hoodie and stood in front of the floor mirror. Ellis was right, there was a mark there, three marks. Scratches. It wasn't Jasper. He'd only scratched her a handful of times, always on her hands, and always whilst playing. He'd never try to hurt her on her neck, and the marks were too far apart for cat scratches and parallel all the way along their length.

These were fingernails.

9

St Anns was a picturesque church in the middle of Ainsdale. Built over a hundred years ago in an intensive red brick, it had stood as the centre of the village for decades until the community expanded, leaving it a silent sentinel on the edge of the current habitations. Its modest tower was still high enough to reach over all the surrounding buildings and pigeons sheltered from the wind on the deep-set ledges around the tower's windows.

Judy parked and nodded at a middle-aged couple carrying flower displays heading for the back entrance.

Malc was waiting by the porch and embraced her warmly.

It had been weeks since they'd last met up. Like Seth, Malc was also a member of the mysterious occult organisation known as the Vigilance Society, but unlike Seth, Malc was still willing to see her. From what little she understood about Vigilance, they were a force for good, fighting against those that would use the occult to harm. But they operated under a strict code of secrecy, so much so that Malc had kept his association with them hidden from his wife, a contributing factor to the breakdown of his marriage.

"Great to see you," she said, and meant it.

"You're looking well." A polite lie but she appreciated it all the same.

"How's Joe?"

"Doing good. He had his last session with the counsellor last week. He's making friends again."

"Are you getting enough support from the school?"

"On the whole, they've been good. But, it's tough. There are things Joe can't talk about without things getting worse for him."

She could imagine that it would be difficult.

Joe was Malc's son and had been kidnapped by an infamous occultist called Adam Cowl, an experience that they were all still trying to process.

Malc led Judy inside. It had been months since she'd been in a church. The last time had been for Phil's funeral and despite not being a religious woman, she found the surroundings offered her some comfort.

The pews had recently been replaced as part of a refurbishment and rows of comfortable seating had been arranged in readiness for the evening service. Bibles had already been placed on the seat of each chair, and an overpowering aroma of furniture polish hit her as they walked down the nave. That smell, with the remnants of the incense from the last service tickled her nose, and she resisted the urge to sneeze.

Behind the altar, the couple she'd seen in the car park were replacing floral arrangements, whilst the sunlight streamed through the main window above them, hitting the crossing in front of the altar with a rich golden blaze.

"How's Georgia?" Judy asked. Malc's wife had moved out of the vicarage and into a flat with Joe. When Malc's secret life with the Vigilance Society had come out, it had proven one thing too much for her to handle.

"She's doing better."

"Good."

"What about you? What's going on with you and Jemma?"

"Jemma's doing well in school. She seems to have made a few new friends. Keeping on top of her homework."

"And there's not been anything strange happening in your house?"

"It's been quiet."

"No doors?"

She shook her head. "It's hard to think that was only a few weeks ago. Do you think they've gone for good?"

"The Adherents were excellent at knowing when to take a step back and regroup. Adam will be holed up somewhere, deciding on his next move. Now that he knows that Vigilance is looking for him, he will be even more cautious. Remember, the adherents kept off the radar for thirty years. He's used to waiting for the right time and choosing his moments."

It bothered her that he was still out there with his followers. So far, there'd not been so much as a sniff they were seeking retribution for Judy being involved in thwarting their latest plans. If she had the funds, she'd leave the area for good, but her financial position didn't make that easy. Perhaps if she could make a go of this new venture, she'd be better able to make a fresh start somewhere else. But that would also mean saying goodbye to friends like Malc who understood her situation. Who else could she talk to about all of this? Who else would protect her when the Adherents came after her?

"And have you heard from Seth?"

"I hear he's doing well, but he's still being as difficult as ever to work with."

"He's not returning my messages. I worry that he's in something bigger than he can handle."

"Vigilance are good people. They understand where he's coming from and they will make sure he's comfortable."

"But what's he doing with them? Are they going after Adam and his Adherents?"

Malc shrugged. "There's more out there than one cult. More dangers that you don't want to know about."

"I don't see how any of it could be any worse than what I've already experienced."

"You went through a lot. I know that. If Vigilance were in a stronger position, Ravenmeols would never have happened. But now that they have Seth, they might have a chance to stop something like that from happening again."

"I hope so."

"Have you been in touch with the others?"

He meant the others at Ravenmeols, the survivors. The ones that had seen all that the Adherents had thrown at them. They'd paid to attend a ghost hunt at Ravenmeols, an abandoned psychiatric hospital, but instead they'd witnessed blood, ritual, and murder. They'd made it through to the other side, but they were far from unscathed. Whilst Judy had the benefit of a friendship with Malc and Seth, people who knew what was happening, the survivors didn't. All they understood was that a group of psychopaths had tried to hurt them.

"We've reached the point in our relationships where they would sooner not keep in touch. It doesn't help that they see me as someone still in contact with the man they partially blame for what happened."

"Understandable, I suppose."

"Unfair."

"Whatever helps them cope. I guess we should be grateful. They could make things very difficult."

"For whom? For Vigilance?"

"They did help save them."

"They weren't there. There was only you." Then she realised what she'd said. Obviously, Malc was part of Vigilance. In a way, Vigilance had saved them.

Malc suggested two seats in the middle of the church and Judy accepted. "It's very peaceful here."

"Always is. And you're welcome any time. You don't need to be religious. No one will try to convert you."

"How do you do it? You've got your beliefs laid down for you in the bible. The last I heard, there was nothing in there about the Almost Realm and Almost Doors. Nothing about cultists and possessed paintings. How does this fit into your worldview?"

"None of this conflicts the bible. Just because it doesn't mention these things, it doesn't mean I can't experience them. There are a lot of things I have to deal with daily that aren't covered by the bible."

"You've got to admit, it's an unusual position to find yourself in."

He shrugged. "I wouldn't change anything, though."

Except perhaps the relationship with Georgia. I'm sure you'd change that if you could, she thought.

He tried to smile, but it was an effort and she wondered whether he was thinking along similar lines to herself.

"Why did you want to see me?" he asked. "I don't wish to put you off coming here, but when you called me earlier, I got the sense that there was more going on than you wanted to say on the phone."

She shuffled on her seat and considered how best to broach the subject. It's just advice, you're not asking him for anything more than advice.

"What's up? You know I'll help with whatever I can."

"Something unusual is happening with my sister-in-law. I went around to her house a couple of nights ago and sensed a presence."

Malc leaned in. The smile faded. "What kind of presence?"

"It was belligerent. It wasn't happy that I was there."

"How did it show itself?"

"It didn't. I was alone for only a few moments, but during those moments, I wasn't actually alone. Nothing visible. Just a feeling."

"You think it was a spirit? A shadowman?"

She shook her head. "No. Not a shadowman. It was curious. It felt like it was checking me out. Seeing who this different person was in her house."

"Her house? You think this entity lived in your sister-in-law's house previously?"

"I don't know. Possibly. There was definitely a sense of entitlement, like it belonged there when I didn't."

"Did you talk to your sister-in-law about it?"

"Not then. Not that evening. I was surprised, to be honest. It had been a stressful night, and I was tired. I didn't know if what I was feeling was real or just a result of tiredness."

"But you've changed your mind."

Judy slowly nodded. "Lisa spoke to me the next day. She's been worried about someone coming into her room at night."

"You think it's this entity?"

"I'm concerned that it might be."

"Does she live with anyone else?"

"A guy called Ellis. They're housemates."

"Could it be him?"

"She doesn't think so."

"Why has she spoken to you about it? Does she know about—"

"My abilities?"

"I didn't want to put words into your mouth, but yeah."

Judy brushed a strand of hair back behind her ear. Her abilities? What even were her abilities? "Malc, I feel out of my depth here. Lisa knows some of what happened with Adam. Jemma doesn't seem to know when to keep her ideas to herself."

"That must be tricky for you."

"How does Seth manage this?"

"That's he's a medium? He's never tried to hide it. It would be difficult to keep quiet about it and make a living from it at the same time. But he's cautious about who he shares that with. The internet is a great place to advertise. Only people looking for people with his abilities will find him."

"And it never caused trouble with his parents?"

"They had his sister to deal with. Seth grew up under their radar. They noticed nothing different about him, and he didn't tell them."

"And now?"

"Seth doesn't tell me much about it. I saw his dad after he got discharged from hospital. He asked me how things were going with Seth and his thing. He knows. No doubt about it. And I don't think they are particularly bothered." Malc lent back in his chair. He looked older than when she'd last seen him. These last few months hadn't been easy on him. The stresses of dealing with Adam and the Adherents would have been enough for most people, but Malc still had his congregation to consider. She suspected that it couldn't have been much fun knowing how small-minded some church goers could be, with his wife leaving him. Tongues would have wagged. "Seth will be OK, as will his parents. But, what about you? I'm getting the sense that you're not about to let this thing with your sister-in-law lie."

"How can I? She's asked for help, and I don't know who else to turn to."

Malc stayed quiet for a moment. She looked at him for some reassurance that she wasn't crazy in contemplating this.

"If you want my advice, which I know you don't, you'd do better to keep out of it. If there is an entity and you can sense it means you harm, tread warily. You don't know how strong it might be."

"She's family. How can I keep out of it?"

"You should at least be careful."

"We're talking about one entity." And as she said the words, she meant it. She'd taken on far worse and survived. How hard could it be to investigate? "If there is any trouble, I'll call you."

"Yes, you must."

"But in the meantime, I don't suppose you can spare some holy water?"

10

The morning was long and dragged on for at least a week. Lisa could barely keep her eyes open as she slaved over her computer, trying to find a new way to promote double-glazing for one of their regular, albeit lower-paying clients. Nina had kept to her own side of the office and Lisa timed her coffee breaks to make sure there would be no awkward encounters in the kitchen area. Ellis had glanced in her direction a few times but hadn't yet stopped by. If he didn't come over by the end of the day, she'd have to go and break the ice or that evening would be even more awkward.

Lisa had tried applying some foundation to conceal the scratches on her neck, but that experiment hadn't been completely successful. A light scarf had been the only option and, so far, no one had noticed nor commented on it if they had.

At lunch, she left the office, not stopping to chat to anyone, and drove over to her parents' house. Her dad's car wasn't up the driveway. Good, as she wasn't ready to speak to him.

"Oh, darling," her mum said after opening the front door. "I'm so glad to see you."

"Hi, Mum."

They went through to the kitchen and Lisa perched on a stool by the centre island. Her mum hovered by the kitchen sink, looking effortlessly at home there.

"Are you on your lunch? Have you eaten?"

"Only got twenty minutes before I need to head back."

"But you haven't eaten? I can make something."

"No, Mum, don't worry. I'll grab some toast when I get back to work."

Faith's lips thinned. "You will not. I was going to make an omelette for myself. It's no more trouble to make two."

Lisa allowed herself to smile. There was nothing quite like being looked after by her mum. "Thanks, Mum. Can I help?"

Faith had already dragged the frying pan from the cupboard beside the oven. "No. Don't move. You will sit there and let me cook for you. You hardly ever let me do that."

"I don't like imposing."

Faith straightened from grabbing a bottle of oil from another cupboard and faced her daughter. Pan in one hand, oil in the other. "How could you ever impose? This is your house. I'm your mother."

"I know. I just don't want to put you out."

Faith tutted and placed the pan on the hob. "There are some eggs in the fridge."

Lisa went to the utility room where the fridge was kept and dived in for the eggs. Despite it being just the two of them, her mum had never gotten used to it being that way. The fridge was packed. Tubs of coleslaw, bags of lettuce, jars of pickles. It took her a while to locate the eggs.

"How's Dad?" She asked when she returned.

"Fine. At the office."

"I mean, how is he after the meal?"

Faith cracked four eggs in a bowl, then took a fork and started whisking. "He's a little quiet, if that's what you mean."

"I didn't think he'd react like that. I didn't want to hurt him, or you."

"Don't worry about me, love. I've always known that you would want to know about your birth parents, it was always just going to be a matter of when, not if."

"So why can't Dad see that?"

"You took him by surprise, that's all. I guess he thought you'd got to an age where you weren't thinking about it anymore."

"I never stopped thinking about it. It was Phil."

"Yes, I thought as much. You never liked to upset him, did you? You were always the inquisitive one. Even when you were little."

The eggs went into the pan and Lisa excused herself, saying she needed to pay a visit. She did need a wee, but there were things she wanted to do first. Her dad's office was upstairs, next to the bathroom. And in that office, her dad kept most of the paperwork relating to his letting agency. There were several filing cabinets in there, and she knew that he also kept other important documents in there including their passports before she moved out. What was the betting that other important family documents were also kept in there?

Adoption papers?

She flushed the toilet so her mum wouldn't get suspicious, then pushed down on the handle to the office.

Locked.

She'd never known Dad to lock it before. When she'd lived here, the door was almost always ajar, even when Dad was working in there. She didn't even think there had been a lock on the door when she'd last lived here. The handle looked new.

What the hell was going on?

Her mum called up to her. "Lunch is ready."

They ate at the breakfast bar in the kitchen. Faith had poured them both a glass of freshly squeezed orange juice, or at least that's what the carton claimed it to be.

"I've looked into it, the adoption process, I mean," Lisa said. "And I think if you can let me have a look through the original paperwork, I can get in touch with the adoption agency and get them to help."

"It can't be that easy, surely."

"There's no guarantee that my birth parents will want to be contacted, and I'll respect that if that's their choice. But yeah, it is kinda that easy."

"But you need the original paperwork?" Faith set down her knife and fork. "Then you will have to ask your father."

"Would you know where it is?"

"Where we keep all the important documents—in the office."

Of course, it would be.

"Do you mind having a look for it? Now that I'm here. It will save a trip later."

"Don't you need to get back to work?"

Lisa checked her watch. Shit. She only had fifteen minutes to get back into town. It would be a push. Failing that, she'd offer to work later to make up for it. After those late nighters last month, she had a right to expect a little leeway over lunch. "I've got time," she said confidently.

"To be honest, Love, you will have to wait until your father gets home. He's been very security conscious and has put a lock on the office door. I don't think he's left a key here."

"Why did he think to do that?"

"Your guess is as good as mine. You know how he gets. An idea comes from nowhere and takes hold until it's scratched."

"When did he put the lock on?"

Faith looked at Lisa with a curious expression, like what she was explaining didn't matter in the slightest. "He had someone come over on Monday morning to fit it."

Monday morning. The day after Lisa told her dad she would start looking for her birth parents. Now, what are the chances of that? Lisa looked down at her plate and the half-eaten omelette.

"You not hungry, Love?"

"You're right. I need to get back to work, and besides, I've lost my appetite."

11

"How's your day been?" Judy asked as she stepped into Lisa's hallway. Straight away she spotted the marks on her neck and lent in closer. "What happened?"

Lisa straightened and pulled her scarf back around her neck, covering the marks.

"It's nothing. I must have scratched myself sleeping."

Judy noticed her stiffening and caught herself doing the same. Once again, there was a feeling like walking into a room after everyone has done talking about you.

Lisa led the way into the back room, past the open door of the lounge where Judy spotted movement out of the corner of her eye. Ellis must be in there playing on his Xbox. But there was no time to pop her head through and say hello as Lisa seemed on a mission.

Judy followed obediently, then placed her rucksack down. Lisa hurried behind her and closed the door. She was acting even more uptight than she had a few days ago.

"Did you bring your equipment?" Lisa asked.

"I've brought some bits. It's not much, but it's a start. Tell me what's going on though. I said I'd help you, but you need to talk. What's stressing you? What's happened?"

Lisa glanced at the ceiling like she'd heard something, then she met Judy's gaze. "It's not been a great day to be honest."

"Is it your dad?"

Of course, it was her dad. Judy knew that before she'd even asked the question. Lisa's body language was so controlled, her arms folded in front of her chest, and there was a sense of her being a lost child. Judy wanted to grab hold of her and make her realise that despite how it felt now, things would work out OK. Adrian had told her about Lisa's illness and she was cautious about feeding into that with false promises, so she resisted the urge to act overly maternal.

Lisa sniffled then told Judy what had happened at Adrian's house that afternoon with the new lock on the office. It sounded if not suspicious, then at least deeply curious.

"What did your mum say?"

"That he keeps his important documents in there for the business. That she'd speak to him when he gets back and ask him whether he could start looking for the paperwork."

It had surprised Judy that the adoption paperwork hadn't been handed over to Phil or Lisa along with their birth certificates and passports when they'd grown up. It seemed like they would be important documents to want to keep for themselves.

"If she will do that, I don't see that there's any point in worrying yourself over it. Adrian has always been a little—"

"Pig-headed?"

"I would say intense, but we can go with pig-headed if that helps." Judy's spirits lifted as she saw a smile cross Lisa's face.

In the distance, she heard a key turn in the lock then the front door opened and closed. "Lisa, are you home?" Ellis's voice bellowed through the house.

"In here," Lisa shouted back.

Judy rubbed the back of her neck, the fine hair there tingling. Lisa must have noticed. "Are you OK?" she asked.

"Fine. Just thought he was already in the house."

"Probably dropping his new girlfriend off home."

The door opened and Ellis entered, a large bag of takeaway in one hand, the smell wafting through the air. Indian. Judy tried not to think about the bag's contents, realising that she hadn't yet eaten her own tea.

Ellis's face lightened as he saw Judy, then flatlined as he gestured to the bag. "I would have gotten more if I knew you were here. There's plenty though. I always get extra starters."

"No, honestly," Judy replied. "I'll grab something later."

"Where's Jemma?" he asked as he wandered through to the kitchen, flicking the light on, then placing the bag on the counter.

"Her friend's. They're supposed to be finishing a project, but I suspect they're both on Xbox."

"A girl after my own heart," Ellis said.

Judy fiddled with the strap on the backpack. "I could get this set up whilst you eat."

"I'll come with you," Lisa said.

"Honestly, it's not a problem. I'd like to set it up on my own. I need to be comfortable doing this. And to be honest, if you're around, it might interfere with any feelings I may get."

Lisa still didn't look happy about this, so Judy stood and headed for the door with her bag. "Relax, you're making me nervous. And this could be the perfect time to tell Ellis what you're doing."

"Are my ears burning?" Ellis stepped in, carrying a large plate with onion bhaji's and samosas. Judy's stomach was crying at the smell of them. "You going somewhere?" he said as he saw Judy standing by the door.

"I'll let Lisa explain," Judy said as she excused herself, closing the door behind her. She didn't linger to listen in on what Lisa might tell him. Probably making an excuse about being here. Would it help or hinder the situation if they told Ellis that they thought the house might be haunted?

The stairs creaked like old men's bones as she headed upstairs, the rucksack bumping in the small of her back, nudging her along. A single pendant lamp and a fussy fake crystal lampshade illuminated the space, but the bulb must be an energy saving one, an underpowered one for the space it needed to light. As her head met with the floor level of the landing, she could see through the bannisters and scanned all along, from Lisa's bedroom door at the back of the house to Ellis's at the front. The spare bedroom and the main bathroom sat between them; their doors closest to the top of the stairs.

She paused. Then placed her rucksack on the floor and pulled out her pocket notebook. She flicked to the first empty page then wrote 'Lisa' at the top followed by the date and time. Then she did what she had become so practised at when entering new spaces—she counted the doors she could see, paying close attention to the walls between the bedroom doors. There were two. She presumed they were cupboards, their design fitted in too well to be Almost Doors, but she stepped across to them all the same, putting her hand on them carefully, like patting the back of a lion's head. It paid to be cautious. There was no sensation from either of them, so she tried the handles. They opened easily. Inside one, the airing cupboard, the hot water tank sat cladded in thick red insulation. The other was used for storing books and boxes of odds and ends.

She made a note in her notebook that these doors were meant to be here and were harmless.

Above her head was the loft hatch. She took out the LED torch from the rucksack and illuminated the square. There were no signs of anything dangerous. She used the torch to light up the other corners of the room. A few cobwebs but nothing unusual.

But if everything was fine here, why was she finding the impulse to run back downstairs irresistible? Ellis and Lisa had gone quiet, busy eating their tea.

Ignoring the other rooms for now, Judy headed towards the back of the house. The back corridor had a step making it lower than the rest of the landing and she almost missed it, stumbling and swearing under her breath. What maniacs would build a house like this?

As she approached the bedroom door, she realised her breath was almost visible in front of her face. She hadn't felt cold even a moment ago but now the temperature had unmistakably fallen a few degrees.

Her heart was in her mouth by the time she was at the threshold of the room. Was it just her imagination or was the landing light getting even dimmer? She steadied herself against the wall before pushing the bedroom door open with her other hand.

The room was full of shadows and hard edges silhouetted against the moonlight coming in through the windows. The bedroom curtains hadn't yet been closed and wherever the light from the moon hit, objects were kissed with a sliver of silver.

Judy stood and watched, taking the scene in. Seth would have barged straight in and dealt with the consequences later, but he was fearless. Her method, she'd decided, pretty much whilst standing on the threshold, was to take it slowly. This wasn't a race. She wasn't competing with anyone. All she had to do was observe and record.

Music suddenly blasted from a speaker beside Lisa's bed. An old seventies number. Was it Dana? A few bars played, then the speaker fell silent.

"Hello?" Judy asked the darkened bedroom.

In some cases, she knew that acknowledging a spirit was one way to strengthen its position and could be reckless. Judy wasn't thinking of that. "If you're in here and want to communicate, show yourself."

Her mouth was so dry that getting the words out almost made her cough.

If anything was in the room, it wasn't interested in showing itself. "Did you make that music come on?"

Nothing.

Judy entered and placed her backpack against the door so it wouldn't close on her. She'd learnt to always keep your exits clear.

It was an innocuous enough bedroom. A double bed with fine dark lines running across the duvet, a faux fur cover had been set at the end of the bed, a solid band of yellow softening the pattern. A large mirrored wardrobe dominated one wall. Judy thought the mirrors would bother her if she was sleeping in here. Too many opportunities for unexpected movement.

It was simple to spot which side Lisa slept on from the bedside tables. One side was bare apart from a lamp, the other had a half-drunk glass of water on a Harry Potter coaster atop a closed laptop; a Stephen King paperback of Carrie, well-loved telling by the curled-up edges, and a box of tissues.

From her rucksack, Judy removed a small box, about the size of her palm, and she flicked a switch on the side. A row of five LEDs built into the surface flickered into life, glowing a bright red in the darkness. They'd had EM readers like this at Ravenmeols. They'd not been much use at the hospital, and looking at the reviews online had been inconclusive, but it had to be worth a shot, didn't it? Holding it out before her, she stepped gingerly across the room, careful not to stand on any of Lisa's discarded clothes.

Almost as bad as Jemma, she thought.

The five lights extinguished, and she tapped the unit. Testing it before coming here hadn't been high on her priorities. Surely it was just a case of switching it on and searching for the areas where the most lights came on.

One light.

She stood still.

OK, a base reading. Let's call that a base reading.

One light is good. Harmless even.

Five lights.

So, there's that. EM readers would pick up on other signals in the vicinity. Not as useful as she'd hoped then.

One light.

But if she found an area where the reading stayed consistently high and she could discount other signals, then that would indicate something else causing the disturbance.

She swung her arm around, so it was pointing towards the window.

Two lights.

They didn't extinguish.

Why am I holding my breath?

She stepped across the room, heading to the window.

Three lights.

She paused again. Three lights could still be because of phones. Ellis and Lisa could be using theirs now. Judy realised she should have told Lisa what she was doing so they could have cut out as much interference as possible.

A floorboard creaked behind her, somewhere by the door. She spun around, the arm with the reader outstretched like it would protect her.

Nothing.

Four lights.

The door inched shut, her rucksack moving with it, being shoved along by the door. Judy realised the EM reader was a little unnecessary and let her arm drop. How much activity did she need to see to acknowledge that there was something in this room she didn't understand?

"Hello. Can you communicate? Let me know why you're here."

The room dropped several degrees in seconds, and she brought her arms across her chest. Her breath became noticeable in the dim moonlight and she realised one more thing.

She was no longer alone.

12

It had been thirty minutes.

"What's she doing up there? Should you check on her?" Ellis said, picking up the last scrap of poppadom.

"I told you, she's helping me out with my computer."

"But she could bring it downstairs."

"She doesn't like the attention. Prefers to do it with no one looking over her shoulder."

Ellis didn't look convinced, but he didn't press the matter. It had been silent since Judy had left the room to go upstairs. Those sounds she'd heard earlier hadn't come again and with every glance at the clock on the wall, Lisa felt the room close around her as her worry set in.

"I'll just see if she wants a coffee."

"I'll put the kettle on," Ellis replied, then headed for the kitchen.

Lisa closed the dining-room door behind her and peered up the stairs. The landing light was out. She shivered at the chill that seemed to flow down the stairs like a river of freezing air.

"Judy?" Hopefully, she'd get a response and then she could go back and make that coffee and not have to go upstairs and face the darkness at all.

But Judy wasn't answering. She can't have left the house and not told them, could she? No. She'd have heard her come downstairs. Whilst eating her meal, she'd barely been watching the television, her ears straining to hear anything unusual.

She flicked on the light switch. The landing light illuminated. Then, the bulb began to glow brighter, the light quickly becoming too bright to look at directly. Panicked, she flicked the switch back off, but the light stayed on. What the hell? How is it even doing that? Ready to call for Ellis, she had turned her head back to the dining-room door when the light bulb popped and extinguished.

"Judy?"

Lisa took a step on the first tread of the staircase then thought better of heading up into darkness and fetched her phone from the dining room. Ellis put his head through the open kitchen door. "Everything OK. What was that noise?"

"Lightbulb went out."

"I only put that in last month. So much for these energy saving bulbs being cheaper to run. At the rate we go through them, we're burning through any savings on our electricity bill."

She shrugged, grabbed her phone and turned on the torch before heading back out, closing the dining-room door behind her.

Her phone's torch wasn't that great, but it did enough to light up the first couple of feet in front of her. Upon reaching the halfway point, she spotted all the doors were closed. Unusual. They would normally leave the doors open so the cat could wander around unimpeded. Leaving the doors closed would risk leaving the cat locked in one of the rooms, or have him scratching at the carpet in front of a door trying to get in.

"Judy?" her voice echoed along the hallway.

Stepping onto the landing, Lisa shivered. Why was it always so cold? There were no windows on the landing, so with all the doors closed, she was reliant on the torch from her phone.

When it went out, she froze.

Her fingers gripped the phone's casing tighter, her index finger feeling for the fingerprint sensor on the back to unlock it so she could at least use the screen's illumination to find her way.

She turned back to look down the stairs and stifled a scream as she saw the back of a figure enter the dining room. The door closed behind it.

"Ellis!" she yelled.

Nothing. She ran down the steps. The figure hadn't been Judy. It had been wearing a dark dress, with flecks of red in the pattern. It had been the same figure she'd seen in her bedroom the other night. And it was in her house.

Her hand trembled as it reached for the door handle to the back room.

"Ellis?"

She pushed down on the handle then opened the door.

A flame of light cut the darkness. She jumped back, startled by the ghostly face behind the flare, then kicked herself as she realised it was Ellis, using his lighter to light the room.

"I think the consumer unit's tripped," he said. "What's Judy doing up there? She's not plugged in anything dodgy, has she?"

"Hope not." Lisa didn't want to move. It was comforting being with Ellis, despite the disagreement they'd had the other day, she'd take his company to being left in the house in the dark on her own.

But before she could ask him to come upstairs with her, her blood ran cold. There was a shape in the kitchen. A human looking shape. The intruder must have snuck past Ellis whilst the room was in darkness. How had he not even noticed?

"I'll check the consumer unit, but you best see if she's OK. She might have hurt herself."

Ellis's lighter extinguished. "Shit." He flicked the spark wheel again and the flame was back.

And a woman's face was behind his shoulder.

Lisa's scream bounced off the walls and surprised Ellis so much that he let the lighter extinguish.

The main lights came back on. The face was gone. Lisa stepped back until she felt the comforting feel of the sofa behind her legs.

"What the hell?" Ellis's features were caught in a moment between horror and surprise. "Why did you scream?"

"I thought I saw something."

"What?"

"It doesn't matter."

Telling him what she'd seen seemed stupid. Whatever was wrong with her was not worth troubling Ellis over. He would only get upset and start shouting at her again, maybe even call her parents and let them know what a weirdo she was being. The last thing she wanted was for her parents to get involved in this.

"Judy?" Ellis suggested.

"What about her?"

"Perhaps check on her. It must have been a general power cut. Haven't experienced one of those in years."

Lisa hurried upstairs. The landing light was back on, and the doors to the bedrooms were once again open. She couldn't have imagined that. They were closed earlier, she was positive. And the light had popped hadn't it? She'd heard it. Ellis had heard it. That must have happened.

Her own bedroom door was the sole door upstairs that remained closed. Standing outside it, she foolishly lifted a hand to knock.

What the hell are you doing? This is your room. You don't knock to go into your own bedroom.

Instead, she reached for the handle and after taking a deep breath, swung the door open.

The room was dark, and it took Lisa a moment to realise that the figure laying down on the bed was Judy. Her sister-in-law was fast asleep.

*

"Honestly, I don't know what happened." Judy was talking with Lisa in the front room, away from the prying ears of Ellis. Lisa had already admitted to not telling him the truth about Judy's visit and whilst not what Judy wanted, she respected Lisa's decision, for the time being at least.

"You were properly asleep though. It took me ages to wake you up. I thought I would have to get an ambulance."

Judy's face flushed at the thought of paramedics coming in and finding her asleep on the bed with no explanation as to why.

"I remember checking out the room with the EM reader, and then the door started to close, and then... it's like I blacked out."

"But you were on the bed."

Judy shrugged. "I don't know what to tell you. It's ridiculous. I know it is."

Lisa told her about what had happened to the lights when she'd come upstairs to check on her, and then the woman she'd seen standing behind Ellis just before his flame extinguished.

"Did you recognise her?"

"Never seen her before. She looked ordinary. Dark hair, pale skin. But there was something about the eyes."

"What like?"

"Let me put it this way, I wouldn't want to have a conversation with her. There was something there screaming at me to keep away. A look of madness, anger, and malice." Lisa shivered and tugged a throw from the back of the sofa to wrap around herself. "The heating in this place is rubbish. I should probably call someone out."

"Well, unless it's connected to this apparition."

"And that's what we're calling it now?"

"A ghost, an apparition. Don't suppose it matters what you want to call it. You saw somebody in your house that vanished as soon as the lights came on. The same somebody that you've seen leave your room in the middle of the night. I don't think you've got any reason to suspect your house is anything other than haunted."

To her credit, Lisa didn't try to deny it. She must have suspected that was the reason for the disturbances or else she wouldn't have called in Judy. At least this way, she had another person to confirm what she'd seen. At least Lisa could take comfort in knowing she wasn't mad or seeing things.

"What did your equipment tell you in my bedroom?"

"Only what we already know. It picked up strong signals in there. And for a moment, I thought I saw somebody as well."

"This woman?"

"It was dark. Hard to say for certain. And then the door started to close even though I'd propped it open with my rucksack." Judy racked her brain, thinking of the moment the door had closed on her, and that nebulous feeling of not being alone. Had there been anyone else in the room? "Maybe you should move out. Go live with your parents for a bit."

"Not sure that's the best idea. I don't think Dad will want me there. And besides, what would I say? That I need somewhere to stay because my house is haunted?"

"Then come and stay at mine. We've a spare bedroom."

Lisa shook her head. "No. It's fine. This thing is annoying, but I don't see that it can harm me. It's had the opportunity and so far, it's done nothing but show itself a couple of times. Perhaps I'll not find out what it wants unless I stay."

"And what if it wants nothing other than to scare you? Or this might be the first stage of it trying to hurt you. It might not be strong enough yet. They say that some spirits draw their energy from the people and places they inhabit. It might be building strength before it can attack."

"God, do you think so?" Lisa pulled the throw tighter around her.

"You know I've not been doing this very long. I am only getting this from the internet."

A thin smile appeared on Lisa's lips. "You're doing a better job than I am. What happened to you at that hospital you visited? Jemma told me you were there the night it caught fire."

Looked like she'd be needing to have more words with Jemma about who she could talk to about Ravenmeols.

"It was an organised ghost hunt. Only there were some fanatical people behind the event. They'd tricked us to go along."

Lisa frowned. "Oh my God. Who were these people?"

"They were part of a cult. In the seventies they were all over that hospital in positions of authority. Using the patients in their rituals."

"Sounds barbaric. How come that wasn't in the papers?"

Judy shrugged. "If you look in the right places on the internet, you'll be able to read all about it."

"And did they hurt you?"

Judy remembered that night with total recall. The night had ended with being trapped, chained in the occultists' inner sanctum, waiting to be possessed by adherents from the Almost Realm. Suddenly, she felt cold and brought her arms together, bringing them around her front in an act of comfort.

"Yes. They hurt us." She forced a smile, eager to change the subject. "I've got to get going. I promised Jemma I wouldn't be late."

"So, what's next? About my ghost?"

"I've left the EM reader in your room, along with a thermometer and some talcum powder."

"Talcum powder?"

"It will eliminate the possibility of a physical presence causing the interference. Dead people don't leave footprints."

Lisa nodded. Even though they were certain that this had nothing to do with Ellis or his girlfriend anymore, it didn't hurt to make sure that Ellis wasn't contributing to the problem.

"I'd also suggest locking your door at night."

"Can't do that. Jasper needs to get in and out."

"You could lock him in the kitchen. Give him a bed. He's got his food and water and his cat flap. He'll be fine."

"He'll cry like a baby. I won't get any sleep if I do that."

Judy nodded. "OK. But maybe put something behind the door so it won't open all the way."

"Good point."

"And there's one other thing you could do. I tried to find a tape recorder that would record you throughout the night. But I couldn't get hold of one today. How about setting your phone to record? You said you heard someone moving around in your room. Perhaps that will pick up something."

"OK. I'll do that." The pair of them stood and Lisa embraced Judy. "Thank you for believing me."

"Of course, I believe you. And you've no need to thank me. We're family."

After Judy had left, Lisa told Ellis she was off to bed. He looked ready for bed himself but was turning on the Xbox instead.

"Was she OK?" he asked.

"Yeah, fine. Nothing to worry about."

"Great."

And that was that. Her housemate didn't seem concerned about anything. The strange behaviour with the lights earlier had been put down to some unknown thing that Judy had done to Lisa's laptop—a dodgy power pack tripping the consumer unit. Lisa hadn't bothered to point out that if the consumer unit had tripped, it would have needed resetting, but the lights had come back on before that had happened. Whatever helped Ellis cope with the oddity of the situation was fine with her. She wasn't ready to tell him it all now. And besides, if this house was haunted, it didn't seem to be causing him any issues. Why put the pressure on him? She needed his contribution to the rent and hated the idea of having to find somebody else to come instead. It was comforting to be around Ellis, despite everything that had happened between them.

Upstairs, she found the EM reader and the bottle of talc on the bedside table. She picked up the talc then thought better of it. If she sprinkled that on the floor, Jasper would walk his footprints across her room and out onto the landing. Ellis would notice and that would lead to more silly questions. Idly, she switched on the EM reader, and her heart raced a little as all five lights illuminated before extinguishing. Judy hadn't even explained to her what to do with it. What good would it do to use this to detect any paranormal presence? She already knew that there was a presence. She set that device aside as well.

Recording her whilst sleeping was the least worst idea Judy had suggested. She could use her voice recording app that came pre-installed onto the phone, but that would mean having to play back all seven or so hours of her sleeping to find out if it had picked up anything interesting. She didn't have the time nor patience for that.

Instead, she flicked through other recording apps, and came across a sleep recorder app. The rating wasn't great, three and a half stars out of five, but they were mainly complaining about too many ads in the app. She didn't care about that. The feature that she most cared about was that the app was sound activated, only retaining sections of audio above a certain volume threshold. It was meant to help people who talked in their sleep to understand how bad a problem they had, or those with snoring problems.

Yes, that app sounded like just the thing. She hit install and watched the progress bar fill up.

13

There was someone close. She could almost feel their breath on her neck. It smelt of all the bad things she could think of. The last bits of bin juice when emptying the bins, the stench of rancid meat left at the bottom of the meat drawer in the fridge. And the smell was all over her.

"Stop it."

The someone was closer now.

Lisa's eyes snapped open and she couldn't see a thing. The blackness of her vision was darker than the darkness of the night. Her heart was beating so fast, too fast, and she could feel it, no she could hear it smashing against the inside of her ribs, like a desperate animal trying to escape its cage. She'd felt like this before. The night terrors that used to wake her up screaming as a young girl. Those nights were over thirty years ago and since leaving home, she'd not had them since. She'd always put it down to wanting her freedom.

Medication helped.

But she wasn't taking anything new now. Her collection of drugs had decreased this last year and she no longer felt like she was rattling around in the morning.

But this darkness. She tried to move, but it was no good. Of course, it would be no good. What was the point of a night terror that you could escape from by leaving the bed? She was trapped, immobile under her duvet, her arms pinned down by her sides.

Pinned down.

That's what it felt like. Pressure above her elbows, right on the fleshy part of her upper arm, but not just any pressure. Not some random weight, but a real presence pinning her down. Her perception focused on that part of the terror and she discerned hands, then fingers. And that weight on her chest. It shifted like someone was on top of her.

She failed to scream.

She was still paralysed.

The entity. The thing that she'd been seeing these last few weeks. The presence that Judy had felt too, was in here now and sitting on top of her, pinning her down. And she knew only one thing about it.

That it meant to hurt her.

Lisa screamed and this time it snapped her out of the dream.

She howled and fumbled for the light switch on the cable of the lamp by her bed, failed and knocked over her glass of water. Sound was still coming out of her mouth, a loose wailing that could have been pain or laughter, but felt like the world was ending and she was the only one to realise it.

The door barged open and the main light flicked on and Ellis stood in the doorway wearing just his boxer shorts. He took in the mess of her bedside table, the spilt drink.

"What's happening?" His muscles were taut—he didn't stop looking around. Then he ran to the window and checked it was closed, checked all the corners of the room. "What's happening?" he repeated, then lowered his voice as he began to realise that Lisa, the mad housemate, had just had another bad dream.

"Someone, here," she croaked.

And he looked confused at that. He stepped out into the landing, then back into the bedroom. He bent down to pick up the dropped glass, and to right the knocked over lamp, switching it on as he did so. Then he went back to the main light switch and turned that off, leaving them with a level of light they didn't have to blink against.

"There's no one here," he said. "You've had a bad dream."

"It was in here. I felt it on me."

Ellis sat down beside her and let her lean against his bare upper body. She was acutely aware that she was leaning into his naked muscles, but his strength gave her some comfort. To know that there was someone else in the house, real and strong enough to protect her. That was what she needed right now. His arm wrapped around her shoulders and he pulled her onto his shoulder. Letting her sobs subside.

"You're OK. A night terror. I've had a couple in my time. You'll be able to laugh about it in the morning."

She was still sobbing. Her chest was tight, and the sobs came out like half formed gasps, like she was drowning and desperate for air.

After a couple of minutes, Lisa sat back upright and took several deep gulps of air.

"Nina's not here is she?"

"No."

"Thank God."

"Yeah, I don't think she'd have been best pleased that I'm not dressed and in your room."

"I'm sorry."

"You don't need to be."

"I am though. I thought there was someone in here." She turned and sat back in her bed, keeping her eyes level with Ellis's face. The room looked different now. The corners seemed so much closer and so much darker. The shadows were sated for now at least, keeping their distance, watching and waiting.

"It's a night terror. I've had them. Pretty sure everyone's had one."

"I used to get them as a girl. But it was less embarrassing when you only had your parents and brother to convince you weren't mad."

"I don't think you're mad."

"Thank you." But you barely even know me. Not really.

She didn't feel like she was properly in the room yet. Like half of her was still trapped in the dreamworld, unable to escape. Night terrors or sleep paralysis was well enough understood, her parents had taken their time to explain what this all meant to a confused little girl who was convinced that every night someone was in her room trying to hurt her. And she'd had it all, the hands gripping her in the bed, the dark figures standing at the end of the bed watching her. None of this was made any better by their explanations. The part of your brain that can recall this information is suppressed when caught in the middle of the experience, refusing to let the physical reality of the moment interfere with the fear.

But what had irked her the most, was that Phil had experienced the same problems as a child. And she knew he had them because on those rare occasions when she wasn't having them, she'd hear him whimper from across the landing. She'd sometimes be the first one in his room and she'd try to wake him, but her presence was never enough to do that. It would take her dad's reassuring grip to shake him back into the real world.

Phil had never been the centre of her parents' attention when it came to sleep paralysis. Once he'd woken, he would sit and look startled, then nod when he realised what had just happened, before turning the light off himself and rolling over to go back to sleep.

It was never that way with Lisa. It would not be that way with her tonight. She would stay awake with the light on for most of the night and not even try to go back to sleep. With her head the way it was she didn't trust herself that it wouldn't send her back into that terrifying world.

But, things had changed hadn't they? She knew that this wasn't just some random brain quirk that was causing these night terrors. Something caught her eye at the other side of the room. On the dressing table opposite the bed, five solid red lights were illuminated on the EM reader that Judy had brought into the room when she was sweeping for paranormal activity. The lights went out as she looked at them.

"Honestly, Ellis, thank you for checking on me. But I will be fine. I'm just overly tired, and a little hot. It happens the most when I'm hot."

"Do you want me to open the window?"

She nodded, and he complied. Lingering by the open window a moment.

"What's up?" she asked.

"Thought I heard Jasper out there."

She looked around the room. "He's normally in here. I closed the kitchen door. You didn't open it did you? He shouldn't be able to get outside."

"No, I left it open. Well, I think I did. I'll check."

"Thanks," she replied.

Ellis started to leave, then noticed something on her arms and stopped in his tracks. "What are those?"

"What?" Lisa was confused. Ellis was gesturing at her upper arms and only when she looked did she realise what had caught his eye. "Hell. I don't know. What is it?"

Five white marks, spread out like the fingers of a hand. Marks that appeared on both her upper arms, exactly where she'd felt the entity pinning her down.

14

Judy had left Jemma at the church hall for her singing lessons. Her daughter had been enrolled with the same talent group since she was in the first year of primary school and had come such a long way. They say that kids today only want to spend time in front of YouTube and video games, but Judy had never found that to be the case. Yes, Jemma was overly fond of her phone but from what little she could tell, Judy guessed most of that was group chats with her friends. Since coming to the talent group, she'd grown more confident and had a friendship circle outside of her school. Judy wished her parents had cared as much for her own mental health when she was little. Having different social networks was so important, especially today. But whenever she dropped her off and saw how easily she integrated with another group of friends, it made Judy realise how lacking her own social network was. When you hit adulthood, it was so hard to make friends at all. When you had a husband like Phil, it was even harder.

The main shopping area wasn't too busy this morning. Ever since they'd pedestrianised the main shopping street, fewer and fewer people were venturing to the town. It didn't help that Liverpool had its new sprawling shopping mall with the designer stores to entice the public.

The quiet streets suited Judy, and she ambled along. She only had an hour to kill before she needed to pick up Jemma but after entering the third shop and having zero interest in any of the clothes on the rack and being very aware of the state of her bank balance, she resigned to avoid the rest of the shops and wait it out back in the church gardens.

Lisa hadn't been in touch yet, and even though it concerned Judy she assumed that no news was good news in this case. If anything had happened, Lisa would get in touch. If she hadn't heard from her by the end of the weekend, she promised herself she'd get in touch anyway.

Falling asleep on the job was not what she'd imagined her first night as a ghost detective would be like. The bedroom had unnerved her. The entity that had been in the room with her had unnerved her even more. But after the shadowmen and the painting, Judy felt she was tougher than she once was.

Would Seth have done anything differently? She thought he would have been more prepared than she'd been, would have found a way to communicate with the entity. Let it know that it wasn't OK to be lurking around Lisa's bedroom. She pulled out her phone and checked for messages. Would today be the today that he'd return her calls?

No. Judging by her missed calls list, that hadn't yet happened.

On the way to the church, the wind picked up and the light spattering of rain suddenly turned into the worst downpour she'd seen this year, and she hadn't thought to bring a coat. She ducked into the first shop doorway she could find and hid in the porch.

A gentle bell sounded, and the door opened.

"Come inside. You'll get soaked standing there." The voice belonged to a middle-aged man, slim in a well-cut suit and a blue shirt and yellow tie. He wore black-rimmed glasses and there was a hint of stubble that reminded her of those action movie actors that raced around in fast cars. She hated those movies, but thought the actors were pleasant enough on the eye.

Judy hurried inside, the rain still catching her back until the man closed the door. "Where did that come from? The forecast promised blue skies today. Well, at least one of my weather apps did. The other two are often in disagreement."

"Thanks."

"Grab a seat if you like. We're dead today. I don't think we'll get any more customers. Especially not with that going on out there."

Judy was standing in the smallest estate agents she'd probably ever stood in. She hadn't even realised this shop was on this street.

"Don't suppose you're looking to buy?"

"I'm afraid not."

"Shame. I've got some nice properties here." He gestured to the side wall where the particulars for a dozen properties were on display. "And there's more on the website. It's getting harder to get people on the books, though. So many love set fees and want to do it all online, never having to speak to an actual human being. What ever happened to the personal touch? How am I meant to compete with these firms with venture capital money and no staff to speak of? Some days make me wonder why I bother." Then realising that he'd just spent the last two minutes ranting about a business Judy couldn't possibly be interested in, he apologised. "Sorry to bore you. I guess I'm happy to have someone to talk to."

"Just you then?"

"Can't afford anyone else. Carol used to help with all the admin and bookings and could keep the office open whilst I showed houses to people or gave valuations. But things have been slow. It became impossible to justify keeping her on. She was nice about it I suppose. Only threw coffee at me the once and called me a bastard, but it could have been worse I suppose."

Judy couldn't help but smile. "How could it have been worse?"

The man seemed to consider this like it hadn't occurred to him before now. "Could have been hot coffee?" He smiled back, then put out his hand. "Richard Calvert."

He looked at her again, his head tilted. "And now I'm wondering whether we already know each other? Did you go to Ainsdale High School?"

Oh my God, that's where she recognised him from.

"Richard? From Mrs Forbes class? Friends with Russell Brooks?"

He nodded.

"You're Judy Armitage, aren't you? I never forget a face."

The years were ripped away, and she tried to reconcile the middle-aged man before her with the slight skinny image she had of the geek that had been Richard Calvert. She felt the heat of a blush on her cheeks as she remembered the names they used to call him.

Judy took his hand. "It's Judy Doyle now," she replied. "You look great."

"Nope, but you're very kind. You on the other hand haven't aged a day." He had a twinkle in his eye that she couldn't evade. "The rain's not letting off yet. Don't suppose I can get you a coffee."

"You don't have to go out in this. You'll get soaked."

"I wasn't planning to." He was smiling. "I've got a kettle back here. I was going to offer you a cup of instant. Or tea, if you'd prefer. I steer clear of coffee shops. Never know what to order in one of those places. Always feel under pressure to get the right thing but I don't even understand the menu. Truth be told, the last time I tried to order one I couldn't even see the menu, so just grabbed the first thing that came to hand on the counter. Who knew that a gluten-free, nut free, dairy free, breakfast bar could taste as appalling as it sounds. And it cost me the best part of two pounds. Never again. But you will stay for a coffee?"

How could she say no to that? "I've got to pick my daughter up in twenty minutes."

"It's instant. I can have it ready for you in two, and I'll even pour it into a styrofoam cup so you can take it with you."

She nodded. "Thanks, but a mug will be fine."

"One mug of cheap instant coffee it is." And Richard headed out to the back room, leaving the door to the back room open. Judy stepped forwards to get a better look and saw a small corridor with a couple of kitchen cupboards and a kettle and fridge. Another door led off to the side.

That's three doors in this space. She reached for her bag and took out her notebook, then quickly scribbled down the number, date and location. He noticed the notepad. "If you're writing your telephone number, that's a bit soon for me."

He was joking again and even though his sense of humour belonged to the dark ages, she couldn't help but smile at him. It had been a long time since she'd felt this comfortable in another man's company. Too long. She racked her memories, trying to remember what kind of person Richard had been in school. He used to keep apart from the bigger kids, she remembered, preferring to keep his head down and do well in his lessons so he wouldn't have to spend time with the more disruptive kids in the lower sets. If she had been forced to come up with a list of the people she'd been to high school with, she doubted whether Richard would even have made the list.

She moved to the next empty page of her notebook, wrote her name and mobile number, and then tore it carefully from the book.

"You can have my number. Might be fun to catch up." Why not? He was funny. And made her feel relaxed. The casual warmth that came from him melted the gulf of time since they'd last seen each other.

The coffee came quickly as promised. He handed her a mug with giant cartoon letters spelling 'Boss Lady'. She raised an eyebrow. "I don't suppose this was the offending weapon?"

"You'd suppose correctly. So, where's your daughter?"

"She goes to a drama group. Dreams of becoming an actress."

"Good for her. There aren't enough dreamers anymore. Everyone seems so stuck in the fear that it's all doom and gloom and everything will only get worse. We need a bit of hope in our world."

"I didn't say she was any good."

"I'm sure she's perfect. With a mum as charming as you, she'll go far."

Charming. That was only one step away from saying that he found her attractive. She could feel her ear lobes prickling at the thought of Spotty Dicky finding her attractive. Those awkward teenage years were long past him and she realised he wasn't at all bad looking. The suit wasn't what she'd have chosen for him, but at least it fitted him well and wasn't hanging too baggy or too tight. And he looked well-groomed in that old-fashioned sense. There was a light smell of aftershave that she found not unpleasant.

"And you? Have you got any kids?"

She felt herself going red again at being so forward. That was only one question away from asking if there was a significant other, and there was only one reason she might ask such a question.

He didn't even bat an eyelid.

"No. No kids. No wife. No girlfriend. No boyfriend come to that. I'm desperately lonely. Wedded to the business I suppose. Never have any energy left to find someone."

"That's a shame. You know, to be honest, I didn't even realise this shop was here. It's very..."

"Tiny?"

"I would say it blends in with its surroundings. Perhaps a little too well. Maybe a paint job on the outside would be enough to bring more attention."

He shrugged. "Maybe. I could do with selling a few more properties before I put money into the building though."

"I wish I could help you with that."

He took a sip from his own drink and nodded. "Have you got any selling experience?"

"None. I used to work in a school."

"Teacher?"

"Primary children. Put it on hold whilst I started a family." And kept it on hold, she wanted to add, but that came with a layer of bitterness she didn't feel comfortable conveying. A little too personal.

"That's great. Such a hard job I imagine. All league tables and snotty noses isn't it?"

"Something like that."

"You used to do that? What about now?"

"Oh, I'm a lady of leisure now. Trying to get back into it, but to be honest, the job market isn't what it was. School budgets keep getting cut, there's less hiring going on. And my skills are a little out of date."

"I'm sorry. That sucks. And your other half?" He glanced aside as if this wasn't an important question.

"He passed away last year. I don't think you knew Phil. He was in the first year when we were in the fifth."

"I'm sorry to hear that. I mean, no, I didn't know him. Wait, though. Not related to Adrian Doyle at Doyle Lettings?"

"Adrian's my father-in-law. Do you know him?"

"He sometimes uses me to advertise his flats." Richard was frowning.

"What's wrong?"

"Nothing, just, this is all a bit unexpected. I don't keep in touch with anyone from high school."

"No. I know what you mean."

It was unexpected, but that didn't mean she wasn't having a nice time.

She checked her watch. "I'm sorry, but I guess I should pick up Jemma."

"Right. Sorry. Didn't mean to keep you."

But you really weren't.

She set her cup down. "Maybe next time I can get you a drink. Show you around the menu board of the coffee shop."

"I'd like that."

He put out a hand for her to shake, then rather awkwardly, she did that. An odd formal way to end what had turned out to be a friendly chat with another lonely soul.

He held the door open for her. "At least the rain has eased off."

The remaining drizzle didn't look like it would go away any time soon. Richard hurried to the back kitchen and returned with a black umbrella. "Here you go. Take this."

"Oh no, it's fine. Just a bit of rain."

"It's not mine. A customer left it. Can't bear umbrellas. Always getting blown inside out and getting lost. What's the point? But you can take it. I don't think she's coming back for it."

"Thank you."

And then he surprised her by patting her on the back lightly as she left the shop. She walked the next few metres, heading for the church with a lightness to her step, despite the puddles underfoot and the grey sky overhead, today wasn't proving to be as miserable as it had first appeared.

Then she noticed the car three shops down on the opposite side of the road. Adrian's car. He was in there, on his phone. It didn't look like he had noticed her, and she angled her newly acquired umbrella to hide her face as she went past.

But as she went past, she couldn't help but feel that there was something odd about seeing him there. They were nowhere near his office, and he'd never seemed the kind of man to head into town for a bit of light shopping on a Saturday.

That left her with only one niggling thought.

Was Adrian keeping tabs on her?

15

Ellis had gone out to play five-a-side leaving Lisa in the house on her own. It had taken her a while to find Jasper and when she did; he was outside, sat by the shed, licking his paws. He looked like he'd been out here all night. His fur was wet and his face dropped into that petulant standoffish face that only cats could pull off.

The kitchen door had been open when she'd got up so she couldn't think of any reason he would have kept away. She picked him up. His paws were black with dirt and smudged on her dressing gown, but he compliantly let her tip him onto his back to hold him like a baby and give him a cuddle. Taking him towards the house, he got fidgety and started to kick up a stink, wrestling free of her grip. She let him drop and watched him wander to the shed where he resumed his skulking by its base, eyeing her distrustfully.

"What's wrong with you, puss?" Lisa continued watching the cat for a few seconds, curious to see what he might do next. Was he ill? They'd always had cats when she was growing up and they'd keep to themselves if they were feeling ill. The girl cats when having bladder problems could be very vocal and would keep themselves close to the litter tray. Jasper didn't have a tray, preferring to use outside. Was that why he was being so keen to stay out? She'd have to monitor him.

Inside, she showered and put on some fresh clothes, thinking of what had happened last night with the lights and Judy. In her naivety, Lisa had hoped that simply by having Judy come over, she'd get to the bottom of the problem. Even now, she didn't want to call it a haunting, but that's what it was, wasn't it? There was no point in denying that the activity they'd seen over the last week could be anything other than paranormal.

As she tidied her room she called out, "Are you here now? What do you want?"

She paused in making the bed, listening for any stray sound that might indicate she wasn't alone. The shower head across the landing dripped, a light wind ruffled the bushes below her window, but there was nothing out of the ordinary. It was disappointing in a way. Making peace with the entity was not what she wanted. It had to go. She couldn't continue living in the same house as a ghost.

Ellis had only briefly mentioned last night's events before he'd gone out. He was more amused than anything about Judy—Lisa had told him Judy had fallen asleep on her bed. But he was also concerned that the wiring would need to be checked and if found to need replacing, he reckoned they were looking at several thousand pounds, not including all the hassle of the mess and needing to decorate afterwards. He was at least honest with her when he said that he didn't think he'd renew his house sharing agreement if it came to that.

Who would blame him? He was still all over Nina from the office and wanted her to stay over this weekend. Lisa didn't object and promised to be on her best behaviour.

Her phone beeped a notification, and she picked it up from the bedside table. The app she'd used last night to record her sleeping was reminding her that she hadn't reviewed the recording yet and there were three points of interest.

Three? Right. She sat down and unlocked the screen. The app was still open and running. She stopped it and saw the three points listed with stars on the first page of the app.

What was she expecting to hear? She'd already seen enough to know that the house was haunted. This proved nothing she didn't already know. And then with shame she checked the time on the first moment of interest. Just when she'd been screaming and scared Ellis into her bedroom. She skipped that point and checked out the other two. In the first, she could hear herself snoring rather loudly. Embarrassing. She hoped that it wasn't loud enough to ever disturb Ellis. He'd said nothing, but she left the bedroom door open so there was no chance of him missing it.

The last starred moment was an hour before she woke up. Tentatively, she pressed the playback button and listened.

There was heavy breathing. God, was that what she sounded like when asleep? That was not a good sound. It was like an asthmatic air conditioning unit. If she were to ever find a boyfriend, she'd have to find some way to put a stop to that. Next came a noise she couldn't quite hear but thought it might be the creak of the door opening. She paused playback and searched in her bottom drawer for a pair of headphones. She normally kept some in here for when she went running.

She plugged them in and rewound the playback to the beginning. The breathing sounded worse this time, now that she could hear it so well. And next came the noise. Definitely the door opening. Maybe it was Jasper. He sometimes did things like that, rubbing his cheeks on the hard surface, not caring what he might knock over as a consequence. A floorboard creaked. Not Jasper then. Even he with his overeating wasn't heavy enough to make the floorboards creak in her room. She shivered, and pushed back against the headboard, pulling a pillow from behind her to hold in front of her. Despite this being a recording, it was still disturbing to hear the sounds from her room from last night. A kind of minor time travel was happening here. Same location different time. There was a noise that sounded like someone talking. She couldn't be sure so paused the playback and increased the volume to maximum, then cued the recording back a few seconds.

When she heard the words again, she almost cried out, but instead she clamped a hand in front of her mouth to stop her own panic escaping. The words were clear, but worse than that, they were familiar.

"Go back to sleep," the voice said.

Lisa shut the app down and hid under the duvet cover.

Jemma frowned. "Is it about what happened with the woman last year?"

"What woman?" Judy said, acting like she'd forgotten the woman who'd followed Jemma home then threatened her. That had been the week of the Adherents' painting and no charges had been brought against anybody. She'd reported the incident to police, but they hadn't got back to her and Jemma hadn't been pushing for a resolution. As far as she was concerned, it had been a one off from some nut job who'd wanted to scare a schoolgirl.

"Don't mess. We both know who I'm talking about."

Judy nodded. "I know you think I'm overprotective, but you know as well as I that we've been involved in some scary situations this year. I don't want to risk you getting into anything dangerous. I like to know where you are. I'd take you to school every day if you'd let me."

Jemma didn't argue. They'd had the conversation before, and Jemma had pointed out that parents didn't drop their kids off at high school unless they wanted their kids to get bullied. Besides, going to school with her friends gave them the chance to catch up before going into lessons. It was a good thing that Judy wasn't prepared to risk. Friends were important and Judy was determined that Jemma make as many as possible.

"I just feel that sometimes I'm a burden. That you're just sat waiting around for me."

"Never think that. You're never a burden. You're my special girl. Always will be. You know I'd do anything for you."

For a while, they ate in silence, content to simply be in each other's company. Nothing more needed saying.

*

Back home, Jemma got straight on the Xbox and loaded up Fortnite, putting a headset on and joining three friends already online. It had become a regular Saturday afternoon ritual and despite it being a socialising she'd never experienced when at school, Judy didn't mind it at all. If this meant she could spend time with her friends doing something they all enjoyed, and she knew where her daughter was, she considered that a win-win situation.

Judy had something she wanted to do. It had been on her mind since the dinner with the in-laws and now seemed as good a time as any to get it over with. She fetched the pole she kept in the airing cupboard and unhooked the loft panel before lowering the ladder.

Phil's stuff was in the loft and she wanted to check something out.

She climbed the ladder and poked her head into the darkness as she reached for the light switch. Whoever had installed the loft hatch had placed the switch on the roof framing inside the loft itself meaning you had to embrace the darkness for a few seconds whilst finding it. She flicked it on and the single bulb above her head banished the shadows.

She normally only came up here at Christmas to get the decorations down. Phil had no interest in helping decorate the house at Christmas and would always leave for the pub when the first weekend of December arrived. He would only ever get in the way, so Judy was glad that he didn't interfere. The way they operated was Judy would decorate, buy whatever new decorations she wanted for the year, then Phil would return, inebriated and nod at what she'd done. There was never any praise or thank yous. It was just a job that needed doing and he didn't mind the house looking like a grotto for a few weeks as long as he didn't have to lift a finger to help.

This last Christmas had been their first without him. Adrian and Faith had invited Judy and Jemma around to spend the day with them, but even without asking Judy knew that would not work. A full day for Jemma away from her own things would be more stressful and less fun. And frankly, Judy could do without the pressure to look happy in their presence.

The loft had been mostly boarded, so Judy was free to move around up here. Under the eaves, the insulation looked like it could do with replacing. A faded yellow that looked like the birds had been in here stealing bits for nests. It was only head height in the exact middle of the loft and as she moved to the edges, she needed to stoop.

She didn't know exactly what she was looking for, only that Phil had kept some of his private papers up here, where he could keep them safe. It wasn't that he didn't trust her not to go through them, that was always an unspoken rule. But Phil had been a great one for his own privacy and he'd often be taking his own boxes of papers up into the loft. If there was anything about the adoption that might help Lisa, it would be in one of his boxes. Judy just needed to find it.

Music blasted from beneath her. Sounds from the eighties crashed through the ceiling under her feet and into her space, disorientating her.

"Jemma, do you need it that loud?" Judy shouted down and considered stamping her feet on the loft boards, but she had no idea how strong they were or how well fixed to the joists they were. Falling through the ceiling was not on her bucket list.

The music didn't stop. Judy rolled her eyes and sighed, trying not to get annoyed. It didn't matter. Choose your battles.

Past the boxes of Christmas decorations, she stumbled across a collection of empty packaging from the various computers and televisions they'd bought over the years. They never seemed to get rid of these, keeping them in case the equipment needed to go back under warranty. In reality that never happened, and the empty boxes kept piling up. Some old carpet, leftovers from Jemma's bedroom, and a section from the lounge had been rolled up and dropped under the eaves, resting on top of the roof insulation. God only knows why they kept it. If the carpet in either of those rooms got damaged enough to need bits replacing, there wasn't enough here to replace the whole thing, and neither Judy nor Phil had ever been skilled enough to know how to patch up. It was just one of those things that people kept in their lofts. Remnants. Preparing for the worst.

At the back of the loft, on the far wall above Judy's bedroom, Phil had installed some stacked shelving. There was plenty of clutter on here as well. Boxes of photos from a time when they'd get their photos developed rather than staring at them on an iPad. Idly, she lifted the lid from one box and pulled out an album. It was from a holiday they'd taken to Greece over twenty years ago, way before Jemma had been born. The smiles in the photo had been genuine enough. They'd been good together. A relationship that held to certain rules and boundaries, but that was needed to keep it all moving in the right direction. Phil had been a firm believer in household roles, and she knew that within weeks of first meeting him. That hadn't put her off him, in fact, she enjoyed the idea that he was such a traditionalist, that he wanted to be the family provider, the breadwinner. Nothing wrong with wanting to look after my family, he'd say. And for a time, he was right. There was nothing wrong with it at all.

She put the album back and replaced the lid. It was depressing to see the colours on those photos, aging even in their albums in the loft. They were from a different time, a different place. And it made her uneasy.

Scanning along the shelves, she passed other objects she'd forgotten about. The box with Jemma's baby clothes from her first week, a bag with pressed flowers from her wedding bouquet. souvenirs from their honeymoon. There was so much here that she'd forgotten or had pretended had never existed.

The music stopped from Jemma's room and the silence was even more disconcerting.

"You should see some of this stuff, Jemma. Come up if you want." She spoke loudly enough for Jemma to hear her through the open hatch, but there was no reply. She must have gone back down, another round of Fortnite.

The box she'd been looking for was on the bottom shelf. She paused before pulling it out. This was one of Phil's boxes she'd left alone, thinking that Jemma might appreciate some of her dad's things when she was older.

A car alarm sounded on the street outside, the clamour travelling easily into the loft through the roof. She heard voices from the street, then the beep of a car remote and the alarm stopped. Despite knowing there were people so close, she suddenly felt very removed from the world.

She carried the box closer to the hatch and the single light bulb. The light from the bulb wasn't bright enough to illuminate the loft space completely. There were curtains of blackness around the periphery and the bulb's glare remained a faint glow by the shelving. She needed to go through this box carefully, and she'd do that downstairs in the kitchen. But her curiosity was such, that she couldn't resist peeking now.

Inside the box, on the very top, was a notebook. A plain black moleskine. Phil had used these every day of his working life. He never completely trusted gadgets to record his appointments or his notes, so notebooks became very much an extension of him. A habit he said he'd picked up from his dad.

Her fingers brushed against the cover and a tingle ran across her spine. It had been a while since she'd touched anything so personal to her husband.

A creak from the ladder made her catch her breath. "Jemma, are you coming up?"

No reply. Judy stood, almost knocking her head on one of the overhead joists, then stood to peer over the edge. There was no one there.

A whisper across the back of her neck made her spin around. What was that by the far wall? A shadow? The shadow moved and Judy almost fell down the loft opening in her haste to move away.

But it was nothing. Just shadows as she got in the way of the loft's single light bulb.

Stop overreacting.

Settling back down again, she flicked open the notebook. It was his most recent.

The dates were neatly recorded on the top line of each page in his tiny black handwriting. Looked like he was using this as a diary with his appointments for the day. Working for his dad, he had a lot of appointments to show clients around letting properties, but he was also involved in managing renovation projects on newly acquired properties.

She flicked through the pages, curious as to this part of Phil's life that she never had a chance to investigate. Then she saw the comments under a heading called 'Reflections'.

Dad was being an arse with me again. Called me a dickhead in front of the rest of the office.

Then a few days later.

Surprised to find Hampton Street listed in an old ledger. I thought we'd got rid of those rentals years ago and couldn't see any record of any rentals. Asked Dad about it and he screamed at me like I'd just scratched his car. Furious that I'd gone through his filing cabinet. Seriously, I don't know why I carry on with his shit.

Judy's stomach dropped, and she wanted to sit down and take it in. She'd always suspected Adrian treated Phil badly, but they never spoke about it. This was an insight into her dead husband's mind, and she wasn't sure she liked what she was reading.

She thought about putting the book back and forgetting about his notebooks. That's not what she was looking for, she was after paperwork relating to the adoption. Something that she could pass onto Lisa. But she flicked through, not able to stop herself. She found the blank pages at the end and flicked through the week before.

Then her heart shuddered at the words she'd caught in his reflections paragraph.

The woman was in my room again tonight. I think she wants me dead.

17

Judy had brought Phil's box from the loft and into the kitchen. Jemma hadn't shifted from her Xbox game and despite that making it a couple of hours play, Judy didn't feel the need to ask her to take a break. She didn't want Jemma to see her dad's stuff, not until Judy had had the chance to go through it and filter away anything she thought might caught upset.

The woman was in my room again tonight.

That line bothered her the most. It was bizarre to think he might be talking about the same thing Lisa was experiencing at her house, but it almost made perfect sense at the same time. How long had this been going on? And how many nights had she spent in the same bed as him when he was scared by this thing haunting him?

And he never ever said a word to her about it.

Was that just like Phil, keeping his feelings to himself until it suited him? No one knew her husband like she did. Not his parents, not his twin sister. But now it seemed that she didn't know him as well as she thought she did.

After making a drink, she took the book out from the box and sat down, taking more time to read through the contents. The book covered a little under six months, from the last year of his life, the period before he gave up because of his cancer. She found only one reference to his terminal condition. The 7th May, a note:

Cancer. Crap.

And a week later, the entries stopped completely. She continued looking and found another two entries relating to the woman in the bedroom. Both were factual, neither revealing what he might have experienced or how he felt about things. The first read:

She watched me from the end of the bed. She didn't move. We stared each other out. Then I fell asleep again.

The second read:

I saw her in the early evening. I'd come out of the shower and she was there in the bathroom mirror. I dropped my shaving mirror and cut myself on the glass.

Judy remembered that evening. Phil had been getting ready to go out with his running club and had come down looking for plasters in the first aid box, getting irritated when the only ones he could find had Fortnite characters on them. That almost escalated to a row but Peter, his running buddy rang the doorbell and distracted him. Upstairs in the bathroom, he'd left the broken mirror by the sink. The useless oaf hadn't even bothered to tidy it away, not minding that Judy or Jemma could have cut themselves on the glass. And had she felt something that evening? Even knowing that Phil had left the house, there had been a pressure, a weight on her mind that she couldn't quite nail down. Like the idle worry of going shopping and not remembering the last thing on the shopping list, the thing that had driven you to go shopping in the first place. That bathroom should have still been warm with the steam from the near-scalding showers that Phil liked to take. There was mist still on the bathroom mirrors built into the medicine cabinet. And the windows were closed despite it helping to get rid of the inevitable condensation that would form.

It had been freezing.

Judy had picked up the broken pieces of mirror and wrapped them as carefully as she could in folded toilet tissue, before depositing them in the bathroom bin. Only, she hadn't been careful enough as she'd cut her finger on the edge of one of the shards where a thin sliver of crimson appeared. And when she'd sucked the blood from her finger and taken a fresh sheet of toilet paper to stem the blood, hadn't there been a moment when she'd convinced herself she wasn't alone? Hadn't she called out to Jemma, thinking that she must have just walked past the open bathroom door?

Whatever had happened in that room, she'd dismissed it and never mentioned it to Phil or Jemma.

How many other times had she almost caught sight of something out of the corner of her eye? Or heard a noise from one room in the house, thinking it had been Jemma, only to discover that Jemma had been in another part of the house entirely?

She put down the journal. She didn't want to see anymore. Was her house haunted?

The doorbell rang.

Malc was standing there with a concerned look. "Can I come in?"

*

He refused a drink, but Judy took some biscuits out the cupboard anyway. She needed some sugar after going through Phil's notebook—a little bit of a pick me up.

"How's things?" she asked.

"They've been better," he admitted. "Georgia has been keeping her distance from me this week. She cancelled my time with Joe. Said she had too much on and Joe was getting upset with all the toing and froing. I told her that he could stay at the vicarage for a couple of nights and I'd drop him at school on Monday morning but that didn't go down well at all. She is becoming a complete test."

"She probably didn't want him in the vicarage. Truth be told, it gives me the creeps going there knowing what happened. From her point of view, it makes total sense to keep away."

"But it will never go away." He scratched his eyebrow. "I've thought of leaving the area, starting again with Georgia. Ask to be transferred to a new parish."

"Do you think that will make any difference?"

He shrugged and she could see the tiredness there. The lazy movement that reminded her of an older man. "Maybe."

"I don't think it's the vicarage that's the problem. You were keeping a pretty big secret from her for most of your marriage."

"I did that to protect her."

"I guess we all find reasons why we keep things secret. The other party doesn't want to hear excuses though. They just want things back to how they were with the secrets excised from memory."

It was then that Malc seemed to consider the box on the table and gestured. "I've interrupted you."

"Just some of Phil's things. I found it in the loft." And then she wondered how much she should share with Malc. It was personal, but it was in his specialist subject and whilst she thought she knew what she was doing, her experience at Lisa's house showed that she didn't know half as much as she thought she did.

Carefully, she took out Phil's notebook and passed it to Malc, who took it surprised. "And you're showing me this because?"

"Phil always kept his notebooks. When he worked for his dad at the letting company, he used them for appointments and observations about the day. I'd never seen inside them before."

Malc raised an eyebrow. "Until today."

"Uh-huh, that's right. I wanted to see whether he had anything related to his adoption. Something that I could pass onto Lisa that might help her find her birth parents."

"What did you find?"

She shook her head. "I didn't even get that far. I brought it down out of the loft when I read some things I didn't much like." She leaned across and flicked through to the notebook pages she'd folded the topmost corners on. Handy bookmarks so she could remind herself she hadn't been dreaming. She told Malc to read each of the notes on the three pages she'd marked and then watched his expression as he did so.

He looked up at her when he'd finished. "Was he recording his dreams?"

"No. Not the type. Too pragmatic for that. These things happened to him." And she told him about the time in the bathroom when she'd been convinced she hadn't been alone.

"Do you think maybe you've got a little too caught up in your sister-in-law's problems?"

"I saw something at Lisa's house as well. And earlier, when I was in the loft, I don't think I was alone."

His face pinched in alarm. "Not shadowmen?"

But she had already anticipated his question and was shaking her head. "No. Not at all. I've felt a presence in this house several times, but I've always put it down to stress or an over active imagination. Malc, I think Phil was haunted by the same entity that's haunting his sister now. I think it might be haunting us both."

If she'd expected Malc to leap to his feet and jump to her rescue, perhaps grabbing a bottle of holy water and a bible before blessing the house, she was disappointed.

"You think your house is haunted?"

"Do you?"

He shook his head. "I'm sorry, but I'm not feeling anything unusual here. What about Jemma?"

"I'm sure as hell not going to mention any of this to Jemma."

"You don't have to tell her what you've told me. Ask her if she's seen anything odd."

She thought about it. "After what we've been through, there is no way I could broach the subject and not have her freak out on me. It was problematic enough getting her back here after last time."

"But, if she'd experienced anything unusual, she'd have told you?"

There was a long pause, then Judy said, "Yes, I suppose she would."

"And she hasn't."

"No, she hasn't."

Malc put the notebook back on top of the collection of papers then stood as if to leave. But he wasn't about to leave.

He'd come around for a reason and it wasn't to moan about his wife. There was something else going on here. Should she nudge him or let him broach what was troubling him in his own time?

"I don't suppose you've heard from Seth?"

The question surprised her. Not so much that it was about Seth, but because of what it implied. Something's happened, she thought, and you're worried about your friend.

"Not a peep. I'd ask you the same but I'm guessing you haven't either."

"It's probably nothing. Just unusual for him to remain out of contact."

"Do you think he's OK?"

"He's working for Vigilance. I'm hopeful they'll be looking after him."

"Hopeful isn't resounding reassurance."

He looked at her and slipped a hand into his pocket, fetching his car keys. "I'll drop by the house. The collection needs him."

The collection. A dangerous basement full of occult artefacts that Seth's uncle had collected over most of the later part of his life. The entire collection was bequeathed to Seth when his uncle died but since Seth had been in contact with the Vigilance Society, the responsibility for looking after the artefacts should have been shared between them and Seth.

Judy had dropped by several times at his house and had yet to find Seth there. Usually an officious guy would answer the door and claim that Seth wasn't at home, but he'd relay a message. She'd taken the hint after a few wasted trips and followed up with Seth with a few angry text messages. The replies came but had become shorter and less meaningful.

Judy told Malc all of this, and he listened and looked thoughtful, then his face crumpled in concern.

"You're still in contact with him though?"

"I guess so, barely," she answered, although a dark thought had crept into her mind. What if those messages weren't even coming from him?

18

"There's someone to see you." Meg from reception said, her voice full of the Monday sadness that usually surrounded the girl. She was probably on minimum wage and yet still managed to get hammered every single weekend. If you were foolish enough to stop and shoot the breeze with her on a Monday morning, she would hit you with every story.

Lisa had avoided that today and had slunk into work feeling dreadful and empty at the same time. It was as if her insides had been scooped out and she'd been left with a shell of a human to animate and play house in. She hated this feeling. She hated the weird atmosphere that had developed between her and Ellis, and worst of all she was hating herself again. Previous bouts of depression had taken her months to come around from. She'd only been on a reduced dose of Setraline for the last three months and that had been against her doctor's advice. She'd threatened her that if she didn't reduce the dosage she was going to reduce the dosage herself and see where that would end.

Lisa knew full well where it would end, and she did not want to get readmitted to the sad farm again. Once was quite enough. Enough with the quietly spoken nurses and doctors who always wanted the best for you and wanted you to share your feelings. But then the pills would come around and the group therapy sessions would be encouraged, and before you knew it, you were acclimatised.

Lisa didn't want to be acclimatised ever again.

The person waiting for her was her dad. Her first thought was that something bad had happened to Mum. His sad eyes glanced at her when she entered reception before fixating once again on the envelope in his hand. Her second thought was that he was here to apologise for his short behaviour at the restaurant.

"Hi, I was passing, thought I'd drop in."

"It's a little early for me to take a lunch break, but if you want to grab a coffee?"

She hugged him and the embrace was good. In that precious few seconds, she was safe again.

Downstairs, there was a decent coffee shop that the other offices in the building all shared.

"I'll just fetch my pass."

Ellis spotted her as she was heading back out and she told him she had a quick errand to run but would take it out of her lunch. He spotted her dad in the reception area, leaning against the reception desk, talking to Meg and he raised an eyebrow. "Take your time."

Lisa's dad paid for the drinks, and he even bought her a huge slice of cheesecake whilst abstaining like she was some baby who needed treating. It all stunk of something not being right between them.

It could be an apology, she thought. But when had he ever last apologised for anything?

"I'm sorry," he said.

And there it was.

"Sorry?"

"You're going to make me spell it out, aren't you? I can't say I blame you. I know I wasn't especially nice to you at dinner and that it must have been a big deal for you to want to talk about it." He picked up a sachet of sugar and ripped off the end before upending it into his black Americano. "I'm sorry I made it awkward for you. If I could turn back time, I would."

He looked up at her, searching for something in her expression, but she was careful not to give anything away.

"You've nothing to apologise for." Apart from humiliating me in front of Phil's wife and my niece. Neither of whom will look at me again without pity in their eyes for as long as they live.

"You're being polite, and I appreciate that, but you've got to let me take the blame for this. I hate that this has become a thing between us," he pressed.

"This thing is a big deal for me."

"Yes. I know."

"I don't want to upset you or Mum."

"I know that too."

"And you should know that I will continue looking for my birth parents with or without your help."

He shifted his weight on the chair and adjusted his tie. Why did he wear a tie to work when he owned the business? If Lisa ever got her own digital marketing company, she would ensure that everyone felt comfortable in what they wore. The tie was just another attempt at keeping authority pressing down on his employees. Besides, it was a ghastly tie. Mum must have bought it.

"And you're right to do that. It's what I would do if I was in your position."

"Right. So, we're agreed then, that I should continue looking?" Damnit, why did that slip out? She would not ask for his permission.

"This is your life we're talking about. I'll do what I can to help."

She wanted to ask him about the locked office, but that would only let him know that she'd tried to look around his personal space without his permission. There was no way she'd come away from that looking good.

"Great. Thank you."

She put her hand out to his and their fingers met, his curling around her hand. She liked that feeling and hated herself for thinking badly of him. He wasn't a bad man. He'd done all he could to provide for them. Hell, not even just provide. He'd given them all a great life through working hard at his business. She was too young to remember him in the early days when he was struggling to pay the bills and the repayment of the business loan he'd taken out to get the letting agency started. But even then, they'd spent as much time as possible away enjoying the caravan, making sure they all had good quality family time together.

Adrian gestured at the cheesecake. "Are you going to eat that or not? It's killing me to wait."

"You could have got your own piece."

"Your mum is watching my figure for me. I wouldn't get through the front door before confessing."

Lisa smiled and picked up her fork. The cheesecake looked delicious. A vanilla filling with a layer of sliced raspberries tumbling over the edge. This wouldn't last more than a minute. Her stomach grumbled in anticipation as she sliced the edge of her fork through the cushiony cakey goodness.

"Are you not going to ask me what I've got here?" Adrian lifted his hand up from the envelope he'd had with him since the office and had been placed beside his coffee on the table with no explanation.

The cheesecake never made it to her lips. Instead, she lowered her fork and stared at the envelope, her heart beating a little faster as she contemplated its contents.

"What's in the envelope?" she asked.

"It's all I have on the adoption. It's the paperwork you've been asking for."

Lisa struggled to keep from bursting into tears. With her right hand, she brushed aside the plate with the cheesecake and stared into her father's eyes.

"I can see it?"

"You can have it. It's nothing I need to keep physical copies of now. I've copies of all of it on my computer."

"And this is what you got when you adopted me?"

"That's what I said. It's the paperwork from your adoption. All of it, in there to help you out."

She didn't know what to say. The tears still wanted to come, but she held them back with a Herculean effort. The tears would slow her down when she had a million questions to ask.

Adrian pushed the envelope across the table with the tip of his finger. She noticed the bit nail and the scratched skin around the edges of his finger. A nervous habit that he'd had since a child. It had always freaked her out a little when she was growing up as there were rarely any days when there wasn't a speck of blood on his finger, or a lifted fleck of white skin, ready for him to scratch off with the nail of his other hand.

Then he tapped the envelope with the same finger. "It's all in there, what we have. All of it. But—"

But? What do you mean there's a but? There can't be a but. That's not fair.

Adrian continued. "We used a private adoption agency. They were starting to become a thing in certain parts of the country in an effort to support social services's rather inadequate offering. Social services weren't interested in placing anybody with us as your mother had foolishly admitted in our initial interview that we were still trying for a child of our own. She thought it would show how dedicated we were to wanting kids, that despite all the miscarriages, we were determined and would do whatever it took.

"Whatever it took is not what the social services wanted to hear. It took a while for us both to realise that we wouldn't get very much farther with the social services adoption process, but I wasn't about to let your mother down. It wasn't her fault they are a bunch of wankers."

Lisa winced. It was rare to hear her dad swear.

"What did you do?" Because there was something coming that she didn't want to hear. But she had to hear it because if she didn't, she might just explode.

The lights flickered in the cafe. They were using those trendy antique light bulbs, hanging them low over each table with a copper shade around each one. It was barely enough light as it was but when the lights flickered, she squinted towards the back of the shop where the owners were looking at each other in surprise. Then just as she was turning her head back to her dad, she saw the figure in the shadows through the open doorway leading to the back kitchen. She froze at the sight and a chill ran across her back.

"Lisa?"

Her dad's voice pulled her back and she frowned, wondering whether she would need to call work and tell them she would take the afternoon off sick. There was a delicate tension in the front of her head, right between the eyes, that threatened to become something far worse if she didn't get herself into a darkened room and lie down.

"Lisa?" Her dad again, this time the insistent voice was accompanied by a touch of his hand on her forearm. "What's the matter?"

"Nothing," she said, "I'm fine."

"You look pale."

"I might be coming down with something."

"Let me get you home."

"No. Please, tell me what you were going to tell me."

He hesitated, and she thought he would ignore her request and manhandle her out of the cafe and back home like she was a little girl being disobedient in a public place. But you still have this thing you want to tell me. No, not want, you NEED to tell me.

"Let me know if I can get you anything."

"I will. Now, back to the adoption. What did you do when you realised social services weren't going to proceed with you?"

"I lied to your mum. You mustn't tell her. She has always believed I pulled some strings with a friend I knew at university and got us back moving down the approved channel with social services, but I didn't. I found us a private adoption company instead. Don't tell her. It's not worth upsetting her."

"But why does it matter?"

"Because she's always found reasons to blame herself for not being able to have children. I don't want her to think I went to extra expense to get us children. I don't want her to think that I bought you."

I know he didn't literally mean that he bought us, but is that what this amounts to? Isn't that effectively what the super-rich celebrities do? Make generous donations to poor adoption companies to get their names to the top of the list?

Maybe it wasn't like that at all. Maybe it was just a simple case of using a new private adoption company. But still, Lisa felt uneasy. Was this what he meant when he said there wouldn't be the happy ending to this story?

"We never met your parents. But we know that they were struggling for a long time with employment and that money was always tight. Their family was not the kind they could have gone to for support either. Adoption to them, was a way of getting you and Phillip into a new life that they couldn't afford to show you, and, maybe it would get them out of the financial abyss they'd stumbled into."

"Where were they from? Were they local?"

"No. They came over from Ireland. They were living in South Manchester. He was a factory worker, laid off three weeks after they found out she was pregnant."

"And my mother? What did she do?"

"Occasional bar work. Lots of short-term part-time jobs. They were living hand-to-mouth. They had big loans to pay off and a landlord who had tied them into an unfair long-term contract. They were trapped."

"Are they still there? In South Manchester? Are all the contact details for the adoption agency in that paperwork?"

"The agency folded less than a year after we'd completed the adoption. The owner died suddenly and there was no one ready to take over."

Lisa's heart skipped a beat. That wasn't fair. How am I meant to track down my parents now?

"But there's something else." Her father took her hands again in his and looked her in the eye. This was a look she'd not seen from him before. The eyes were no longer emotionless vacuums but were brimming with tears. "Your parents died in a car crash just four months after you and Phillip were born."

"What?"

"They're gone, Lisa. There is no one to find. I'm so sorry."

19

"Can I come in?"

It was Lisa on the doorstep, drenched to the skin with the rain that hadn't stopped lashing down since the middle of the afternoon.

Judy opened the door wide and Lisa stepped in, water already dripping off her onto the carpet.

"I'll get you a towel. You'll catch your death." But it hadn't escaped Judy's notice that Lisa looked a little like she was halfway there already.

Jemma came out into the hallway as Judy passed on the way to the stairs.

"Hey, Lisa. Raining then."

"I hadn't noticed."

By the time Judy had returned with a towel, Jemma had brought her auntie into the front room and sat her down on the sofa. The Xbox was on, much to Judy's chagrin, but the console was on the main launch screen. Her friends must have ducked out to do other activities. Jemma rarely played alone, preferring multiplayer over single every time.

"Have you got your homework done?" Judy asked, not wanting to sound too harsh.

"Yeah, just got a bit more to finish. I'll do it now."

"Thanks."

Jemma left them alone, leaving Judy to drape the towel around Lisa and sit on the edge of the sofa opposite. The woman must be freezing but she wasn't showing any sign that the wet was bothering her in the slightest.

"Has something happened? Have you seen her again?"

Lisa's eyes sought Judy's, and they were piercing points of blue. "I saw Dad."

"And how was he?"

"He wanted to give me this."

From within the folds of the towel, she retrieved an envelope that she must have had stashed up her jacket on the doorstep. She handed it to Judy who accepted it, her fingers tingling at the weirdness of the situation. The envelope was new, the protective tape over the adhesive was still in place so this had never been sent through the mail. On the front, written in the thin black scrawl of a ball-point pen were the words:

Lisa's adoption

"The adoption papers you were looking for. That's excellent." She slipped her hand inside and pulled out several documents, all much older than the containing envelope. These looked official. The topmost had the legend Premier Adoption Services typed across the top of the page in black typewritten ink. There were the postal details, and phone number, Judy noting the Southport address and the Southport number with the missing prefix that had been introduced much later. She turned to the next page and saw a letter outlining the confirmation that the adoption process had been successful and that the legal documentation followed.

"It's all he has. I didn't have to ask him for it. He met me this morning then handed it over."

"That's good. Does it have the details of your birth parents?"

"No. That's not in there."

"But you can contact the adoption agency and put a request in?"

"No. The adoption agency doesn't exist anymore."

Judy felt that there was something else she wasn't being told. Lisa was talking, but it was a distant Lisa, almost a parody of the person she'd known all these years.

"Have you tried ringing the number?"

"What would be the point? The place has shut down."

"Maybe you'll get through to someone who can pass your details on. Maybe it got incorporated into another company."

But even as she was saying these words, she didn't believe what she saying. This had all happened years ago. She felt sad and understood why Lisa was here, looking the way she looked. To be so close and yet so far must hurt like hell.

"There's something else. Dad said that my parents died in a car crash when I was only a few months old. There's no one to look for. Dad was trying to protect me at the restaurant. That's why he never wanted me to investigate because the moment I did, he would have to tell me what I didn't want to hear. And there goes my dream of finding them. It would have been better to not have tried. At least that way, I could have held onto the illusion that they were doing OK and were missing me as much as I wanted to see them."

Dead.

"I'm so sorry." Judy didn't know what else to say. Could there be any worse blow to suffer? Sure, there was always the chance that she would never have been able to find them, and Lisa was in her forties now, so her parents were likely to have been hitting old age, but to have that hope destroyed by the news that they'd died in a car crash was devastating. "Let me get you a drink."

"I don't want a drink."

"A cup of tea."

Lisa threw Judy a look that silenced any more suggestions. "I don't want tea. I don't want anything. I don't want this bloody towel. I don't even know why I'm here. This has got nothing to do with anyone else."

Judy paused. She'd never seen her sister-in-law act like this.

You're reminding me of Phil, she thought. And I don't like it.

Judy glanced up at the ceiling and listened for the sounds of Jemma. The only good thing to come out of her marriage with Phil. Years of doting on him, then serving him, then fearing him. And here was his twin sister, in the same room that he'd sulk in, acting in the same petulant manner.

"You're right. I'm sorry." Judy sat back in her chair and waited to see what Lisa would say next. Let her lead the conversation. Adrian had alluded to her poor mental health and she felt she'd seen a hint of that just now.

"I should go."

"You don't have to. Stay and have something to eat. I don't think you should be on your own."

"You think I'll hurt myself?"

"No. But, you're upset. I wouldn't want you to feel sad on your own."

"I've just found out my parents are dead. I've got every right to grieve for them."

But you didn't even know them. They've been dead for almost as long as you've been alive. Harsh. Too harsh.

"Yes, you have. But you don't need to be on your own."

"I think I want to be, though." Lisa stood up suddenly and let the towel drop from her shoulders to the sofa. "I'm going. You can keep those. I don't need them anymore."

"I'll look after them for you."

"Do what you like with them. It doesn't matter. That's no use to me. I'm not looking for them anymore."

20

After dropping Jemma off at school, Judy drove back into town. She parked up on the promenade, got herself a coffee from the first coffee shop she passed, and strolled along the gardens, thinking.

Lisa had been right to be upset upon the news of her parents' death. Just because it had happened over forty years ago, it didn't diminish the feelings. It wasn't even knowing they were dead, it would also be having to give up on the dream she'd been harbouring for these years. Without her parents, what could she find out about her background?

It would not be easy with the adoption company closed, but Judy promised that she would do what she could to help. Lisa had left the papers with her and wasn't in a good enough place to make enquiries herself, but that didn't mean that Judy couldn't.

She hadn't even mentioned any more disturbances. It was possible the activity had stopped, but not likely.

Malc hadn't had the answers she'd been hoping for and that left her on her own again.

Half an hour later, she found herself staring at the properties on display in the window of Richard's estate agents.

"Hello, again." His voice made her jump. "Sorry, didn't mean to startle you."

"No, I'm sorry. I'm just a bit distracted." A bit distracted and in need of some company.

"Come in. Take the weight off your feet."

"No really, I didn't mean to disturb you."

"It's not a disturbance. I'd be glad for someone to talk to."

"Not much happening today?"

"A few phone calls. Got to do a viewing later. That's it."

She followed him inside and immediately felt like she'd stepped back into a safe space. There was nothing unsettling about this simple setup. She did a quick count of the doors, but everything was as she'd remembered. Richard was wearing a different shirt but the same tie. He had a smell of an aftershave she couldn't place and despite him being a tad generous with it, she didn't mind it at all.

She'd thought of what he'd been like at school but again all she could think about was how much he'd been teased. How much of that was me? she thought.

"So, what's distracting you?"

"Oh, just the usual. Life." She smiled.

"Anything I can help with?"

"Not unless you know of any primary teaching jobs going." He frowned. "I'm afraid not."

"Then I guess I'll just have to suck it up and carry on."

"Having money troubles?"

Such a personal question, so quickly. Judy found herself not caring in the slightest.

"Phil's life assurance paid off the mortgage but it's a big house. There are maintenance issues around every corner. I've just had a quote to replace a section of the roof and it will take quite a dent to the savings. I could do with getting some work before the problem gets any worse."

"I'd offer you some hours here if it would help. Wouldn't be very much, but it would be something."

"I didn't come here asking for work. I know you can't afford to take anyone on. No, I need to find something more permanent."

He sat on the edge of the desk, his leg brushed against hers and he apologised. "You say it's a big house. Have you thought of downsizing?"

"No. I couldn't. That's the only house my daughter's ever lived in. It's the family home."

But how many years had it been a happy family home? Maybe moving to a new house might be the fresh start she needed. Somewhere where she could start new memories with Jemma.

"I couldn't. That wouldn't be the right thing. It's just buying time again."

"Maybe it will buy you enough time until you're properly settled with a new job. I've helped lots of customers do the same thing."

"Old customers?"

He laughed. She liked the sound of it. "Well, yes, mainly they're older, but it doesn't change the maths behind it. If it's just you and your daughter, you've got lots of options. I've got a few nice properties in Hillside. What school does your daughter go to? She's at high school, isn't she?"

"Hillside High."

"Right, I think you'll do well to get a house in that area. They're rising in value faster than any other part of Southport. Think of it as an investment."

She shook her head. It was just pie in the sky. There was no way she could sell her house. Adrian had helped get that house for them, even paid the deposit. He wouldn't be happy to see her sell it and move on.

But it's none of his business what I do with my house. It's not as if he's reaching out to help.

"It's just an idea. Don't worry about it. I'll keep my eyes open for any full-time jobs that might suit."

"It's not a terrible idea. It's just something I've given no thought to."

"Scary?"

She nodded. "A little."

"And whilst you're also looking for work, it's a lot to take on. I understand."

He smiled and went to the kitchen. "Do you want a drink?"

Judy lifted her takeaway cup, realised it was empty, then set it down on the desk. "OK, that would be good."

Richard grinned and disappeared. The kettle clicked on, and she heard cups clinking together as he grabbed a pair from the cupboard.

Judy settled in her chair and found that the anxiety she'd been feeling all morning had left her. There was something about this man that calmed her. Did he ever get worried by anything?

She gazed to look out of the window and found her eyes drawn to the spot Adrian had been parked at the other day. Had he really been there for his own reasons or had he been keeping tabs on her?

Richard placed a mug in front of her.

"Milk no sugar?"

"Yeah, perfect."

"Is it just the money that's distracting you? If you don't mind me saying, you seem to be someplace else."

"I'm just thinking about Phil."

"Do you want to talk about it?"

"I've not talked to anyone about him, not in the way things really were. Not about how things were in the end."

"OK. So—"

"But, I think maybe I do, I mean—"

The awkwardness was a chasm that spanned between them.

"If you don't want to now, you can drop in another time, or maybe over a drink."

"Phil was a control freak," she blurted out. "His family think he was a saint who worked hard to provide for me and Jemma, but the truth was he could never see us living any part of our life without his input. I never wanted to give up my teaching career, but Phil convinced me that with the salary from his dad and the promise of a future partnership in the business, there was no need for me to work. The best place for me was at home, raising Jemma.

"And to be honest, after having Jemma, that sounded like the ideal. I'd be free of all the pressures that most mums have of trying to occupy their children and find them the best childcare they could afford but still making it worthwhile going back to work. Only, I didn't realise that I was giving up my colleagues. They were my main social network, and I became isolated. By the time it would have been appropriate to let the school know whether I was going to go back, I'd changed my mind and was ready to return, but Phil had already made his mind up. In his eyes, we'd agreed months before that we would do things the way he'd laid down and a deviation wouldn't work out."

"Sounds like a bit of an idiot."

"That was just the start of it."

Suddenly, music blared from the little kitchen at the back of the office. Dire Straits, Money for Nothing. Richard hurried to turn the radio off. "I don't know what happened there. Sorry."

When he sat back down, Judy had fallen silent. The interruption had come at the right time. She'd said too much and couldn't continue talking about her private life to a stranger.

"What's the matter?" Richard asked.

"Nothing, just spooked me." But she was thinking of darker thoughts. Of the kinds of thoughts that a woman who'd been on the brink of spilling the secrets of her marriage. But there was something else.

That was Phil's favourite song.

Coincidences. You're finding coincidences and looking for patterns in things that aren't there.

"Did you ever get married?" Judy asked.

Richard shook his head. "There's been a few possible contenders over the years, but never got the nerve to actually propose or anything. Guess, that was never meant to be. I think I'm a bit too set in my ways now to settle down with someone."

"People are getting married for the first time later and later. And besides, who says marriage is all that, anyway? Nothing to stop you finding the right someone and just being with them. You don't need a marriage certificate to have a great relationship. Trust me, that piece of paper is more a burden than the weight of being single."

"You don't regret getting married do you?"

Did she regret it? Judy had asked herself that a few times in her life. And there was never an easy answer. If I'd never have married, I wouldn't have stuck around long enough to have Jemma. And Jemma was the world to her. The cost would be too great.

"I'd have got married," she replied. "But I'd have kept my options open. It's important to remember that you have a life before marriage, and you can have one after marriage."

The office phone rang and startled them both. Richard reached over to pick up the receiver and spoke to the caller, his professional brusque business tone taking charge.

Why have I come here? she thought. Is it really just to talk to someone who will not judge me?

"I'll get going," she said lightly, then before he could get to his feet and stop her, she was gone, letting the shop door close behind her.

21

The figure in her room was on top of her again, breathing that death breath into her lungs, letting the foetid stench of decay and soil and rot spray over her. Lisa tried to scream, but her mouth was frozen. She tried to force back against the skeletal hands that had pinned her arms to the bed, tried to push back with all her strength. But all she managed was tiring her muscles until she could fight no more.

The dream ended as it had to, with Lisa reaching for the light and fighting for her breath and wanting to scream out to Ellis for help.

Had she screamed? There had been a noise that had woken her, had that been her own struggling sounds or something else?

A cry like a baby's painful sobs came from outside. Lisa froze in her bed, trapped beneath the sheets, not wanting to move, not sure whether she could. The sound repeated, a desperate sad wailing noise. She knew what it was.

Jasper was in pain. Her phone said it was a little after two and she held onto it like it was a lifeline. Ellis was out. He'd texted earlier to say he was staying at Nina's flat. Who could blame him? But that meant she was in the house on her own and she didn't like that.

Nor had she let the cat out.

It might not have been Jasper. She turned the bedside light on and checked his radiator hammock where he'd be asleep when not on the bed. But it was empty.

"Jasper?" She hated how desperate her voice sounded in an empty house. What would she do if she heard someone reply?

The noises continued. It could be the noise he made when defending his territory. He would do that if trapped inside and seeing a strange cat cross the garden. It was a clear warning to the intruder to vacate the space quickly before he unleashed a cat hell upon them.

She'd locked the kitchen door. He couldn't get to the cat flap. He couldn't be outside.

But you know that's him. You can't just ignore it; you will have to go and look. He sounds in pain. You can't wait until morning.

Shit and damn and buggery bollocks. Yes, OK. Right then. She hurried out of bed, grabbed her stripy dressing gown and switched on her phone's torch. At the threshold of her bedroom, she hesitated. Ellis's bedroom door was open. Had it been like that earlier when she'd gone to bed? She couldn't be certain.

The light switch was at the end of the short passage from her bedroom to the landing proper. Only about three metres, the length of the wall of the bathroom that adjoined her bedroom. But those three metres were in darkness. There was minimal light seepage coming through the open doorway of Ellis's bedroom. That room was on the front of the house with windows looking out onto the street. The amber glow from the streetlamps should be seeping into the house, but there was nothing. It was like a sponge was soaking up all the residual light.

At the light switch, she flicked on the main landing light, and relaxed as the illumination cast away the shadows.

She was on my chest. The woman that's been visiting me in my room. The entity living in my house.

A chill ran through her and she pulled the belt of her dressing gown around her before slipping her phone into the dressing gown pocket. This entity didn't feel benevolent. It wanted something. Did it want her gone? Was that all it was? Because, she couldn't see herself moving out anytime soon. She'd never had to look for a place on her own without her dad and going back to him to ask for help wasn't an option. It might not have been his fault that her birth parents were dead, but he'd kept the news from her until he could keep it no longer. How long would he have stayed quiet if she hadn't started looking into her past? She knew the answer to that. It would still have been a secret.

She stood at the top of the stairs and flicked the light switch that should have turned on the light at the base of the stairs.

Nothing.

Shit. Her heart rate sped up, and she swallowed, suddenly thirsty.

There was an unfamiliar noise coming from somewhere downstairs. It took her a moment to place it, then she realised it was running water. She once again retrieved her phone and turned on the torch, before taking those steps downstairs.

A sudden burst of wind rattled the letterbox. She startled, then caught herself being ridiculous and continued, trying to focus on her mission. Get Jasper safe.

At the bottom of the stairs, the light from her phone's torch cast a strange focused light on her surroundings. A stark white halo leading all too quickly to a falling umbra and then the unknowable shadows.

A louder insistent meowing sounded and she hurried along the hallway, stopping as soon as she entered the back room. The door to the kitchen was wide open. But more worryingly, so was the back door to the house. The noise she was hearing was the hose pipe fixed to the outside tap. It had been turned on, but the tap leaked and sprayed out at the point of connection, making it a wet job to turn the thing on or off.

There's someone in the house. An intruder has broken in. That's why Ellis's door was open.

The panic hit her then. She listened but couldn't hear anybody moving around upstairs.

They'll have heard you moving around, they know you're awake. They're probably shitting themselves now, thinking how they can get away with whatever they've nicked without being caught.

But had they targeted her house? Did they know that she was here on her own? If they'd been in Ellis's bedroom, they knew that at least one of the house's occupants was absent.

Without thinking through the possible outcomes of a burglary gone wrong, Lisa ran out into the garden, no longer feeling safe within her home. Spray from the leaking tap caught her as she stepped barefoot onto the patio and she cursed at the cold.

Everything felt different in the garden in the night-time.

"Jasper?" she hissed into the indistinct shapes of the garden. Her eyes hadn't yet adjusted to the gloom, but she didn't have time to do that, anyway. She needed to find her cat and get the hell out of here.

Burglars usually have someone on watch outside the house.

Shit. Hadn't thought of that. She spun around, throwing the light about her, wondering whether to shout to the neighbours for help.

Call the police.

She would do that. But that would mean giving up the light from her phone and she wasn't prepared to do that yet.

The spray from the leaking tap was noisy now that she was outside. It would help to obscure anyone that might be out here. Decisively, she went to the tap and turned it off. Then with the water off, she looked at the hosepipe and realised it had been unravelled.

Strange thing for a burglar to do.

The cat meowed again. Outside, it sounded different to how it had sounded from her bedroom. There was something not right about it, like the acoustics were distorted somehow.

The unravelled hosepipe trailed to the back of the garden, leading away from the house. She followed it, shining the torch along its path to see where it led. The garden shed was sited several metres from the fence at the back of the garden, twenty metres from the house and the hosepipe led all the way around to the far side of the shed.

Where the cat noises were coming from.

Suddenly, it came to her why Jasper didn't sound right.

She ran across the grass, ignoring the cold on her feet. At the corner of the shed, she turned and almost bumped into the water butt, a huge blue plastic container that had been fixed in place to catch the runoff water from the shed and should be used to water the plants. Not that Lisa ever did any of that. The butt was a relic from the previous owner.

But the lid was off, and the end of the hosepipe had been draped over the top, leading down inside.

"Jasper?"

The cat replied, and Lisa peered over the top of the water butt, shining her light inside.

Jasper was standing on his back legs, pawing to get enough purchase to get out. When he dropped back, she could see the water was three inches high, enough to cover most of his legs. Jasper was soaked.

What bastard would do this to a cat?

It was no accident. The lid was never removed. There was never a need to. A tap at the bottom was used to drain the barrel. She turned the tap now and saw the slow drizzle of water emerge. It would take it down to an inch. But she still had to get him out. The butt was huge and heavier than it looked being made from heavy grade plastic, but eventually, Lisa got it to tip onto its side, supporting it all the way.

Jasper darted out, not interested in staying behind for hugs. From the speed of him, she guessed he was OK, only his pride had been injured.

She turned back towards the house, aware that this was the middle of the night and she was very exposed in her nightclothes in the garden. You need to get back inside and call someone. This wasn't an accident. Someone wants to scare you. Now she'd finished rescuing Jasper, she could feel her heart thudding in her chest, expanding and falling and her ribs strained under the pressure. Her airways felt constricted, it was difficult to breathe.

I'm having a panic attack, she thought, a bloody panic attack. She'd never suffered with asthma but knew from her experience with panic attacks the pure fear of not being able to draw enough air into your lungs. That's what this felt like now, that someone had sucked all the air out of the night, leaving her drawing down on void.

She staggered to the back door, then halted in her tracks. Someone was standing in the kitchen. A figure different in stature to the one she'd seen in her room. This was broader shouldered. It was a man. The face hidden by shadow, the light coming from behind him, then that light shut off leaving the man-silhouette hard-framed in the doorway. He was in her house and she was stuck in the garden with no way out. In these terraces, there was no way round to the front without going through the house. Her only option would be to go over the fence at the back or the sides into her neighbours.

Anger hit her like a jab in the arm, and she pushed aside the fear.

"Get the hell out of my house!" she shouted, her voice cutting across the distance between them, to her ear, not sounding brave enough or strong enough to have any meaning. What if he came after her? What if this wasn't a burglar? What if there were other things on his mind?

The kitchen door started to close, and she ran for it, picking up a fallen spade from the garden where she'd planted a bush. Brandishing that, she felt more confident, but she would not reach the door in time.

The door slammed, the handle raised, and she heard the lock turn as she banged into it. Her shoulder stung with the impact.

"Bastard!" she called through the glass.

Then she gasped.

A face obscured by the frosted glass flashed in the window half of the door. The intruder was only an inch away from her and she dropped the spade in shock, realising that she had been so close to being stuck in the house on her own with the intruder.

Her panic reasserted herself and the outside suddenly seemed very large again, too large, pressing down on her with its openness, threatening to engulf her with the dark open space.

Stumbling backwards, she stepped back out onto the grass, ignoring her cold feet on the wet grass.

The face slunk back from the glass. Movement caught her eye above, and she looked up to her bedroom window.

There, a second figure stood framed in the window, this silhouette was surely the woman. There were two of them, working together. What the hell did they want with her?

That figure moved backwards, hiding into the reaches of her room where she couldn't see because of the angle. She moved back, further into the garden, straining her neck to see further into the bedroom, trying to make out the figure.

A noise from behind her made her spin around. On the ground, just a hand's reach away from the shadows was the teddy bear she'd thrown out in the rubbish the other day.

Lisa's brain reacted to the adrenaline and light breathing and took the only action it had available.

Lisa fainted.

22

Judy pulled up by the curb on the opposite side of the office block. She was on the other side of Southport to where she lived, much closer to Marshside and an area she wasn't that familiar with. It was just after lunch and her stomach was still full of the sub she'd treated herself to from Subway. Her chat with Richard had made her look at things afresh. What if she did put the house on the market? Would that be such a bad thing?

Maybe getting rid of the house was the way to get rid of the problems that came with the house as well then. She wasn't naïve enough to think that every house only carried good memories, but what if her time with Phil had tainted the property? Could feelings be trapped in bricks and mortar?

Richard had been helpful in making her see there were other options available. And wouldn't it be nice to start somewhere new and make a whole new world of memories? Being close to Jemma's school would be a bonus and getting out of the house that Adrian had helped find for them would also be a clear sign of her independence. She didn't need anyone. She could sort her life out on her own.

There were no signs she was at the right place. Adrian had told her that the adoption agency was long gone so she hadn't expected to see any signs advertising it, but there was an aura about the place that she didn't like, and as she got out of the car and walked closer to it, she felt a bad trembling in her stomach, like she was delving into something she had no right messing with.

This was the right address. Hosforth House. She'd double-checked the papers and Google maps.

She walked through the nearly empty car park and headed for the main entrance. The doors were locked, and she checked the intercom for a clue as to how to get in. There was no main reception, so she tried the button for the unit number that matched the adoption agency on Lisa's paperwork.

"Massive Dynamics, can I help?" The man's voice was polite and precise.

"Hi, I wanted to speak to someone at Premier Adoption Services. I wonder if you could help."

There was a pause. Then, "This is Massive Dynamics."

"Yes, I know."

Another pause. "This isn't an adoption agency."

"I know, but you might still be able to help."

"Have you tried the other offices? I'm not sure if there is any adoption company here."

"No, there isn't. It closed."

"I'm confused. Why are you here?"

"Perhaps you could let me in. You could still help me."

She imagined the person on the other end of the intercom looking through the built-in camera and sighing, wondering what they'd done to deserve such a visitor.

Just as she was about to give up with Massive Dynamic and try another business, the door buzzed. Before they could change their mind, she shoved open the door and let herself into the building.

It was roasting inside. Heat rose from the antiquated cast iron radiators, filling the space with a dry heat that made her reach for the top button of her coat. There was a staircase by the entrance, its carpet threadbare. A stripe of warning tape was holding down the carpet on the first two steps. The floor in the reception was a black industrial lino well beyond its natural lifespan. You could see every scuff and mark and scratch, and it told the story of a thousand souls coming to work.

Just as she was debating whether to head for the stairs, the double doors opposite the entrance opened and a thin gangly man stepped through into the reception area and smiled.

"I'm sorry, but I honestly don't know what you're after. You said you were after an adoption company."

"Premier Adoption Services. I know they're closed, but they had offices here in the seventies."

"Goodness. That's before my time."

"Is there anyone here that might have been here then?"

He shrugged. "Matt Hodgson's been here a while. I think he was here back then."

Judy's heart lifted at the news. This suddenly didn't feel like the complete waste of time it had a moment ago. "I don't suppose I could speak to him."

"I don't work with him directly. He's the maintenance guy. He's employed by the landlords. He comes in once a week or as work is needed. I can ask him to call you when I next see him."

"Do you have any idea when that might be?"

"You might be lucky. He normally pops in on a Tuesday afternoon."

"Excellent. Let me give you my details."

*

Judy spent the rest of the morning at home, tidying, making lunch, a pitiful jacket potato she wazzed in the microwave for ten minutes until its sides sagged like an old wet sack, then she put herself in front of her laptop and checked out the house prices in her area.

Richard's words had struck a chord with her and since he'd mentioned it, her mind kept returning to the idea that she could do much better off by downsizing. It only took a couple of minutes to find Richard's estate agents online. There weren't many properties listed and none from her estate.

Damn it, she thought. That's the second time today I've come back to thinking about you and your business. The thought of working for someone like Richard appealed in a way she hadn't imagined. How much nicer would it be dealing with people who wanted you to help them sell their property than dealing with thirty unruly children and their apathetic parents? It would make it much easier to come home and leave work at the door. But it wasn't just the thought of working in an estate agent that was appealing, it was working with Richard. A light rush of heat lifted her cheeks, and she clicked onto another website instead, banishing the idea of agreeing to go out for a drink with Richard. She had more baggage than he knew and there were things she wasn't ready to tell anyone just yet. About the time she'd spent with Phil and how he'd changed her. Not even Jemma had seen the change in her and that was how she wanted it to stay.

After clearing away her lunch plates, she went upstairs to change the sheets and stopped in Jemma's doorway. The bedroom was your typical messy twelve-year-old's domain.

But I tidied you this morning.

The drawers in her desk had been pulled out. The wardrobe doors were open as well. Tentatively, she stepped into the room and pushed the drawers closed. She had closed the drawers that morning. She was sure of it. Inside the wardrobe, the clothes had been squished to one side, compacted up against the wall leaving a space on the right.

A space big enough to stand in, she thought.

Brusquely, she swiped the clothes back across the rail, distributing them evenly before slamming the doors closed and heading to her own room.

She was thrown from her thoughts by her mobile ringing.

"Hello, is that Mrs Doyle?" It was an older gent, gruffly spoken.

"Hi. This is Judy, are you Mr Hodgson?"

"Call me Matt. Someone left me a message to call you. Something about adopting. I don't know why you'd want to speak to me; you must have got the wrong end of the stick. I'm the maintenance man, just a part-time caretaker. I have nothing to do with the businesses that rent office space, that's not my department see. I'm just employed by the landlord. Nothing to do with me."

"That's fine. I know that."

"Oh. You do, right then. What am I calling you for? There's not much in the message see."

"The man I spoke to said that you'd worked in that building for a long time. I wanted to speak to someone about a company that had office space there in the seventies."

"I was working back then right enough. But my memory is not what it was. I don't think I'll be able to help you."

Not if you won't let me get a word in edge ways.

She pressed on. "It was an adoption agency called Premier Adoption Services."

"And?"

"And I wondered whether you were there back when they were running."

"They're not operating now? Have you tried calling them?"

"Yes. The number is old, before the area codes were changed even."

"Well don't you just put a leading zero before the number you've got? Maybe also a seven after the area code."

You are a fountain of knowledge. She sighed. This was going nowhere. She was wasting his time and her own sanity was slipping away every second she remained on the call.

"The number is disconnected. I'm trying to find anyone that might have been working at the offices when the company was there. You're my only name so far. If you could remember anyone else that might have been there I could get in touch with them instead."

"I'm afraid you might have to do that."

She paused. "Can you think of any other companies that had office space then?"

"I'd suggest ringing the landlord, only that building has changed hands half a dozen times at least in the time I've worked there. I doubt you'll get any—" he broke off suddenly.

"Hello, Matt? Mr Hodgson? Are you still there?"

"Just looking at the note that was left for me. Judy Doyle right?"

"Yes."

"Are you related to Adrian Doyle by any chance?"

Her heart skipped a beat. "He's my father-in-law."

When Matt next spoke, he sounded like he'd just solved one of the world's greatest riddles. "Well that makes life simple then. Speak to your father-in-law. His company had offices in the building."

"Their offices are on Dukes Street."

"Is that right? Well, back in the seventies, they were Hosforth House. They moved out in the eighties. I'm telling you, you're best speaking to Mr Doyle. He'll be able to sort this out for you."

She thanked him and hung up. Then sat there for a minute before wandering back to the kitchen and switching the kettle on. She'd had enough tea today, but the ritual gave her mind a way to focus. Adrian's company had been in the same building as the adoption agency they'd used to adopt Lisa and Phil. She didn't know much about the state of the adoption service industry now, and nothing about how it was in the seventies, but surely there can't have been many. Didn't the health service look after things like that back then? What were the chances of an adoption agency being in the same building?

23

Thirty years ago

They'd gone out again and left them in the caravan on their own. Not unusual for a Friday evening. Lisa and Phil had grown used to it, just as Lisa had grown used to being dragged up here every weekend and being forced to share a bedroom with her stinking brother. Much as she liked having a twin, she'd often wished that it was a girl she shared the same DNA with. Having a brother who barely washed, farted loudly in the night, and was generally mean to her during daylight hours was enough to justify that she thought.

Today had been no exception. Whilst she'd wanted to stay in their shared bedroom and finish her book, he'd wanted to go exploring and Dad had thought that a good idea. If they didn't go too far, it was fine with him. He'd brought a stack of paperwork with him and had taken over the dining room table with it. Mum was out shopping at the local grocers and wouldn't be back for an hour at least—a trip to the grocers for Mum meant a trip to the local village, and that entailed going to pretty much every shop along the village high street, whether she had plans to buy anything or not. Lisa guessed it was her way of socialising, but she was sure that Mum made it deliberately onerous to ensure that neither of the kids would want to come with her, giving her an hour or two of alone time.

Exploring with Phil was dull as usual. There weren't any places left to explore. They'd spent a little time running around the main road, seeing who could get to the next junction the fastest. Lisa could easily beat Phil at this but he never took it very well and would find additional ways to torment her later on, usually by encouraging her to look out into the dark woods at night when their parents had left to go socialising at the bar.

But after half an hour of this, it seemed that Phil had something else on his mind. He'd stopped by the side track leading deeper into the woods—the track that led to the holiday lets. There were five small houses in their own plots through the woodland, part of the caravan site, but marketed at the richer families who considered caravans beneath them. Lisa wondered why her dad didn't let them stay in one of those whilst they were up here, and he'd told her that staying in a caravan was part of the fun of getting away. Where was the fun in staying in a house? They might as well just stay back at home. Lisa wanted to tell him she thought that was a terrific idea but that would only hurt him and deep down, really deep down, she actually enjoyed having this second home to come up to every weekend. Even if it was a caravan. It was something her friends didn't have and when she wanted to elevate herself above them, which she needed to do from time to time what with Lucy being so melodramatic, she'd drop into conversation that she was going up to their second home for the weekend. That was enough to shut them up or bring the conversation back to her. Better than the attention being on Lucy.

"I don't think I want to go that way," she told Phil. He was raring to go, eager to explore the holiday lets. There were two problems with his plan. Firstly, the track was surrounded by heavier trees blocking more light than she was comfortable with. It didn't feel part of the caravan park; it felt like crossing over into some place different, somewhere other. She'd gone that way with Phil once a few months ago and he'd tricked her by letting her walk ahead whilst hiding in the bushes, making crying sounds like the foxes at night. She'd promised herself that she wouldn't let herself be tricked by him again.

Secondly, Dad had asked them not to wander up to the holiday lets. The families staying there didn't want kids running around, disturbing their peace. They were paying more for the seclusion, to get away from it all. Lisa wondered what kind of family would pay to spend time in the darkest part of the woods, away from the sights of the rest of the caravan site, right where the animals ruled.

But there was also one property that had been left in a rundown state. Dad knew Phil was interested in exploring the house and he'd made it explicitly clear that he wasn't to go near the place. There just weren't enough richer families wanting those properties to bother refurbishing them all. It was unsafe to walk around, he'd tell the children. Lisa didn't care about going to see it, but to Phil it had always sounded like a fun thing to do. On their caravan site with little else to amuse them, hell they'd just spent the morning running around the roads seeing who could get to the next bin the fastest, it was an exciting distraction for Phil.

"Come on you wuss. It's only a couple of minutes down here. I know you want to see it."

"I don't. I just want to go home. You're so boring, Phil."

He was affronted by that. "Am not."

"Boring." And she patted her hand to her open mouth in an exaggerated yawn. "I'm going home."

"Dad's hiding something up there."

That caught her attention.

"What do you mean?"

"Come and see and I'll show you."

"You're so full of bullshit." She never swore in front of her parents but actively swore in front of her brother. They both swore at each other and thought nothing of it anymore.

"I'm not full of bullshit. You're just a bloody chicken. So scared of what might happen if you don't do what Dad tells you." He stormed up to her and had his face almost in hers. Almost mind, as despite being twins, she was in the middle of a growth spurt and was an inch higher than her brother. A fact that she'd remind him of whenever he got too annoying. She leant forward, not scared of him. This was familiar territory and took her mind away from the track ahead of them.

"I'm not scared. I just don't do what I'm told by annoying brothers."

"If you're not scared, prove it."

"No."

"You are scared."

"I'm bored. I'm going back home." She turned to go back to the caravan, wondering whether Mum would finally be home. Maybe she'd brought them something nice to eat, or maybe she could persuade her to take them out for the rest of the day. Keswick wasn't too far away and had a decent bookshop. If Dad would be busy with paperwork for the rest of the afternoon, he'd probably even give her some pocket money to get something new to read.

"I saw Dad come up here last night when he thought we were all asleep. Why would he do that?"

Lisa paused. It wasn't unusual for Phil to make up stories to get her into trouble, but she couldn't fathom why he would make up something so odd. "Why would Dad come up here? And how do you even know? You can't see this track from our caravan." She could think of several reasons herself but wanted to hear what Phil had to say. Back home, at their real home, she knew that Dad was a restless sleeper, often talking in his sleep or wandering downstairs when sleep wouldn't come. And despite promising Mum that he'd given up smoking, she'd caught him in the back garden in the middle of the night, chuffing away on a cigarette. If Dad had gotten up in the middle of the night, it would have been to take a walk to clear his head and sneak a cigarette to help him sleep.

"I followed him, dumbass. I let him get a little ahead and then I followed him."

"Why would you do that? What made you think that was a smart idea?"

"He was talking in his sleep. It woke me up. He came into our room and was watching us for a bit, but I pretended to be asleep. I thought he was still mad at us."

He had been particularly shouty at them yesterday, the argument started from nowhere, something and nothing as is always the case. They'd been playing outside with Phil's football when he'd knocked the ball against the side of Dad's car. Dad threw the ball into the boot of the car with the promise that they wouldn't see it until they got back home. Phil had almost called him a bastard. Lisa had seen the word form on his lips, but he'd held it in and took the ear bashing like he always did. Despite Lisa being a part of the game, Dad only gave her a cursory telling off, leaving his anger for his son.

"I don't remember him being in the room."

"It was late. You were asleep. Your snoring and muttering were almost as bad as Dad's. It's almost like you're having a conversation with each other in the night."

"I don't snore."

Phil smirked. "Of course you don't."

"I don't."

"Whatever, it doesn't matter. Like I said, I was awake, and I couldn't get back to sleep."

Lisa's interest was piqued, she couldn't lie. She no longer wanted to go back to the caravan. She wanted to hear what her brother had to say. Lisa turned to face him. "How long did you follow him for?"

"About half an hour. It was bloody freezing."

"And he came up here?"

"Yep, further. Up to the fifth house. The one at the end of the track."

The fifth house was the one they'd been warned about. The one that hadn't been refurbished.

"What did he do up there?"

It was a strange thing to leave the caravan in the middle of the night. Lisa could have settled on that if it was just because he wanted a walk and a cigarette, but coming up to the holiday houses meant coming through the more intense parts of the wood where it was harder to see and the animals were closer.

"I'll tell you more if you come up to the house with me now."

"No. You're tricking me. I'm not stupid."

"You are stupid. You're as stupid as I am, but I know you, we think alike. You want to know what Dad was doing here as much as I do. Who was he meeting?"

"Wait, he was meeting someone?"

A flash of annoyance hit her brother's face. But he recovered quickly. "Maybe, and maybe I'll tell you if you come up to the house. There's no one in the other houses. They're empty now. No one will see us. No one will be complaining to Dad."

She was torn. A strange tingling had begun in her belly and she wanted it to stop. But how could she go back to the caravan and look at her dad in the same way knowing that Phil had this secret about him that she didn't know? It would be torture.

But there was something she hadn't noticed about Phil's behaviour until now. He wasn't just taunting her; he was pleading with her. He was scared about something, but he was refusing to show it. But as he'd said, they were twins and she could sometimes feel what he was feeling. It was a strange gift they shared between them, something they rarely acknowledged and would never mention to their parents.

She couldn't let him down now.

"If you're tricking me, I swear to God I'll make the rest of your life a living hell."

His face lit up. "You'll come?" He sounded surprised and relieved.

"Yes. But let's be quick. I don't fancy Mum coming home and not being able to find us." There was a chance she'd drive around the caravan site looking for them and she didn't want her to find them coming out from the track with the holiday houses. She knew the rules as well as the kids.

During the trek up the access road, Lisa's apprehension increased exponentially. It started as a simple increase in her heart rate, she could feel her chest vibrating as the muscle became more frenzied. Her mouth had dried as well and when she swallowed, there was an uncomfortable sensation at the back of her throat. It made her want to gag, but she held herself back and coughed instead.

Phil had gone quiet. The boy who'd only minutes ago had been antagonising her, was subdued, almost sullen. His face had gone pale, the colour drained leaving him sickly white. She walked beside him, keeping close, their arms brushing against each other. Ordinarily, that would have been more than enough to cause an argument between them, but Phil said nothing.

A narrower track split off to the left. Shortly after, a second track split to the right. The house they were going to was all the way along the road at the end.

The woods were quiet. Lisa listened for wildlife, but it was eerily quiet, no birdsong to disturb the calm. A gentle breeze whispered along the edge of the foliage on either side. In the trees above, the branches moved in rolling waves, bending on the whim of the wind. Lisa looked up and saw the patches of sky above seemed darker. A grey blanket of cloud had moved in since they'd started playing outside, taking the remaining warmth out of the day. Lisa wrapped her arms around her and resisted the urge to shiver.

It took a few minutes to reach the sign for the fifth house—the forbidden house. Lisa glanced behind and could no longer make out where the track had broken off from the main road around the caravan site.

"Did you follow him all the way down here?" she asked.

"Yes."

"And he didn't notice you?"

Phil shook his head. "I walked through the undergrowth, keeping low."

Lisa glanced at the shrubbery and realised that her brother was braver than she thought. The bushes looked uncomfortable and in the dark, it would have been impossible to walk through and see exactly where your feet were going. Phil could have disturbed any number of wild creatures.

They stopped by the wooden sign. A chain had been looped around the sign and a tree on the other side of the access track. A metal sign, rusting with age, flapped lazily in the middle.

No entry

Lisa knew they would step over the chain, but she hesitated. Something was wrong and she couldn't work out what. It wasn't just that her dad had told them not to come to this part of the site, or that she was bothered by what might be lurking in the woods. It was more a sense that she'd been here before. Deja vu?

But I haven't been here before.

It was possible though, wasn't it? They'd been coming to the site since she could remember. It was very possible that in that time, her dad had brought her up here.

Possible.

"He went up the track?" she asked.

"Yes, all the way up to the house. Come on," Phil said, his voice getting a hint of enthusiasm back, "I'll show you. It's pretty great."

"After you."

Phil stepped over the chain and began trudging up to the house. When he realised his sister wasn't following, he paused and called back to her. "Come on."

She gritted her teeth and stepped over the chain.

Nothing happened. Did she really think it would? There was nothing unusual about this place. If Dad really was here last night, and she'd yet to convince herself that Phil was telling her the truth, then he probably had good reason.

When she turned the corner of the track and saw the house ahead of her, she stumbled and almost fell to the ground. Phil was there to catch her. "You OK?"

"Must have tripped on a rock."

But there were no rocks. It wasn't her footing that was causing her imbalance, it was seeing the house for the first time.

Only it wasn't the first time.

She'd seen this house before, in her dreams.

"Phil, has Dad ever brought us here?"

He shook his head. "You've seen it before, haven't you?"

24

Lisa's head ached like she'd been drinking heavily, except she would never do that. She had a moment of blissful ignorance, then the events of last night snapped back into her consciousness and she gasped, sitting bolt upright in bed, putting her hand on her belly, and reaching for the first thing she could use as a weapon. The kindle wasn't going to be much use against an intruder, so she shamefully dropped it on the bed.

How the hell did I get here?

The last thing she could remember was seeing a face behind the glass of the kitchen door, and another figure upstairs in her bedroom.

The room you're lying in.

Her heart pounded, and she forced her eyes to focus across the room, blinking away the sleep from her eyes. There was no one here.

The idea that she might have dreamt the whole thing occurred to her. It would explain a lot. The cat falling into the water butt was the most ridiculous notion. Jasper would not do that, and he wasn't fond of strangers. He wouldn't have let a stranger get close enough to pick him and drop him inside.

The bedroom door was closed. She hadn't closed it. So, who had?

She checked her phone for the time then saw it was ten past nine. She was already late for work.

A noise from the kitchen made her pause. There was still someone in the house.

Last night hadn't been a dream. Lifting the bed covers, she understood why she was so cold. Her pyjamas weren't sweaty, they were damp. She'd fainted on the grass hadn't she? And someone must have brought her up here.

Cautiously, she made her way downstairs.

"How you doing?" Ellis asked. He was leaning against the open door to the back room.

At the sound of his voice, her legs trembled, and she turned and grabbed onto the bannisters.

"Hey, easy. I've got you," he said, and helped lower her into a seating position. The hallway was spinning, and the back of her neck felt too hot, like she was coming down with something.

"I thought you were a burglar."

He chuckled. "I'm sorry if I scared you. I came back late last night and found the back door open and the lights on. I thought we had been robbed. Then I saw you out on the grass and brought you inside. I think you'd fainted."

"I did. I went outside. There was someone in the house."

"Oh my God! Really? You mean we did have burglars? What did they take?"

But she was shaking her head. "I'm not sure they were. I think they were just messing with me." Then she told Ellis about waking up and finding Jasper in the water butt and the people she'd seen in the house.

"We should call the police," he suggested.

"Is anything missing?"

He hesitated. "I don't think so. I haven't been in all the rooms though." He put his head through into the lounge. "Xbox and television are still there."

"Was there any sign of a break-in?"

He shook his head. "No. It was all locked up."

Lisa didn't like the way Ellis was looking at her, like she was making all of this up. But it had felt so real. She couldn't have been asleep. "Have you seen Jasper?"

"Just now, in the kitchen. I put some more food out for him. He seemed hungry."

She went through to the kitchen, Ellis following behind, and found Jasper finished, sitting by his dish, licking his paws. He trotted up to her when she entered, and she scooped him up into her arms and looked him over. "He's OK."

"You said he was stuck in the water butt."

"Wait, I tipped it over." Then she unlocked the back door and stepped into the garden. The butt was still over on its side. "It happened." A pain in her stomach, like someone had pinched her. She hurried back inside and locked the door again as if she was being followed. "The water butt has been tipped over. That's what I did to get Jasper out."

"We should call the police then. This happened. Oh my God, I'm sorry I wasn't here. Maybe they wouldn't have targeted the house if they'd seen a second person inside."

"You think that's what it was, a targeted burglary?"

"Well, what else could it have been?"

She thought of telling him about the things she'd seen, and the things Judy had seen in the house. The reason that Judy had been round the other day. But, would it make any difference?

"Have you seen anything out of the ordinary? Like, I mean around the house?"

He shot her a quizzical look. "Like what? Is this your way of saying I'm not tidying the house enough, because I'm keeping up with the rota."

"Nothing like that," she said, taking a deep breath. "I think there might be something in the house with us. Something dangerous."

This time the look he gave her was not just quizzical but one of downright bafflement. "Like cockroaches?"

Again, she shook her head. "I've seen strange things happen. That night I woke up screaming, I thought there was someone in my room, and when Judy came over, with the lights."

"That's the electrics. It's an old house. The landlord needs to sort it out." Then, remembering that the landlord was Lisa's dad, he added, "And I'm sure he will, just as soon as we let him know."

"I don't think we're alone in here. I sense someone with us."

"You will feel that though. It's only natural after someone's tried to burgle your house."

"But I'm not convinced that anyone did."

"Come again."

"I think the house is haunted."

The pause that sat between them could have been as long as the titanic and heading for icy parts as easily. "No, I don't think that's right. I think you've been too busy at work and upset about your dad. I know you don't think you can talk to me about family stuff, but if it will upset you this much, I think I've got a right to know what's going on. I can't help if I don't know."

"It's not because of my dad. I've been having these feelings for weeks."

"Is it your medication? When did you last go to the doctor?"

That's bloody typical isn't it? Blame the nutcase on the anti-depressants, she thought. Yes, I may take a wonderful cocktail of drugs, but at least they're all prescribed. What the hell were you taking with Nina the other day. That wasn't just booze that was making you like that.

"I've been on the same medication for three months. I'm not due a check-up for another fortnight. The drugs are working just fine."

"But perhaps you're under more stress than usual. The Bodeman contract is a big deal. It might be too much to give you right now. I could slide it over to Nina and give you more breathing space."

And this is breaking cardinal rule number one of living together. There's a reason the No Talking Shop sign had been hung in the hallway. They could only carry on living together if they kept their work and home lives separate. If they didn't, and they didn't allow each other to shut off, then they would surely both go mad.

"I really don't think it's anything to do with the medication."

"But you don't really think we're haunted." He searched for a clue in her expression that might suggest she was just making this up. God knows why he'd think that, but she understood the scepticism. It had taken a while to get used to the idea herself.

"You can call it whatever you like, but I'm telling you there's something in this house that isn't normal."

"What happened to you last night wasn't because of a ghost. A ghost didn't try to drown your cat, then lock you outside."

"Why would burglars break into our house, oh and by the way, with no sign of forced entry, how exactly did they get in?" She held a hand in front to let him know she wasn't expecting an answer.

"But ghosts isn't the answer either. We might have left the back door unlocked."

"Did you?"

He shook his head. "No, of course not."

"And neither did I."

"But the point is." He ran his hand through his hair, trying to calm down. "The point is, there are dozens more likely explanations than the house being haunted."

"I'm all ears."

She didn't intend to get mad at Ellis. He was after all the reason she was back safe in the house and not still laying outside on the grass. "Wait, why didn't you call a doctor for me?"

"A doctor? Why? Do you need a doctor?"

"You found me outside on the grass. I'd fainted. I could have been injured. I don't remember going to bed. Did you carry me all that way?"

His eyes widened. "Lisa, you weren't outside in the garden. I found you asleep on the sofa. The back door was locked. I went to put a blanket over you, but you mumbled something about going back to sleep, then stumbled upstairs on your own. I didn't carry you anywhere. Trust me, I'm not as strong as I look."

She let the cheap jibe about her weight go by. What was important was that she didn't remember coming back into the house at all. The last thing she'd remembered was the teddy bear on the ground, then… nothing.

What the hell had happened to her?

25

After debating for two hours over what to wear, Judy settled on the outfit she was most comfortable in, her smart jeans and a decent top from H&M. It was probably a bit young for her, but it came with long sleeves and she could wear a smart jacket over the top. It had been a couple of decades since she'd last been on a date…

Jesus, is that what this is, a date?

She drove herself to the restaurant, then without overthinking things, she got out of the car and found Richard waiting outside the restaurant, wearing a nice shirt and jacket.

"You look great," he said, and for a horrible moment, she thought he would lean in and shake her hand, but instead, he pecked her on the cheek. "Do you like Nandos? I know it's a bit obvious."

"It's great."

And was Jemma's favourite place to eat.

Judy knew the menu back to front and that at least took the pressure off tonight. The casual atmosphere was also what she needed. God forbid Richard might have suggested fine dining. That had never been her style and would just have piled on more pressure. At least this way they could have a nice meal and not worry about it taking forever in case it didn't go as planned.

They took a table at the back of the restaurant. The place was pretty full, and the noise was chatty but friendly. A group of ladies had taken a table a couple away from theirs, but apart from them, they had a good barrier of privacy.

Do we look like we're on a date? Judy thought. Does it look sad people our age being on a date?

"So, do you come here often?" Judy said, smiling at the inaneness of her comment. The ice needed to be broken.

"Never. Someone recommended it, but I'm not sure if they were pulling my leg."

"I'm sure they weren't. It's all good."

"The waiter hasn't even acknowledged us yet."

She looked across the table at him, wondering whether he was being serious, then saw the cheeky look in his eye and realised he wasn't.

"You had me going for a minute."

"Just a minute? I must try harder."

The guy was hard not to like.

"Just a minute."

"Do you know what you'd like? I'll order."

Half an hour later, when they'd both devoured their meals, Judy brought up the thing that had been on her mind ever since her last meeting with Richard in his shop.

"You think you could help find me a good place in Hillside?"

"Well, sure. Are you thinking of moving?"

"Don't be so surprised, it was your idea."

"I just was talking a lot the other day. I do that. Sometimes the spiel gets mixed up with the small talk."

"Was that spiel then? Do you think I should stay where I am?"

"You said it's a big house and you're looking for work. Downsizing would give you some more money in the bank, but you'll still be stung with the cost of moving. There's the legal fees, removal fees, and of course the estate agent fees." He smiled. "But I might know someone who could help you out with those. You also need to think about whether you really do want to move out. It's only been a year since Phil passed. I'm guessing you've a lot of memories tied up in that place. You and your daughter. Maybe you should give it a little more time before deciding what to do."

Yes, there were certainly memories, she thought. Just a shame you can't strip away the bad ones to leave only the good behind.

The house had been their first together. Until then, Judy had been living on her own in a flat in Maghull, close to the school she was working at. Phil had been the most charming guy she'd ever dated and getting hitched was never in doubt from the moment they'd first met at Bethan's Halloween party. He'd come as a zombie, with so much green face paint that it had already brushed off onto his pleasingly tight t-shirt, making the most of his muscles. She'd come as a vampire, plastic fangs that dug into her gums, and fake blood dripping down her chin.

Four months later, they'd moved into the house, and a month after that, they'd gotten married. Fast. In hindsight, too fast. No wonder his parents had always been a little cautious with her. Before meeting Judy, Phil was known as a bit of a lady's man, but that had never bothered her. What he got up to before, was in the past. What mattered was how he treated her.

Turns out, you treated me like shit, she thought.

"The house isn't important. It's what we hold on to in our memories that's important," Judy said.

Nice. Is that what you think he wants to hear? Will that make you sound less like a psycho?

"Have you mentioned it to your daughter?"

"No. Not yet. Let's just see how we get on. I take it I don't have to have a board outside the house if I don't want to."

"Entirely up to you, although it would help sell the place."

"Give me two weeks. I'll find the right time to broach it with Jemma."

"OK. Take it at your own pace. None of this needs to happen straightaway. Look at the areas you're interested to move to. See what you can get for your money. Then let me know, and I'll start putting some feelers out."

The lights flickered in the restaurant, and the conversation around them stuttered. A chill breezed across the back of Judy's neck and she glanced at the door, wondering whether somebody had left it open.

"Hey, are you OK? You look pale."

"I'm fine. Just tired."

"I didn't mean to talk shop, but that's me all over, I guess. Never do know when to keep my mouth shut."

"It's not you. I'm having a nice time." And as if to prove it, she stood up, and headed for the bar. "Same again?"

"Yeah, sure."

At the counter, she ordered another couple of drinks. The restaurant was less busy now and she could get served straight away. Was she having a nice time? Talking about Phil had brought back some thoughts she didn't want to be feeling. That she could sit having a nice meal with a nice guy after her marriage was something she couldn't have thought of just a few weeks ago.

So, what's changed Judy? What's so different now that you're ready to move on with your life?

The money situation was a big issue. She'd grown so used to having Phil take care of all the finances, that she was lost when he died. It had taken her a few weeks to get her head around what needed paying and when money would be leaving the account.

And Jemma was growing up fast. In the second year at high school already, she was becoming more and more independent. There would only be a few years until she went onto university, and if that meant she was moving away, Judy would suddenly find herself living on her own in the house that Phil had chosen for her.

The lights flickered again, and that made Judy think of Seth. She sighed, and her stomach rumbled. The time she'd spent with Seth at Ravenmeols had been the most terrifying of her life, and yet she'd survived it. Not just survived, but thrived, taking the obstacles thrown at her, and overcoming them, transforming into someone else.

And she thought she quite liked this person. No longer the widow of a man she'd sooner forget, but as a strong woman who could forge her own path in life. Moving house was just a stage in that journey. Maybe it wasn't about the money at all, maybe just getting away from the house where she'd nursed

Phil over those last few weeks before he finally moved into the hospice was what she needed to start healing.

Or maybe it's the guilt. You could have helped him, but you didn't.

As she walked back to the table with the drinks, a smashing sounded behind her. A plate had been dropped. Somebody swore. Another voice asked where the brush pan was kept. And there standing behind the floor to ceiling windows, on the pavement outside, lit only by the amber light from the car park lighting, was the indistinct shape of a man. His frame was all too familiar.

Judy froze.

It's not real. This is just your imagination messing with you. Your head is all over the place. What do you expect will happen when you start thinking of the dead?

Not that they will show up and spy on your date.

A hand touched her arm.

"Need help?" Richard said, "you looked a million miles away. What are you looking at?"

He peered across the restaurant, checking where Judy was watching.

She tore herself away from the figure, then forced a smile. "I'm sorry, just thought I saw someone I recognised. But I got it wrong. It's nobody."

As they walked back to the table, she checked again, but the figure had gone.

26

Something woke her. Jemma's heart was thudding, and she dared to take a breath. Her arms had broken out in goosebumps and she felt freezing. She didn't think she'd left the window open, but couldn't think of why else it could be so cold.

She listened for signs that there were others in the house and caught the sound of her mum's heavy breathing, almost a snore. Unlike her but reassuring all the same. It had been a long time since she'd felt the need to call out to her mum in the middle of the night but that was exactly what she felt like doing now.

If she wasn't so scared that the something that had woken her was still here and would know for certain she was now awake.

Beyond the noise of the snoring, there was another noise that she picked up on. It wasn't the sound of the wind knocking the bay tree into the fence panels, or the tumble drier downstairs on its crease prevention cycle.

It was the noise of someone under her bed.

There was barely any room under her bed which had become a storage area for boxes and toys she'd grown out of but wasn't prepared to part with. The toys that if her friends found in her room, she'd laugh them off and say they were on their way to the charity shop.

But something was under her bed and it was moving.

The bedroom door was ajar. The curtains were closed. There was only the faint glimmer of moonlight coming through the crack in the curtains and the night light her mum turned on every night on the landing. Nothing was out of place.

Except, was the door a little wider than she'd left it? And had her clothes shifted from their place on the back of her desk chair? It looked like something had fallen to the floor. And the photo frame on the dressing table had moved hadn't it? The one with her and dad had been turned around so it faced the wall. She would never have left it like that.

Was that breathing she could hear coming from under the bed?

If she screamed out for help, the something wouldn't let her get out of the room without grabbing her. She'd seen enough horror movies—always at her friend's house, never here—to know that the monsters under the bed would always try to grab the feet of the person in the bed.

Jemma drew her feet up slowly, ever so slowly, so eventually, her knees were up against her chest.

Then she looked at the floor. The bed was in the middle of the room. She stared at the carpet, and the rug, trying to distinguish what was pattern and what didn't belong.

But it was difficult from where she was positioned. She would have to move to a better spot to know for sure. There was always the chance she'd made a mistake and that the things that had been moved had been because of her mum when she came to check on her, and nothing at all to do with the imaginary thing under her bed.

Because it was imaginary. Monsters didn't exist.

Ghosts didn't exist.

But she'd seen things these last few months that made a mockery of that argument.

The monsters are real.

Jemma closed her eyes and counted to ten. That should work. That will banish the thing from under her bed.

One, two...

A swish as something brushed against carpet.

Three, four...

She shivered as the temperature in the room dropped even further.

Five, six, seven...

A new sound to her right, about an arm's reach from her.
This isn't working.
Eight, nine...
She opened her eyes. The woman was standing beside her bed. Her clothes were dirty. The denim dress she was wearing looking dirty, and the splotches she thought were just dirt could just as easily have been dried blood. Her hair was long, down past the shoulder, dark, but that could have been more mud clinging to it, shaping it into rats' tails.

But it was her face that scared Jemma the most. The skin, what there was of it, was pale like paper, but there were injuries, bits were missing, and in those missing bits, she could see the shadowy stains beneath that could have been muscle or bone.

The thing was smiling.

Jemma screamed and ran for the door which slammed shut before she could reach it. With desperate force, she slammed her fists into the wood, drumming away, and screamed for help. But she still couldn't take her eyes away from the creature, it was not a woman, only a creature, the monster from under her bed. The monster in her room that wanted to hurt her.

"Mum!" she screamed, but now she pressed her back against the door, trying to pour herself into the wood in an effort to get away from the intruder.

The creature's smile had gone, replaced by a scowl that froze Jemma's blood. It tilted its head then it moved towards her. A stumbling movement, like it was only just learning how to walk again after an injury. And she might well have been injured. Whatever had happened to this creature in life must have been horrendous. Jemma knew she wasn't in a nightmare, and she knew that the creature in her room wasn't alive. No more than the shadowmen had been alive. But being alive was unnecessary if the thing wanted to hurt you badly enough.

The door shook behind her. "Jemma!" Her mum's voice was panicked and high pitched. Then, there was another voice she didn't recognise, a man's voice. The creature wasn't reacting to the voices from the other side of the door. Its fixation was her and it stumbled to the edge of her bed. If it wanted, it could reach her in seconds, and yet it was taking its time. Jemma's heart was beating so hard it was hurting her chest, making it difficult to breathe.

"There's someone in here." Her voice didn't sound like her own.

"Stand back from the door." Again the man's voice.

Then another impact, heavier this time. The door burst open and Jemma turned to see a strange man charge into the room, followed by her mum. Both were dressed only in their underwear.

"Watch out for the—" Jemma tried to warn them both, but as she glanced back into her room, she saw the creature had disappeared, like it had never been there at all.

27

Well this is awkward, Judy thought as she passed a glass of milk across the table to Jemma. Both her and Richard were sat at the kitchen table, Richard having taken the time to get dressed and therefore looking terribly out of place in his shirt and trousers whilst Jemma and Judy were both in their dressing gowns. He was the impostor, and it embarrassed Judy to think she'd snuck him in whilst Jemma was asleep.

This isn't like me. I don't do these kinds of things.

The kettle boiled, and she poured water into two mugs, stirring away, delaying the moment when she'd have to join them at the table and explain what was going on. Thankfully, Jemma pulled the plaster on that particular cut.

"How long have you been seeing my mum?"

Judy glanced and caught Richard's expression. How truthful was he about to be? They'd known each other a matter of days and had ended up in bed together.

Did that make Judy a slut? Was that what Jemma would think of her? This was the first time since Phil had died that she'd ever been with another man and the first time Jemma had ever known her to be in a relationship with anyone else.

What had begun as a night of passionate healing for them both had been turned into some ugly thing that she just wanted to forget.

Perhaps I should ask Richard to leave. This should be something to work through with Jemma on our own as a family.

"Not long," Richard replied diplomatically. That should save a few blushes.

"How long is not long?"

"Less than a week. Your mum came into my shop on Saturday when you were at your singing group."

"It's a drama club."

"OK. Sorry, at your drama club. We just seemed to hit it off."

"Getting together with someone in a few days seems pretty quick to me."

"It is. But, I guess, we've known each other from school, and sometimes that's the way things work out."

"You're her first boyfriend."

"Oh. Right."

Is that what he is? A boyfriend?

"So, you'd better be nice to her."

"I will. I promise."

"Promising will have to do. You're a stranger and you're in my house but Mum wanted you here, so that's OK, I guess."

"Right."

"But, you're on a warning."

Judy came to stand beside her daughter and flashed an admonishing look at her. "Jemma! You don't get to talk like that."

Jemma looked up at her mum and there was still that fear in her eyes from the bedroom earlier. "I mean it. You've been through enough with dad and—" her voice trailed off, but she recovered and said, "—the other things. You can't have a boyfriend mess you around. Men aren't worth it."

Richard couldn't contain his laugh, well more of a chuckle than a laugh, but Jemma threw him a suspicious look all the same. "I'll let that pass because you got me out of my bedroom."

"I'm sorry." Talk of the bedroom seemed to suck warmth from the room.

Judy sat and curled her hands around her mug. "What did you see in there?"

Jemma didn't look like she much wanted to talk about it and Judy found it difficult to blame her for that. Shutting the fears inside was one way of dealing with it, but it wouldn't help them in the long-term.

"Did you not see it?"

"I didn't see anything," Richard said. "I'm sorry. What did you see? Was it a nightmare?"

This time, both Judy and Jemma gave him a look as if to say that that was just about the stupidest thing they'd heard in a long time.

"It wasn't a nightmare," Judy said. "Tell us."

Jemma closed her eyes for a moment, then opened them and they glistened like melting ice. Judy wanted to hug her and tell her not to worry about it, but she knew that if they didn't worry about it, the problem was unlikely to go away. Jemma glanced at the kitchen door. "Do you mind if we shut that and turn on the big light?"

Richard hurried to his feet, glad to be of some use, and did as instructed. When he settled back down again, Jemma talked. She held nothing back, starting with the noise under her bed that had woken her, and ending with the moment Richard knocked open the door and found her braced against the wall, hands up protectively in front of her face.

Eventually, Richard spoke. "There wasn't anyone in your room. It must have been a dream."

"It wasn't a dream," Judy replied. "I've been sensing something around me for a few days, ever since Lisa got in touch and invited us out to dinner."

"Who's Lisa?"

"My sister-in-law."

"What've you seen, Mum?"

What had she seen? Pulling apart the emotion from the physical was tricky.

"Felt more than seen. Like I'm not alone when the house is empty."

Richard looked confused. "You're serious, aren't you?"

"Yes."

"But you're talking as if stuff like this is real. Only it's not real."

Judy almost rolled her eyes, but instead she exchanged a look with Jemma. "It's not important whether you believe this. But you need to realise that what both Jemma and myself have experienced is real. You can come up with explanations that will make you feel better about it all, but that's for you to do. I won't do that for you."

Richard didn't respond, only took a sip from his coffee and glanced up at the ceiling. You're not sure though are you? Judy thought. You've sensed something as well, but you can't quite put your finger on what.

Judy wondered if it was safe to stay in the house. It had been on her mind ever since she'd seen the shadowmen, but that had been months ago, and the Almost Doors hadn't made an appearance since Adam Cowl had been sent into hiding. Jemma had expressed no interest in moving out of the house but then why would she? This was the only home she'd ever known. Her ties to it were far stronger than Judy's own.

"I'm listening. Tell me what you've experienced," Richard said. His tone was less confrontational, and she thanked him silently for that.

"I was looking into Lisa and Phil's adoption. Lisa's been trying to track down the adoption agency that her dad used back in the seventies. I wondered whether Phil had kept any paperwork that he hadn't mentioned. I was going through his stuff. But, when I was up there, I got a sense that I wasn't alone. It was dark, and I was only using a torch, but the attic fell cold, and across the space, at the back of the attic, I thought I saw someone."

"There's someone in our attic and you didn't tell me?"

"No. Absolutely not. There's no one up there. But for a moment, I wasn't sure."

"You thought you saw, or you actually saw?"

It was a key difference and a consideration that Judy hadn't been concerned with. Deciding whether it had been a figment of her imagination or something more real would have a bearing on how she felt about living in the house.

"I saw it," she concluded.

"What did it do? Did it try to communicate?"

Judy shook her head. "It was just a shadow. I looked away, and it had gone. But I don't think it meant to hurt me. I don't think it can." But was she willing to bet the wellbeing of her child on that hunch? The shadowmen had been able to hurt people when such a thing seemed incredulous.

"I think you're wrong, Mum. I think it wants to hurt us. It came after me in my room, it was hiding under my bed. Why would it do that if not to hurt me?"

Judy threw a look at Richard, but he shrugged as if to say I have nothing. This was not what he was expecting on their first night together. I've probably scared you off for good now haven't I?

"It disappeared when we came into your room. That's a good thing. That means it doesn't like us being able to see it. I don't think you have anything to worry about."

"I'm not going back in my bedroom."

"That's fine. You can sleep with me."

Jemma glanced across the table at Richard.

"I can get going."

"No. I don't want you to go," Jemma replied then to her mum said, "Could he sleep in the spare room?"

"You'd be very welcome."

Please don't hate me, but please don't leave us.

He grinned awkwardly like it was masking something else, fear perhaps.

"Sure," he said. "No problem."

28

The next morning, Judy found Richard in the kitchen, washing the mugs from last night in the sink, whilst staring out into the garden.

"Thank you," she said, and wandered over to give him a peck on the cheek. His stubble scratched and he could have done with a shower, but there was a manliness to it she enjoyed.

"Did you get any sleep?"

"None. I kept the light on all night." He chuckled. "I'm sorry that Jemma had to meet me like that. I shouldn't have stayed over."

"But I wanted you to stay over. Jemma's tougher than she looks. And besides, she appreciated you being here after what happened. We both appreciated it."

"I didn't help. I don't know what happened. Last night, we spoke about things that I can't even begin to think about."

Judy opened the back door and let the cool air wake her up some more.

"The way you were talking last night... You were taking it all in your stride like that was something normal."

"There's nothing normal about it, but I guess you could say I'm getting used to strange things happening."

"Do you think Jemma was maybe making things up?"

"No," she said firmly. "Not at all. She had no reason to lie."

"And the things you described. The ghost you saw in the attic?"

"I'm not sure if it was a ghost, but I saw something."

"But you're still not sure."

She sighed, then closed the door and went to the fridge, retrieving a carton of eggs and a pack of bacon. "Something happened to me last year, shortly after Phil died. I met someone who helped me see that I have a certain affinity for these kinds of phenomena."

"You see dead people?" he said it then frowned. The idea must be so strange to you, she thought. She remembered when it was so strange to her as well.

"I know it sounds ridiculous, but it's true."

"And Jemma?"

"Are you asking whether she can see dead people too?"

Richard nodded.

"If she says she saw something in her room last night, I have to believe her. Based on what I know, I don't have any reason to think she'd make it up."

When Richard didn't answer, she went and slipped an arm around his waist. "I'm sorry. It feels like I've dragged you into my weird excuse for a life."

"You don't need to apologise. It's OK. I'm fine. I just don't know what to make of it all."

"Do you believe?" she asked tentatively.

"Honestly, I don't know. Is that a problem?"

"No."

I guess not, she thought, but it would make life a hell of a lot easier if you did.

She let him go and began to make breakfast for all three of them, checking the clock to see when she needed to give Jemma a call. Her daughter had fallen asleep quickly beside her, but she'd been tossing and turning all night. Every time Judy nodded off, Jemma would wake her by turning over or muttering indecipherable utterances. Today would be a struggle for both of them to stay awake.

When the clock hit seven, Judy went to nudge Jemma but found that she was already up and dressed for school.

"I've made breakfast," Judy said.

"Thanks. I'm starving."

When Jemma saw that Richard was still here and sat at the kitchen table, finishing his breakfast, there was a noticeable reaction as if she'd forgotten he was in the house. But she sat down and asked politely for him to pass the salt.

"Jemma, I'm sorry for surprising you last night? I know it must have been upsetting to find a strange man in your house."

Jemma looked to her mum. What was that expression? Amusement? "You weren't as scary as seeing that thing in my room."

"Granted. But even so, I'm sorry."

Jemma shrugged. "So is Richard your boyfriend?"

The two adults exchanged glances. This was something they hadn't discussed. Richard was a nice guy, and it had been a long time since she'd spent any time at all with a nice guy, let alone shared her bed with one. But did this fling even have a future beyond last night? After the commotion with Jemma's room and having Richard sleep in the spare room, probably not. Judy felt sad at the thought.

"We're good friends," Richard replied. "And we'll be seeing each other again. Is that a problem?" he asked gently.

"No problem. If it makes Mum happy."

"Yes," Judy replied. "It does."

"Then enough with the questions or I will be late for school." She continued tucking into her breakfast, Judy and Richard both exchanging looks. Richard didn't have kids of his own and Judy wondered what he made of the breeziness that Jemma accepted him in their house. It was so casual that it released a little of the guilt she was holding onto.

"I best be going," Richard said, taking his plate to the sink. "It was nice to meet you, Jemma."

She nodded, her mouth still full of toast and bacon. Judy led Richard to the front door. When she spoke, she kept her voice low to make sure that Jemma couldn't overhear them.

"Thank you," she said.

"For what?"

"For not being a jerk. I didn't know how she'd take to me bringing someone around."

"She's a good kid. She had a traumatic night."

"We all did. What time do you need to be at the shop?"

He glanced at his watch, then grimaced. "I like to be there for nine. It's never good form to open late. But I need to get back to the house first, get a change of clothes."

"You look fine."

"I don't smell fine, but it's kind of you to say so." And then he gave her a peck on the cheek and turned to go. "I'll call you later, if that's OK."

"Of course." She closed the door and leant back against it, looking around the hallway, wondering whether the last few hours had even happened. She returned to find Jemma in the kitchen on her phone. She kissed the top of her head. "How you doing? Did you get any sleep?"

"Funny dreams."

"I bet."

"And no more sign of—"

"The thing in my room? No. Nothing. Do you think it was a dream? A night terror like you used to have?"

"I'm sure of it. There's nothing in this house that could hurt either of us." The lie was an easy one. The lies said to protect the ones we love usually are. There was a chance that what Jemma had seen had resulted from a bad dream or a night terror. Although Judy had done her best to keep her from the details of what had happened with Seth and at Ravenmeols, Jemma had undoubtedly overheard conversations between her and Seth or Malc. And there had been the time at Seth's new house with the occult collection—that morning she'd been convinced she'd heard her dead father calling to her from the basement.

"I am sorry that you found out about Richard like that. I didn't mean that to happen."

"It's fine."

"Yeah, you say that, but I want you to know that I didn't mean it. I got carried away."

Jemma's face was difficult to read. She finished her breakfast and was focused on her phone, only half in the conversation. This was typical of her, never quite being all there.

"If you like him, I don't see the problem."

Judy cleared Jemma's plate from the table. "How about I set up a meal together, give you a chance to get to know him."

"If you like."

Don't push it. If she doesn't want to talk about it, don't force her. You might not like what she has to say. Give her a chance to process it.

"If you're too tired for school, I don't mind calling and telling them you're sick."

Jemma glanced up ever so briefly, an eyebrow raised, before returning to her phone. "I'm good. I guess I'd rather be at school right now."

"OK. If you change your mind when you get there, tell them you're not feeling well, and I can come and pick you up."

Later, after Jemma had left for school, Judy reflected on that morning and thought things could have been a lot worse. At least Jemma wasn't giving her a hard time, and they'd addressed Richard staying over. Judy wondered how she'd feel if Richard became a regular fixture of her life. Judy wasn't even sure she wanted Richard to be a regular fixture. The time in bed had been fun. He'd been gentle and held her afterwards. But she barely knew the man. After twenty years of marriage to Phil, she'd still never uncovered all his secrets. How many did a man she'd never met have?

There was one thing she needed to get to the bottom of, and quickly. As much as she'd like to think that what Jemma had seen had been a figment of her imagination, from recent experience, Judy doubted it. This life she'd been exposed to, with its strangeness and scariness, and unimaginable horror, was her thing. It wasn't meant to be something that could hurt the people she cared about most in her life. Was this what Seth and Malc had had to experience? Seth had spent most of his adult life away from his parents, barely speaking to them. At first, she'd assumed it was because of the bad feeling between them over the death of Kelly, his sister. And Malc—he'd separated from Georgia after their last run-in with the Adherents. How much of that was Georgia wanting to get away from the horrors that gravitated towards her husband, and how much of that was Malc letting his wife and son move away so they would no longer be in the line of fire?

Upstairs, Judy paused on the landing, listening to the sounds of the house. "Is there anyone here?" she asked.

The house was silent. She could almost hear the air moving through the rooms like it was breathing. She counted the doors she could see and confirmed the number with the number she knew to be correct. There were no Almost Doors here. Those mysterious portals hid in plain sight with the strange property of people not being able to notice them unless they concentrated hard or had them pointed out by someone like Seth.

At the threshold of Jemma's room, she hesitated. The door was open, the bedroom itself that of a typical teenager, bedclothes rumpled still, hanging half off the bed. Pyjamas on the floor, scrunched up. The dressing table with a tipped-over can of deodorant and cleansing wipes, used and discarded. Condensation clung to the window, masking the outside.

The door was high quality, solid wood and painted white. Last night, she'd tried to open it, but it had felt locked, despite not having a lock fitted. Jemma wasn't strong enough to block the door herself, and it had taken Richard's strength to get it open. That bit wasn't imagined. That had happened. So, even if what Jemma had experienced had been a night terror, that didn't explain away the door that wouldn't open.

"Are you in here?" she asked the empty room.

There was no sign of anything unusual happening. No sudden chills. No shadows moving in the corners. She carefully lowered herself and checked under the bed for any sign that someone had been there. The bed was a simple bed frame from IKEA with a hollow space underneath. That hollow space was filled with under-the-bed container boxes that Jemma had used to store away things she didn't use every day but didn't yet need moving up into the loft. Nothing could have got under the bed without disturbing the boxes.

But a ghost wouldn't be bothered by physical objects.

Judy went to the bedside table and reached behind the unit, feeling for the edge of the duct tape she knew was there. Carefully, she removed it and retrieved the voice recorder.

The recorder was still recording onto its SD card. This unit could store ten hours' worth of material and that's why she'd bought it, knowing that it would see through the night. Jemma had no idea she'd placed the device there, and she didn't think she'd ever want to tell her. Jemma would no doubt freak out to think her mum had recorded her, but since seeing things at Lisa's house, Judy wasn't about to not investigate her own house.

She quickly made Jemma's bed, then sat on the end of it, looking at the recorder, knowing that she had to do this but also torn at the same time.

You've got to know. If there was something in her room last night, you've got to know.

The unit had an inbuilt display that allowed her to skip back to a point in time. She chose a point about half an hour before the moment they'd burst into her room. That should be enough to listen to.

She clicked play.

There was no hiss from the player, a nice side-effect of going digital, and it meant that she could discern the breathing sounds from her daughter. They were not the calm breathing patterns of a girl in a deep sleep, but restless and inter-cut with almost inaudible moans and half-said words.

Bad dreams, she thought almost with relief. She's having a bad dream.

But what about the locked door?

After a few minutes of the disturbed breathing, there was another sound. Fainter, but definitely there. She set the volume to max and could hear something else alongside Jemma's breathing.

Words.

Mumbles.

No, not mumbling, just quietly spoken. She glanced up at the room and tried to work out from where they might have originated. It was impossible to say.

Although the words weren't spoken in Jemma's voice, they were familiar.

"Go back to sleep," the woman on the recording said.

29

After dropping into a couple of estate agents in Hillside, Judy headed back into town and towards Adrian's office. If Faith and Adrian were happy to take Jemma away for a few days, she wouldn't let the opportunity pass her by. It would do Jemma the world of good getting away from the house.

And seeing how Adrian never offered to pay for anything for Jemma, it was about time he treated her. She thought she'd stop by to let him know in person, but that wasn't the sole reason. She wanted to ask him about Premier Adoption Services. If Adrian's company once held offices in the same building, there was a good chance he knew more about the adoption company than he'd passed onto Lisa. He probably knew some of the people that worked there and Judy wanted to press him on some names. She could track them down and get them to help look up records.

She parked in one of the visitors' spaces at Adrian's office building and approached the reception. Two men were talking animatedly in the main lobby. Instinct more than anything made her hold back, then step behind the tree in front of the building. She didn't want them to see her.

It was Adrian talking to a similarly aged man in a dark blue boiler suit. From this distance, she couldn't make out the second man's features, but there was something about the way he stood that suggested this was not an amicable meeting.

The maintenance guy turned to walk away, but Adrian grabbed his arm, and stopped him in his tracks. Now closer, Judy could see the anger on the stranger's face as he snatched his arm back before storming out the exit.

Judy waited a moment in case Adrian followed him out, but when he turned away and headed deeper into the office building, she came out from behind the tree and hurried to the stranger. He had stopped by the maintenance van and had his key in his hand.

"Excuse me," she started, then noticed the security pass on his lanyard.

Matt Hodgson.

"Yes, do I know you?" he replied, a frown etched deep above his thin eyebrows.

"We spoke on the phone," she continued. "I'm Judy. I was asking about the adoption company. Can we talk?"

"I guess so, but I don't see how I can be of any more help. I told you what I knew on the phone."

She smiled, then ignoring his brusque tone.

"You don't mind, do you?" He pulled out a small tin of tobacco and pulled out a self-rolled cigarette. She waited while he lighted it.

"You're a busy man."

"Come again."

"Working across two sites."

"Oh, yeah, you could say that."

"You do work here though, don't you?"

He glanced at the burning tip of his roll-up as he took a drag. "I work in lots of places."

Not quite a straight answer.

"It's just that I came here to see my father-in-law and I wondered whether that was who you were talking with just now."

He raised an eyebrow. "You been spying on me?"

"I saw you when I parked. I was just about to come into the building when I saw you two talking. I just thought it was funny that we had someone in common."

She could almost see his mind whirling, as he tried to think of a good reason why he was here. She doubted his story about working across two sites but figured it would be an easy enough story to confirm if she could find the contact details for the building management company. And if he didn't work there, it gave him very few reasons to be on site.

Unless he was there to specifically speak to Adrian.

"Yeah, I know Adrian. We go back."

"It's great that you still keep in touch. You must be good friends."

Who were arguing with each other like the bitterest of enemies.

Something about her line of questioning must have alerted his bullshit detector because his whole posture changed. He straightened, tipped his head, and eyed her like this was the first time he'd seen her.

"Why are you here?"

"Dropping in to speak to Adrian. He's taking my daughter away at the weekend. Just wanted to confirm the details."

"You don't have a phone?"

"I was passing."

And then Matt did something unexpected. He stepped close and put his hand on her shoulder. She froze, unsure what was going on and whether she needed to react or just wait it out. She didn't need to wait for more than a second. Matt's face turned. It was like he'd been wearing a mask the whole time they'd been talking and now he'd let it drop so she could see the real him.

He lent in and whispered in her ear. His breath was hot and stank of the roll-up he still held in his hand. "Don't trust him. If I were you, I wouldn't be letting my daughter spend any time with him. He's dangerous."

Then it was over. Matt let go of her arm, opened his van and slipped inside. She stepped back and watched. Much as she didn't think her father-in-law was dangerous, something about Matt's comments resonated.

Don't let your memory trick you, she thought. You saw them together. There was nothing friendly about it. Matt dislikes Adrian for whatever reason, and he's trying to drive a wedge between you. Perhaps that's how he gets his kicks.

Matt reversed his van at speed, and as he switched the gears from reverse back into first, he hesitated and looked at her through the closed window. The look sent a shiver across her back.

30

Judy was waiting on the doorstep at Lisa's for two minutes before she finally appeared, dishevelled like she'd just woken up. Her hair was tied back in a scrunchy.

"Sorry, didn't hear the doorbell," Lisa said.

"Is everything OK? I've not heard from you for days."

"I've been busy."

There was an awkward moment as Judy wondered whether she was going to be let inside.

"Oh, come in," Lisa said, leaving the door wide open as she ambled back into the depths of the house. Judy closed the door and watched her sister-in-law head towards the kitchen. She wanted to get a reading on the house so paused at the bottom of the stairs, looking up into the dark. She couldn't hear anyone upstairs but didn't think Ellis was home.

But that didn't mean they were alone in the house.

"What are you doing?" Lisa was standing by the entrance to the back room, her face impassive. She looked withdrawn.

"Just listening. Has there been anything else happening since I was last here?"

Lisa shook her head. "No, there's been nothing. I think whatever you did the other night must have scared it off."

Judy followed her through to the kitchen where Lisa flicked on the kettle and stood leaning against the kitchen counter.

"Really? Nothing at all?"

"Nothing. It's like that night must have been enough for it. Perhaps it just wanted to give us a scare and now that it's done that, it's just gone."

Judy frowned. Lisa wasn't being truthful, and she couldn't understand why.

What are you hiding? Why aren't you telling me the truth?

"How's Ellis? Has he seen anything unusual?"

"He's at work. He's been busy with that girl of his from the office. He's hardly ever home these days. To be honest, it's a nice break. Gives me time to think."

The kettle boiled and clicked off.

Lisa glanced up at the ceiling, then catching herself, she smiled and got two mugs from the draining board. As she wiped the edges with a tea towel, she asked, "How's Jemma?"

"Good. Keeping busy with Fortnite and somehow squeezing in her homework, but I've got no real reason to complain. I suppose I've got to accept that even though she's not technically a teenager, she's been acting like one for the last couple of years. It could be worse. She could be messing about on the streets like some in her year."

"That's good. I'm pleased. She's such a good girl. And you're a good mum. It's not been easy for you since Phil died."

The observation hit her from left field.

"No. It's been difficult. But I'm over the worst of it."

Lisa poured the water. "The worst of it. You make it sound like an illness you're recovering from." She laughed.

"No. That's not what I meant."

"Like your grief is the flu." She stirred the cups vigorously, the teaspoon smashing away at the sides an unnecessary amount of times.

"I wouldn't have put it like that."

"No. I'm sorry. I guess I'm just missing him."

"It's all right. You should miss him. He was your brother."

"Tell me, do you ever miss him?"

Lisa's eyes looked red, like she'd been crying earlier. Was she really missing Phil? When he was alive, and during Phil and Judy's marriage, it wasn't like he ever kept close contact with Lisa. They probably only saw each other once a month at their parents' house when Faith dragged everyone together for a family meal. And those were hardly the friendliest of times. Phil was never relaxed and that meant the rest of the family couldn't relax.

"Of course I do," Judy said finally, hoping that she sounded convincing. "Why would you think that I wouldn't?"

"Are you seeing someone else?"

Lisa picked out the teaspoon from one of the mugs and dropped it into the sink. The tension was getting thick in here and Judy glanced nervously at the door. Whatever Lisa was going through, she didn't deserve to be made to feel like this.

"Why do you ask that?" Judy replied, keeping her voice calm, forcing her irritation aside.

"I'm interested. I just want you to be happy, obviously." Lisa's smile didn't match her tone and did nothing to settle Judy's concerns about the woman's state of mind.

"Phil's been dead almost a year."

"Eleven months and fourteen days."

"OK."

"The anniversary is in two weeks' time."

"Yes. I knew that. Of course I knew that. But I won't put my life on hold for ever."

"He's not been dead for a year yet, and you're seeing some estate agent."

Judy paused. "How do you know I'm seeing an estate agent?"

Lisa sniffed. "I've seen you."

"When? Where?"

"In town."

"On what day?"

"Does it matter?"

Yes, I think it might matter, she thought. I think it matters because you've not seen me at all have you?

"When did you last speak to your dad?"

"What's dad got to do with anything?"

"I think he's told you I've been seeing someone else and for whatever reason he's told you about it."

For a moment, it looked like Lisa might not answer. She messed with the scrunchy in her hair and took her mug in her hands, not bothering to pass Judy her own drink. "You're right. He mentioned it. But he's only trying to help."

"Help? In what way is spreading gossip about me helping?"

"He doesn't think you're done grieving yet. I don't think you are either. And whilst you're in a difficult place, you're liable to make some hasty decisions."

"I'll grieve to my own timetable thanks; I don't need Adrian or you to tell me what's proper. Jesus, what the hell is wrong with your family?"

"My family?" She raised an eyebrow. "There's nothing wrong with my family. My family has always been good to you. Hell, if it wasn't for my dad, you'd never have got that house you're in now. Phil was always the spoilt one, getting anything he wanted. Look at me in this pokey house, needing to have a stupid lodger to help pay the rent whilst you've got your house all paid for now that my brother's dead."

Was that what this was about? Jealousy? She was jealous of how her dad had been treating Phil compared to herself. Judy had always assumed that the pair had been treated equally, and that Lisa had chosen to live in the smaller house.

"I'm sorry if you think that. But I don't know what arrangements your dad had with Phil. It was all sorted out without my knowledge."

"Great. I'm sure it was all a wonderful surprise for you."

It was. But you've drained away any remaining good thoughts I had about the house.

Judy shivered. There was still more left unsaid. This wasn't just about a house or the fact that Judy was moving on with her life. Lisa was pissed at her about something else.

"I found Phil's journals in the attic. I thought you might be interested to know that he'd seen the same woman you'd seen."

It was like a mask had been lifted. A reminder of what had brought them closer recently. Only now it seems that we couldn't be farther apart.

"What did he say? What had he seen?"

"Someone in my house. A woman in the shadows. The face always indistinct. Even when he couldn't see her, he got the sense that she was there."

"Oh my god, poor Phil. Do you think that's why he was the way he was?"

Judy's chest tightened. "What do you mean?"

Lisa's eyebrows drew close. "I know that you didn't always see eye to eye. I wonder whether this was partly to blame."

Judy thought about the time she'd had to lock herself in the bathroom and wondered whether she should ask Lisa if Phil had gone off the rails that day because he'd seen a ghost. She restrained herself. Unburdening herself like that wouldn't serve any purpose other than further alienate herself from the family, and much as she sometimes didn't want reminding about her in-laws, they were the closest family she had. Lisa, most of the time, was the sister she'd never had.

"Whatever Phil's issues were, I'm sure they weren't because of ghosts."

"But maybe. I mean if he was on edge all the time. It might explain why he was so argumentative."

"I think we need to change the subject. I told you about the journals because I wanted you to know that you weren't the only one who'd seen this woman. What I would like to know is why I'm now seeing her as well."

"You are?"

Judy nodded. "Several times."

"I saw her again the other night. She was in the house. She tried to drown Jasper. And there was this teddy bear. I've seen it before. I don't know how it got into the house." She told Judy how she'd been drawn out of the house only to faint and wake up later on the sofa. Judy listened attentively.

"What happened to the bear?"

"The first time I saw it, I threw it in the rubbish. I couldn't find it again after the second time."

Judy frowned but she dismissed it as unimportant. It was far more important to establish what these entities were.

"And this other figure. The second one. You've not seen them before?"

Lisa shook her head. "No."

"And you're sure it wasn't burglars?"

Lisa sighed. "It wasn't burglars."

If what Lisa was saying was true, and really Judy didn't have a reason to doubt her, that meant that the ghost or ghosts could physically harm them. She thought again about the thing that Jemma had seen in her room, had heard under her bed.

She can't stay there again.

"Maybe you should move out," Judy suggested. "Live with your parents until this settles down."

"What makes you think things will settle down? You were supposed to fix this. I trusted you to make it go away." She was agitated, brushing her arm with her hand, shivering as if it was freezing in the kitchen when it really wasn't.

"I told you I'd look into it with you. I'm no expert."

"You saw things at the hospital. You have all the gear."

"I bought the equipment specifically. I didn't have it lying around." Judy's chest was feeling tight. This wasn't any way to treat her. After going out of her way to try to help, she was being made to feel like the cause of the problems. "Perhaps I should go. Maybe call me if you need help."

But Lisa didn't look like she was about to ask for help from Judy anytime soon. She didn't even come to the front door to show her out.

31

"I want to put the house on the market. How soon do you think you can do that?"

Judy had spent the last ten minutes shaking in her car, the anger from the meeting with Lisa had bubbled to the surface and she'd only just held back tears.

That family are all the same, she thought. Like brother like sister.

She'd not expected such a reaction from Lisa, and she tried to remember what she'd told her she'd do when Lisa had first mentioned her house being haunted. She couldn't have promised getting rid of the ghost because such knowledge was way beyond her.

And she doesn't seem to care that we're now seeing the same ghost in my house. Jemma's seen it and yet it's all about poor poor Lisa and how bloody hard done by she is.

The situation was ridiculous, and Judy couldn't see how it would be resolved until Lisa reached out and offered an apology.

After the confrontation, Judy had driven into town and was sat in Richard's shop, a pack of doughnuts open on the desk between them. Richard was halfway through his second when Judy dropped her request into the conversation.

Slowly, he finished chewing his mouthful, then put the remaining half back down on the desk. He eyed her up, checking to see how serious she was being.

"What's happened?"

"Nothing. I've just let what you said the other day sink in and you're right. It's time to move on. There's no point in being trapped in that house. That won't help build good memories."

And what I need right now is to build good memories.

The house no longer held any appeal for her. She'd mentally listed all the reasons why selling up was the best option. Firstly, and painfully obviously, there was the ghost. It was difficult to find a house comfortable knowing that at any moment, an entity could appear and attack you or your child. Secondly, there were the memories of her life with Phil there. The less said about that, the better. But thirdly, if what Lisa had said was true, then the house had caused a wedge between the family that she'd never even known about. She'd always assumed that Adrian had treated his children fairly, and that was a mistake. Adrian had favoured Phil and Lisa had quietly had to put up with it, the bitterness simmering away throughout her adult life.

"What aren't you telling me?" He sat back in his chair and stared at her, searching for any clue in her expression that would explain what was going on.

"Will you help me sell the house or not?"

"Has Jemma seen more... things?"

"No."

"Have you?"

She didn't answer immediately, wondering whether this was a sign that Richard might believe her if she were to tell him the truth.

Come on then, what is the truth? What do you think is going on?

She reached for a doughnut and took a bite. The caramel topping crunched and a piece of icing dropped onto the carpet. She quickly retrieved it then she bit the bullet.

"Do you believe that Jemma saw something?" Judy asked.

"I think it's only important what Jemma believes. If it scares her to be in the house, you've only got a few options available."

"And they are?"

"Counselling?" He shrugged, then raised his hands in a placating gesture. "Hear me out, I'm not saying there's anything wrong with Jemma, but if she suffers from anxiety, it might help. You told me it's not long since her dad died. She's still going through the grieving process. Who knows what her mind might do?"

"She doesn't need counselling. But you didn't answer my question."

"I know."

"So, what do you believe?"

"I doubt the existence of ghosts. I used to believe in them as a boy, but then I grew up and realised that there is always an explanation."

"I told you I thought I saw something in the loft. I think it's always been there—been in our house. My husband saw it. I read it in one of his journals. I know that when I'm in the house on my own, there is a presence, and it's only been the last few weeks that I appreciate that feeling for what it is. Do you remember the fire at the old hospital last October? Ravenmeols?"

He nodded. "Vaguely. Why?"

"I was there. I'd gone there on the promise of a night of ghost hunting, only the organisers weren't interested in ghost hunting. They were the remnants of a decades' old cult that wanted host bodies for the souls of their departed brothers. They travel to this living realm through portals that manifest like doorways and once here they look like terrible shadow creatures. They can kill you or they can possess you. I think death would be the preferred option."

She paused, took a bite of her doughnut and watched his expression. His eyes had narrowed, and he looked like a teacher whose unruly pupil had crossed the line. It had felt good telling Richard the truth. Or part of the truth. There would be nothing to be gained from over-sharing. If he wasn't scared off by what she'd already told him, she'd consider sharing more. She wasn't yet sure whether she'd try to laugh it off as a joke if he dismissed the story.

Richard picked up his remaining half of doughnut and got off his chair to pace around the shop. A blob of custard dripped onto his tie, and with his spare hand, he wiped it away, or tried to, instead leaving a smear that would require the tie going in the wash.

"I want to think you're making this up, but I can't imagine why you'd be doing that."

"I'm not making it up."

"Then you're either deluded or you're sincere."

"Do I look deluded?"

"I don't know. I don't know what a deluded person looks like."

"What does your gut tell you?"

He paused by the doorway, then turned over the shop sign so it said closed. "My gut is telling me we should get a drink."

"It's not even lunchtime."

"Look what you've driven me to," he said, and a hesitant smile flittered upon his face, then left just as quickly. "But I'm pretty sure it's the only way to sort this out."

*

They headed to the Wetherspoons on the corner of Lord Street. Despite Judy's misgivings over drinking at this time were eased once they stepped inside and she saw others eating brunch with a pint. There really was no helping people.

Who are you to judge? she thought. You're no better than anyone else here. Drinking to forget.

They chose a table by the window, as far away from the diners as they could, but the table hadn't been cleared and still had abandoned plates with scraps. Whilst Richard fetched them both a drink, she slid the plates onto the next table and wiped away some spilt baked bean juice with a spare tissue from her bag.

After Richard sat down, she thought he looked less shocked than he had in the office. The ten minutes had been good for him.

"So, do you want to tell me anything else?"

"There's lots of stuff. How much do you want to know?"

"When did you first see anything you couldn't explain?"

"Start with a hard question then," she said, then smiled. "I suppose there's always been things I've not been able to explain, but I've always dismissed them. Either I'd had a long day and the noise I'd heard upstairs was the creaking of the house expanding after the heating had been turned on. Or the figure at the corner of my eye was a shadow. But, the first time I'd seen something unexplainable was the first time I'd seen an Almost Door."

"An Almost Door? These are those... portals."

She nodded; her face felt hot like she was on the verge of blushing. "I saw the outline of a door at Ravenmeols. A man I was with, Seth, a medium, told me what they were."

"That they're doorways to this other place with the cult people?"

"They're doorways to the Almost Realm. But it's not just people from the cult. It's like a limbo, a place the lost go to before moving on to their better place."

"And they were just in the hospital?"

Judy glanced up and scanned across the pub. It was difficult to know for sure, she'd never been in here until today, and the doors always did their best to blend in with their surroundings. It was like camouflage, difficult to notice them unless you were looking for them.

"What are you doing?" Richard asked, turning around, trying to spot what Judy was looking at.

"They can be anywhere. I guess it depends on how thin the connections are between our realm and the other place." She laughed. "I don't know to be sure. But I've seen them outside the hospital."

"How would I know if I'd seen one?"

She eyed him curiously. The initial scepticism had waned somewhat. Incredulously, he didn't think she was barking mad.

"I don't think everyone can see them. Seth is a medium. He's been able to see them since he was a boy. I've been able to see them since Seth pointed them out to me. I think I've got the same abilities as Seth."

"That you're what? A medium?"

"For my sins."

Richard lifted his pint, but it never reached his lips. He settled it down again. "A medium" he repeated, "like you can talk to the dead?"

"I can't say I've tried, but it would explain a lot of things. About how I'm sensing things, seeing this ghost woman. Hearing things in my house."

She brought out the voice recorder she'd secreted in Jemma's room. It was all cued up ready to go. "And there's this. I left this in Jemma's room the other night."

"Last night?" He raised an eyebrow. "Have you listened to it yet?"

She nodded. "Oh yes. You might be surprised." She put her finger on the play button, but he put his hand on hers.

"Wait."

"What's up?"

"What are we going to hear?"

"You're having doubts?"

He removed his hand and then took a sip from his pint. "No. No doubts. Let's listen."

She pressed play but the background noise in the bar was too loud. She whacked the volume up to its maximum setting, it beeped to let her know she'd reached it, then she set it down on the table between them.

Judy had prepared the playback so it would reach the point she'd listened to within a minute, and she kept flicking her gaze between the LED display with its time display, and Richard's expression. He was focused on listening to the recording. His eyes never leaving the recorder. And then it got to the good bit.

"Go back to sleep," the voice said.

Richard jerked back as if the thing speaking had been right in front of his face rather than a recording. She paused the playback then leaned back in her chair and waited for a reaction.

Eventually, Richard spoke. "What was that?"

"When did you record that?"

"Last night. In Jemma's bedroom, like I said."

"This wasn't the TV or a YouTube video? You're not having me on?"

"Why would I try to trick you?"

He shrugged then picked the recorder up. "Mind if I play it again?"

"Play it as many times as you need."

So he did, and they listened to the words again and again. Judy caught a couple on a table give them an irritated glance, but she ignored them. This was too important to worry about bothering other people.

"Has Jemma heard it?"

Judy shook her head, aghast at the thought of her daughter hearing that voice again. "If she heard that recording, I don't think she'd set foot in our house ever again."

Richard frowned. "There's something else you're not telling me. She's happy to go back into the house after seeing a ghost in her room, but she'd freak out if she heard the voice on the tape."

Judy didn't feel the need to correct him that there was no tape. Instead, she let him have the final piece she'd been keeping from him.

"When my husband used to come back home after a drinking session and wanted to take his frustrations out on me, that's what he'd say to Jemma if she ever woke up. That's not his voice, but it's just so familiar it's uncanny. I'm prepared to put up with a lot, but if the thing haunting my house is going to taunt us like that, then we're not staying there a day longer than we have to."

Richard had put his hand on hers and she was grateful for the warmth and comfort in the gesture. He squeezed tightly.

"You don't need to be scared. I'm here for you."

But who will be there for me when I go back to my house tonight? The first night since the incidents began when I've been in the house on my own?

As if reading her mind, he said, "If you like, I could always come around again tonight." Then he held his hands up. "No funny business. I'll sleep in the spare room again."

She sniffed, then took a napkin from the dispenser on the table and used it to wipe her tears then her nose. "No funny business? Where would the fun be in that?"

He smiled, and she wondered how she had got so lucky. She'd shared all her fears and truths with this man she'd barely known for a week and yet she felt like she'd never been able to trust someone so much in all her life.

He doesn't know everything though does he?

Their conversation was interrupted when a woman stopped by their table and put a hand on Richard's shoulder.

"Hi, long time no see."

"Oh, hi Caroline." Richard seemed to almost flinch from the woman.

"I almost missed you," she said. "Still running?"

"Yeah, not as much. Tore a ligament a few months back. Only getting back into it now."

"You need to come back to the Easy Striders. There are loads of new faces now."

"Will do. When I can keep up." He grinned, but there was a nervousness behind the smile.

What are so afraid of? Judy wondered.

"Not been the same without you and Sam."

His eyes narrowed. "I'll be there soon. Just need to get my legs back."

Caroline frowned, taking in Judy for the first time. "Well, best be going. Nigel's waiting. Promised him a quick breakfast before a bit of shopping. Only way I can tempt him out." She patted Richard on the shoulder again, then to Judy she said, "Nice to meet you."

Judy watched as she left, meeting a man outside, presumably Nigel, before heading off along Lord Street. Judy didn't miss the sly backwards glance she gave to Richard. Did she then say something to Nigel? Judy had a distinct impression they had become the subject of gossip.

"Who was that?" Judy asked.

"Someone from the running group. Not seen her in ages."

"I figured. I never had you down for a runner. What else don't I know about you?"

He smiled. "Plenty. But there's no rush is there?"

Richard's phone rang, and he checked the screen before dismissing it. "Client," he explained. "I suppose we better get going."

As they stood to leave, Judy couldn't help but feel like she'd been lied to. Call that a gift after living with Phil for so many years. She could always spot a lie. But what was Richard hiding from her?

32

Richard closed the shop door and threw his jacket on the coat stand. The morning had been an interesting one, almost ruined by bumping into Caroline in the restaurant. That was a little too close for comfort.

He checked his phone for messages but there had been no more. He'd never planned on hooking up with another woman and the guilt ate away at him like a rotting tooth. Was Caroline likely to see Hannah and if she did, was she likely to mention that she'd seen Richard out with another woman? Damn. When did life get so tricky?

Judy had seemed suspicious, and he didn't blame her but thought that with all the attention on the recording, she was unlikely to focus on it.

And that voice recording was something else wasn't it? He'd been in the house last night but had seen nothing, only heard Jemma crying out for help and her bedroom door being jammed. He'd had plenty of time to think about that when he was tossing and turning in the spare bedroom and by the time he'd headed down for breakfast, had convinced himself that it had all been a play for attention. She was just getting back at her mum for having a man around. Jemma had claimed not to have known that Richard had been there, but she might have noticed his car parked on the front.

But she wasn't lying, was she? The recording proved that.

Hell, the recording proved nothing. Just a voice. It could just as well have been Jemma playing games with her mum. For it to be anything else would mean that ghosts existed, and he wasn't sure whether that was a belief he wanted in his world view.

The spotlights he'd installed around the window to display the property listings to their best, flickered.

He checked the plug. It was firmly into the wall, but the transformer was vibrating.

What the hell?

He unplugged it, then plugged it back again. The vibration didn't reoccur so he let it be.

The lights flickered again, and not just on this window display, but on both sides of the shop.

But they're on different plugs.

Something going on at the consumer board then. Shit, if this place needed an electrician to come and check it he would be pissed.

The consumer unit was in the back, in a small cupboard under the stairs. The stairs were boarded up on his side, leading to a small flat upstairs that had its own entrance. Richard opened the plastic cover and looked inside, realising that he had no idea whether he was looking at a problem. Each trip switch was in the upright position, the main switch to the board was turned on. There was a faint buzzing sound when he put his head closer but wasn't that normal? These things didn't even have fuse wires that could be replaced. If the switches were up and on, then the thing was working.

A crack like a brick dropping came from the shop.

Richard tried to ignore the uncomfortable tightness from his chest, the pain that he'd been to see his doctor about last month. He rushed back and saw precisely nothing. Nobody had entered the shop, nothing looked disturbed, but something was different.

A second crack, this time louder.

And he realised the transformers had blown for the spotlight displays. He picked up one of the transformer units, a small black box a few inches from the plug, and immediately dropped it again. The black casing burnt his hand and the damn thing was still vibrating. A cursory check on the opposite side confirmed that the second unit had blown. He'd had them fitted at the same time so it was conceivable although unlikely that they would both fail within seconds of each other. Would a power surge do something like that? He knew nothing about electrics, but the term power surge gave him some comfort, sounding as it did like a proper technical term that could explain many things.

But you've checked the consumer unit and all the switches are fine. The consumer unit would make sure nothing on your circuit could get damaged.

His rational thought could take a hike. If he wanted to believe that a power surge had done this, then that was what he was sticking to. Thankfully, it wasn't something more extreme. The spotlights had only cost about thirty quid and he could replace these easily enough.

A click came from the front door.

At first, he stared at the door, demanding it to make the noise again. It was a snap, like the click of fingers. He'd heard that noise every time he nipped out to grab some lunch, or when he'd finished for the day.

It was the noise of the snib being clicked off. The door now wouldn't open from the outside.

Richard rationalised—he was getting good at rationalising the unexplained—that in his haste to come back into the office, he might not have set it correctly. A simple gust of wind from outside, might have vibrated the door enough to knock the snib off.

But that sounds like hokum as well, he thought. And if you believed that to be the case, why is your heart beating that little faster right now?

There was a chill in the room. How quickly the temperature had dropped he couldn't say, but it was now cold enough that his fingers had noticed and the hair on the back of his neck was bristling. And he had a feeling that he'd had the previous night when he'd been on Judy's landing, and he'd heard Jemma's cries coming from her room, and he'd heard that voice in his head, the same voice that he'd heard on the recording that Judy had played him less than half an hour ago. When he'd heard, clearly, the words,

"Go back to sleep."

And once the fear appeared, it grew and dug its claws in and made his stomach churn.

Richard was terrified. Perhaps more afraid than he'd been since he was a child.

Stepping across the room, he looked all around, wary of any change in the light or the temperature or sounds. He took the snib off and checked that the door opened. He thought of maybe picking up his jacket and heading home for the day, but he had that one viewing he had to do later on, and the owner would drop off a spare set of keys. It wouldn't be professional to be out.

He closed the door.

"I'm not afraid," he said, although the faint quiver in his voice betrayed him. There was a tremble in the back of his knees and he firmly planted his feet, extending the leg muscles to put some pressure on the joints and stop the tremble.

The snib turned itself. He spun around and tried to turn the snib back again, but this time it wasn't having any of it.

In the reflection of the door's glass, Richard caught sight of a man standing at the back of the office, behind his desk. He yelped in surprise then spun back. There was no man there.

But there had been someone, he thought. He had a large stocky build, dark shirt and trousers, with a lighter coloured tie.

The face was imprinted in his mind. A round face, pockmarked with acne scarring, a day or two's thick stubble growth. And eyes. He shivered. The narrow eyes had been full of hatred.

Richard gulped and inched his way around the perimeter of the room, warily surveying as much as he could. He just wanted to get to his phone, make a phone call, ask for someone to help him with his door. There was no back way out anymore. In his makeshift kitchen was an outside door, but Richard had never needed the back entrance so when the lock broke a couple of years ago, he hadn't replaced it. What was the point in paying a locksmith to replace something that never got used? Besides, it made the place more difficult to break into, didn't it?

But your attempt to save money has cut off your other chance of escape.

Jesus, escape. Richard's mouth went dry, the morning beer forgotten as he realised how ridiculous it was that he was working out how to escape from his own shop.

Richard stopped moving as he spotted something in the reflections from the back of the property listing boards.

The man was still inside the shop, his presence confirmed only by his reflection.

You're tired. There was something funny about that pint. I knew there was. What the hell was I thinking? I should have stopped myself.

For a moment, there was a standoff. The figure in the reflection facing Richard whose body now seemed incapable of any movement at all. The reflection placed the man—When are you going to refer to that as a ghost? It's a ghost. A goddamn fucking ghost and it will hurt you unless you get out of here.

But ghosts couldn't hurt. Their whole raison d'être was to lurk around haunted houses and intimidate the living.

A whirring noise broke his train of thought and Richard looked around, breaking contact with the ghost in the reflection. He knew that sound, but he couldn't place it.

Oh, right. Great.

The shop's metal security shutters were lowering.

It's shutting you inside.

Richard ran for the door again, the metal shutters already a third of the way down. He pulled at the snib, the metal knob slipping through his greasy fingers. People walked past on the street outside. Perhaps he could get their attention, get one of them to stop the shutters and try the door from the outside.

But no matter how hard he banged, nobody stopped or came to his rescue.

Soon, the only light in the room came through a fine crack at the bottom of the door.

He made his way to his desk and flicked the switch on his desk lamp. Nothing. Had he expected anything else?

Nothing can hurt you.

Except Richard didn't believe that was true. Not for one second. If the entity in his shop could lock him in and operate the metal shutters, it could certainly hurt him.

He picked up his mobile and turned its LED torch on, shining it around the room, banishing the shadows from the edges. His heart galloped like he'd just finished a 10k and his chest felt tight. If he'd been out running, that would have been a good sign to pack it in for the day and take a rest.

"Whoever you are, you don't need to scare me. For the record, I'm petrified and totally believe in you. Why not leave me alone? I'm nothing to you."

The room was silent, apart from Richard's ragged breathing.

He turned the phone's light off, then dialled his wife.

It took ten rings for her to answer. Ten rings where he got to enjoy the sound of his racing heart and broken breath.

"What's up?" She sounded like she was speaking from the middle of a crowd. A multitude of voices threatened to swallow her voice.

"I need help. I'm stuck in the office."

"Richard?"

"I'm locked in. Come round. Call a locksmith."

The voices at the other end became louder. Hannah was talking but Richard struggled to hear what she was saying.

"...you're...what's the matter wi—" The line went dead.

Richard glared at the handset in disbelief. He pressed the home button again, but the screen refused to turn on. There was no way the phone hadn't had a full charge. He barely used the thing, and he knew it was on one hundred percent when he'd unplugged it that morning.

Richard ran for the kitchen. There was less space in there, and fewer reflections. Fewer places to hide. And there was a selection of knives. Richard wasn't trying to kid himself that a knife made a great weapon against a ghost, but it was better than using a dead handset.

As he reached the kitchen doorway, he turned, and staggered back in terror.

The man was in front of him. No longer hiding in reflections. He was over six-foot-tall, the facial features, snarled up into a vicious grimace. Richard bumped into his desk, and something knocked over, he didn't care to look to see what it was.

"What do you want?"

The man's mouth opened, and Richard thought he might have heard a sound, a gasp of air that could have been the start of a sentence, or the answer he'd been hoping for.

But there was nothing that he could discern. The thing either couldn't speak or chose not to.

Richard drifted around his desk, never taking his eyes away from the apparition. And the thing took a step into the main part of the shop. Richard could almost hear the thing's footsteps. He thought he could almost smell the thing. and it smelt of all the dead things.

Damn, there was that tightness in his chest again. Worse this time.

"Leave me alone. What do you want with me?" His mouth was painfully dry, the words scratching their way out from his throat.

The ghost continued towards him, cornering him at the back of the office furthest from the door.

His temple pounded like he was coming down with a migraine, and his arm felt peculiar like it no longer belonged to him. The face seemed to be trying to speak, its mouth opened and closed but no words came out.

A terrific pain in the side of his chest suddenly struck Richard. Daggers rising from just below his armpit, driving deep into his abdomen.

I'm having a heart attack, he thought. Oh my God, this is actually happening. I'm having a massive heart attack and I will never be able to tell anyone what I've seen.

33

Despite everything, Judy managed a decent night's sleep. There was no sense that the house would be a problem for either her or Jemma that evening. Jemma was not the scared little girl that the previous night's incident had suggested. If anything, seeing something in her room had made her stronger, more resilient.

Perhaps, she would be OK with them moving to a new house, perhaps she would understand. It wasn't all about the money, families were complicated. But ultimately, this had to be something they decided to do together. It was wrong for Judy to put the house on the market without mentioning it to Jemma first. How would she feel if a 'for sale' board appeared in the front garden?

A pang of guilt hit her as she remembered the confused look on Jemma's face when she saw Richard in the house. Had that been the first time she'd seen a real look of disappointment in her daughter's eyes?

Over breakfast, Jemma had been focused on the day's tests she had coming up. The school was putting their pupils through a week's worth of testing in readiness for their final end of year exams. That meant Jemma had a science test and a geography test, and she was panicking about both of them. This wasn't the right time to talk about house moves so Judy did the right thing and helped Jemma get her bag ready for school, reminding her of the revision cards she'd been using and asking her a few choice questions that Jemma had already highlighted the answers to.

After lunch, she sent a text message to Richard.

Hi. Thanks for listening yesterday. Just promise me you won't turn up with a giant 'for sale' board. I've not had chance to mention any of this to Jemma. She's had enough surprises from you this week ;)

Richard didn't reply straight away, and insanely, she felt that light breeze tickle the back of her neck as soon as she pressed the send button. Something was off but she couldn't place her finger on it.

From beside the kettle, she drew her notepad close and flipped the cover. She'd last made a check in the house yesterday evening whilst Jemma had been ensconced in her bedroom revising. There had been no sign of any unusual activity and no sign of any Almost Doors.

It doesn't mean there won't be any now.

She picked up the pad and went from room to room, focusing on the doors that she knew were real and the spaces between them, tallying them up and making a mark on her pad. On the landing, she paused, her pencil in hand. Had that been a noise from the loft? After seeing the shape in the shadows she would not go up there again on her own.

At the threshold to Jemma's room, she pushed open the door and looked inside. It was difficult to tell where the carpet began and the wardrobe ended. Clothes were strewn over the carpet and continued over the unmade bed. Judy sighed, remembering how quickly Jemma had agreed to tidy her room last night and the casual reply she'd got from her at the kitchen table over breakfast when asked whether she'd done it.

Yeah, it's tidy, she'd told her. But then she'd looked back down at her revision cards and demanded another question from her mum.

There was nothing strange upstairs but the feeling that something was wrong didn't leave her until she was back downstairs in the kitchen, loading the dishwasher.

Her phone buzzed with a notification.

Why were you texting my husband?

Judy's legs no longer wanted to hold her body and she stumbled back into a kitchen chair, almost missing it, needing to reach out a hand for the table to stop herself falling onto her arse.

She stared at the message. Was it a joke? Was Richard messing with her? He hadn't seemed the type to want to play practical jokes on her.

And it wasn't as if the joke was in any way funny.

Why the fuck have you been txting each other all week!!!

Shit. This wasn't a joke. Richard was married.

That feeling wasn't going away. Something else was going on here and it was smothering her senses in a way that made her want to get out of the house and breathe in some fresh air.

Another notification came in, but she couldn't bring herself to look at the handset. Then a minute later, Beyoncé started singing. Judy grabbed the phone, saw that it was Richard calling and swiped to end the call. It wasn't Richard on the end of the phone.

What had happened? It must have been serious for Richard to tell his wife. Or had she found his phone unguarded and looked? How many other women had he been sleeping with?

Don't be so precious as to think you were the only one. Once a cheater.

Had he slept with her just to get her business? No. That was stupid. He might have been desperate, but he couldn't be sleeping with all his clients.

She picked up her turned-off handset and wished she could speak to him, find out why he'd been such a lying devious piece of shit. And the longer she stared at her phone, the worse the feelings became. She imagined tearing a new strip off him, even fantasised about ganging up on him with his wife. After all, they'd both been lied to.

Don't make out you're as much the victim as his wife. Who the hell do you think you are?

The drive to town passed by in a haze of regret and anger. It all made sense. The shifty nature, the reluctance to meet anywhere other than the shop or Judy's place. His claim that he lived in a small flat with a nosey landlady had been another lie intended to keep her away from the truth.

What a fool she'd been.

Judy didn't know how long she stood outside the estate agent's looking at the closed door. The metal security shutters were down around the main windows, only up in front of the shop doorway.

What had happened here? Where was Richard? She stood on the doorstop and peered inside. That was odd, the deskphone was on the floor, like it had been brushed aside and forgotten. From inside the shop, music started to play. She knew instantly what the song was. She'd heard Dire Straits enough to recognise it within a couple of bars.

A woman's voice behind her made her jump.

"I'm afraid it's closed," she said.

Judy spun around and stood facing a woman wearing the uniform of the bakery next door. In a hand, she held a coffee mug. She sipped it as she regarded Judy.

"I was looking for Richard," Judy replied.

A grimace then on the woman's face. It bunched up the lines on her forehead, and there was a hint of reluctance.

"I was the one who called the ambulance."

Judy's heart skipped a beat. "Come again."

"There was a lot of banging, but I had my hands full with a tray of sausage rolls from the oven. I couldn't just stop what I was doing. I thought he'd dropped something. So sad."

Judy wanted to grab the woman by the shoulders but resisted. "I'm sorry, but what are you talking about? Where's Richard? Why did he need an ambulance?"

"I heard them talking as they brought him out. I probably shouldn't say anything."

"Please, you've got to tell me."

"Are you a customer?"

"No, yes. But a friend more than anything."

"I'm sorry then, but it was a heart attack. He was dead by the time the ambulance got here."

34

"I think we're all in the most terrible danger." Judy was standing on the doorstep of Lisa's house. "You should leave. It's not safe for you to be here."

"What are you talking about?" Lisa's posture was that of the sceptical housewife warding off the door-to-door salesman.

"Richard is dead. They say it's a heart attack, but I think he was killed by the thing haunting your house—our houses."

Judy looked up at the sky as she spoke, thinking that might help stop her breaking into tears. She didn't tell Lisa her fear that the ghost might be Phil.

Lisa shook her head. "I don't know what you're talking about. Who is Richard?"

"It doesn't matter who he is. Trust me, he was killed by the ghost. You need to let me in."

Lisa sighed, then pushed open the door and let Judy come inside. The atmosphere was palpably different. The hallway was freezing. "It's still here. I can feel it."

"There's nothing here, Judy. I made a mistake. It's all in your head. I'm still feeling terrible for dragging you into something that you didn't need dragging into."

Judy studied her sister-in-law's face. Something was different about her.

"How are you sleeping?"

"Fine. Much better."

"Good. I'm glad. And how's Ellis?"

"What is this? Twenty questions?"

Judy forced a chuckle. "Sorry. Habit, I guess."

The pair of them walked through to the kitchen, Judy lingered behind a moment and glanced up the staircase. She couldn't see the top of the stairs, let alone the entrance to Lisa's bedroom. The atmosphere in here felt heavier somehow, like stuff was pressing down on her. She hurried back to catch up with Lisa and saw the back room hadn't been tidied. It looked more like a student house-share than the home of two young professionals. A couple of plates with what looked like last night's dinner sat on the coffee table, a scattering of used mugs accompanied the plates. An old towel had been dropped on the back of the armchair, still damp. The kitchen was worse. A smell like rotting potatoes clung in the air. Lisa didn't seem to be aware of the smell. There were more plates and mugs on the side, waiting for someone to wash them, or load them in the dishwasher.

Lisa opened a cupboard and pulled out the only remaining mug, plucking a second from the sink, rinsing it quickly under the tap before setting it down by the first. It still looked filthy and Judy made a note to abstain from drinking from it.

"So, this Richard? Was he a friend?"

"Yeah, an old friend. Someone from the school."

"And he's died of a heart attack? What's that got to do with your ghost?"

"I've got a good reason to believe that the ghost was involved."

"It's sometimes better isn't it, when the death is sudden like a heart attack. I know it's a shock, but it can be better to cope with. Not like when Phil died. That was quite a long painful road, wasn't it?"

"I suppose so."

Where are you going with this? Judy thought. Why do you keep bringing Phil's death back into the conversation? You didn't know him like I knew him. You wouldn't have wanted to know him.

"I've been thinking about him a lot."

"Phil? Why's that?"

"I just get the sense that there was more going on before he died than he ever shared. You've never really spoken about his illness or how difficult it must have been for you."

And there's a good reason for that.

"I wouldn't want to upset you with it."

"I'm not upset." Lisa dropped a tea bag into each mug, then filled the kettle from the tap. "I suppose I regret not taking the time to help you out more."

"There wasn't anything you could have done. You've got no reason to be sorry for anything. Just knowing you were there if I needed to talk to someone was helpful enough."

Lisa laughed. "Don't be stupid. I wasn't talking about helping you. I only ever wanted to help Phil. I know he was Dad's favourite, never going to forget that, and he had a decent job—even if that meant working for Dad—but he was still stuck with you and that weird daughter of yours. It must have been enough to drive him mad."

Where was all this bitterness coming from? "I don't think you're thinking straight. Why do you feel the need to say these things? What's happened to you?"

"Nothing's happened to me. I'm the same Lisa I always was. But what's happened to you? You've changed since my brother died. Can't you see that?"

"In what way?" Judy ear tips were burning.

"In every way. You've let yourself go for starters. I know we all take to grief in different ways, but you've clearly been comfort eating. You will never get a new husband if you carry on the way you are. And thinking you're special in coming around with your cheap electronics, showing off that you know how to deal with a haunting. Well, you didn't get that right, did you? This house is no more haunted than yours. It's all in your mind. My dad's said this plenty of times."

"What has your dad said?"

"That you're a bad influence. You've always been a bad influence on Phil, and you're still influencing our family when you've got no reason to. Why did you come around again? What for? You're nothing to us anymore. Get your own life."

This wasn't Lisa talking, or at least not solely Lisa. Judy knew that there was some resentment from Lisa, especially regarding the house situation, but she loved Jemma. She'd always been a fantastic aunt and a good friend to Judy. Whatever she was saying now wasn't from her.

It's from the thing in this house. The ghost or entity. The woman that I've seen, and Lisa's seen but pretending not to. It's clouding her mind. Making her think thoughts not her own. Or is it the second ghost? Was Phil making her say these things, influencing her somehow?

But knowing that wasn't enough to stop the anger bubbling under the surface. Judy dragged Lisa away from her brew-making.

"We're leaving, now!" Judy thundered.

"What the hell? Get off me!"

As Lisa spoke, pressure dug into Judy's neck, invisible fingers pressing on her windpipe.

Judy dropped Lisa's hand.

"Don't you dare touch me again."

Judy's feet slipped as her invisible assailant dragged her towards the back door. Judy scrambled to stay on her feet as she was pulled up until almost on tiptoes. The tiled floor was impossible to get any purchase on, so Judy reached to her sides, grabbing a kitchen cupboard to stop the backwards momentum.

And Lisa nodded as if this was the most normal everyday occurrence in the world.

"Do you still take sugar?"

Judy had one hand on the cupboard and another at the invisible hands around her neck, trying to pry them away.

"Help..." Her voice was hoarse, and she drew in a quick gasp of air. She would soon lose consciousness. Blackness was already skirting the edge of her vision.

"I've tried to cut back on sugar. They say it's like an addiction, don't they? Maybe they should just ban selling it. It's not like we really need it. Like salt. Why are they still allowed to sell salt if it's so bad for us?"

Lisa glanced up at Judy, a confused smile on her face. The look of a woman who's forgotten what she came into a room for.

Why can't you see what's happening to me?

"Hel—" But she choked on the last utterance. No longer feeling like she was being dragged backwards, Judy released her hold on the cupboard and focused on removing the force from her neck. Lisa wouldn't help, the poor woman didn't have a clue what was happening. Whatever this ghost could do, it had as much a hold on Lisa's mind as it had fingers around Judy's throat.

The grip was getting tighter. She felt the skin around her windpipe stretching against the cartilage.

If she couldn't get the thing to release its grip, she would have to find another way out of this. Judy grabbed for anything on the kitchen counter she could use, her fingertips brushing against a plate. She could just reach the edge of the plate and spun it around, thinking if she could pick it up, she could hit the thing behind her.

But the plate dropped out of her grasp and smashed on the floor.

Lisa glanced at the broken plate, but said nothing, returning to the almost-boiled kettle.

"It's probably time to think about getting a new lodger. I don't think Ellis is right for this house. Or maybe it's time to get myself a fella. I've been out of the dating thing for too long. So, come clean with me, Judy. This Richard was your boyfriend, wasn't he? The man that Dad saw you with. Your new bit of rough."

If I wasn't being strangled, I'd have slapped you.

But the black walls on the edge of her vision were closing in. Her eyes felt like they were ready to pop across the room.

Another plate fell to the floor. Another wasted attempt to attack the entity.

A hiss from the doorway.

Jasper had entered. Judy glanced down and saw his fat tail and arched back. He was stressed but ready to defend himself—not run.

"Hi baby," Lisa called out, and she brushed past Judy, ignoring the wheezing body, and picked up her cat.

"Ow!"

Jasper had struck with his right paw, unsheathed claws had slashed across Lisa's face, leaving clear tracks of blood across her cheek. She dropped him, but he jumped straight back up on to the kitchen counter, keeping his distance from Lisa, with his eyes focused on Judy.

He hissed again.

The fingers around Judy's neck moved. What was this? Was Judy's assailant bothered by a cat?

But cat's claws couldn't attack a ghost.

Judy had another plan though. There was only one person in the room who could help her.

Judy stopped scrabbling at her neck and grabbed Jasper from the kitchen counter instead. He lashed at her hands and got a scratch in, but it was light and easily ignored. She moved her hold until she had one hand tight around the cat's neck and another under its stomach, supporting it.

"Help," she spat at Lisa.

"What are you doing? Let him go." Lisa stepped forward but Judy lifted the cat higher. The pressure around her neck was back at full strength again. She had seconds before she passed out.

"He—."

Judy pinched Jasper's neck tight enough that he let out a howl of pain. That was enough for Lisa. Her eyes widened and colour rushed back into her cheeks.

"What are you doing?" then upon seeing the peril Judy was in, "What's happening to you?"

Lisa drove forward and Judy let Jasper go. He landed awkwardly on the floor but scrambled to his feet and darted into the back room.

"Get the hell off her!" Lisa shouted at Judy's assailant.

The pressure released from around her neck. Lisa grabbed her arm and pulled her close, shielding Judy from the thing that had just tried to kill her.

Finally, able to turn around, Judy did so but there was nobody there, at least nobody that she could see. The kitchen was empty. But then, she glimpsed a woman in the back door's glass. The reflection had a pale angular face, skin stretched tight over pointed cheekbones. The expression was sheer malevolence.

"Come on," Judy said, grabbing her sister-in-law. "We need to get out of here now."

They crashed into the back room just before the door behind them slammed shut. The door leading to the hallway followed, leaving the women trapped.

The vibration in the floor started slowly but Judy felt it grow in intensity through the soles of her feet, quickly becoming uncomfortable. A look from Lisa confirmed she wasn't imagining it.

Jasper hissed. The vibration was driving him mad. He jumped onto the back of the chair. His tail had ballooned in size, and his back was arched. Lisa approached, but he tried to bite as her hand got too close.

Judy shook her head, trying to rid her ears of the thrumming that was building, pressing against her senses. She tried the door to the hallway.

"Locked," she said but didn't give up trying. Lisa had turned and was trying the door back to the kitchen. Jasper jumped down to the floor again, then howling in pain as if the pads on his feet were burning, he jumped at the wall.

A blast of noise from the television made Judy stop trying to force the door. Lisa came and stood beside her.

A black-and-white image, flashes of colour. A house in the trees. The perspective moving along as if from the point of view of a person walking through the wood.

"The house..." Lisa said. "I've seen that."

It meant nothing to Judy. Static flashed across the screen and the image moved on, seconds forgotten. Closer now. Detail in the house could be picked out. A two-story domestic building, a home in the woods. Judy dismissed the notion of a modern-day Hansel and Gretel; the place was too ordinary for that. Or it would have been ordinary if it wasn't for the broken windows and the missing tiles from the roof. Vines had taken hold around the lower right corner of the building, digging into the brickwork, trying to reclaim the man-made structure into the wood, delete it from the Earth.

"Where have you seen it?"

Lisa glanced at Judy, the fear in her eyes raw and new. "In my nightmares."

Before she could respond, Jasper ran across the room in front of them, but as he hit the centre of the carpet, he stopped, like he'd collided with an invisible wall.

Or an invisible person.

And then Jasper was in the air, floating, held by the same hands that had been wrapped around Judy's neck only minutes ago. The cat's back legs dangled as he tried to find something to gain purchase on.

The threat was clear.

If Lisa hadn't moved, things might have been different, but she did what she had to do, anything to save her cat. She lurched forward, hands outstretched, but before she could get there, the unthinkable happened.

Jasper's body turned and lifted in the air, resting horizontally, the legs no longer hanging. It was clear the entity had gripped him from both ends now. The muffled howling confirming a hand was around the cat's throat.

When Jasper was ripped in two, the blood splattered in a crimson arc.

Lisa screamed, and even as the two halves of Jasper were tossed against opposite walls of the room, Judy couldn't take her eyes from the space in the centre. The space where, no doubt, the entity was still watching, observing, demonstrating her power.

Judy tried the door again. The vibration was louder than ever, hurting her ear drums and making her want to put her hands over her ears and curl up in the corner.

This will never stop.

The lounge door burst open, shoving her back into the room.

When she looked up, Ellis was standing in the doorway. His face scrunched up as he heard the vibration.

"What the hell? Turn that down."

He thinks we're playing with the stereo.

The coast was clear.

"Oh my god. Is that... Jasper?"

"We need to get out," Judy shouted above the noise. The picture frames were vibrating in their frames against the walls. A glass that had been left on the edge of a table suddenly fell over, dropping onto the carpet and spilling a small pool of coke into the pile.

Judy grabbed Lisa's arm, slippy now with the blood of her dead cat, and pulled her from the room, pushing Ellis backwards out of the way.

"You need to come too. Trust me."

Ellis looked into the room, then his eyes caught sight of something. "Who's that woman?"

Judy refused to turn and give the entity any more of her fear to feed off. Ellis hurried out onto the front path after them. Judy glanced back at the front door, caught a shape of a figure lurking at the top of the staircase, then she urged the others out onto the street.

"What the hell was that?"

"What did you see?" Judy asked. The absence of the vibration in her ears was a welcome release.

"There was somebody, but they looked vague and indistinct. Shit, is that what you've been seeing in the house?" He addressed this last to Lisa, but the exhausted woman had dropped to the floor, leaning back against the front garden wall, her knees drawn up to her chest, her bloodied arms wrapped tightly against them. She looked like she wanted to disappear into a hole in the ground. She wasn't going to get that luxury.

"You can't go back into the house," Judy told Ellis. "You've seen that entity, that ghost. It's stronger now than it's ever been and for whatever reason it didn't want to let me or Lisa leave. I don't know what it will make of you, but I know that it's angry and I don't think it cares about collateral damage."

He looked like he'd just been told the moon was made of cheese. "I shouldn't believe you, but I do. You're not messing me around, are you? This is the real deal."

"It's the real deal."

"Can you get rid of it?"

Judy shrugged. "I don't know yet. We need to understand why it's here to begin with—what it actually wants."

"It wants me. It's always been about me. I was the first one to see it. It tormented me with Jasper the other night, then when it couldn't get me to stay tonight, it punished me by murdering him." Lisa choked back a sob.

Judy was having a horrible feeling about this whole thing.

It wasn't Lisa that had first seen the woman. It was Phil.

"I want to speak to your dad, Lisa. I need you to come with me."

Ellis nodded. "OK. So what about me? What should I do?"

"Go and stay at your girlfriend's. I'll call you later. Just don't step foot in there again."

35

Things were moving too quickly for Lisa's brain to process. The last twenty-four hours she'd felt this terrible bottled-up anger in the pit of her stomach. Like if she didn't get out of the house she would scream or go mad. But the entity in her house hadn't wanted to let her go and Lisa needed time to understand what that meant.

It wanted me to stay. It wanted me to shut myself away from the outside world.

And it had been partially successful in that regard. The animosity she'd felt towards Judy had been real. Yes, she couldn't forgive Dad for making life so much easier for Phil and Judy than for herself, but none of this was Judy's fault. She hadn't known what financial arrangements were in place.

But still she'd hated her.

That wasn't you. That was the thing in my house.

What did it mean? Did it mean that the entity was controlling her?

Was she being possessed?

Safe in the car speeding a little too fast along the bypass to her parents' house, she felt normal again. Not like how she'd felt in the house earlier. And she didn't feel any hostility to Judy, only sorrow that she'd got her dragged into this.

"I didn't feel myself back there. I'm sorry for what I said. I didn't mean any of it."

"Apart from the putting on weight. You must have meant that." Judy glanced across and then winked. "Don't worry. I could feel it affect me as well. It's powerful. Just look at what it's been able to do. It's gotten much stronger over the last few days. It's able to move things and affect its environment."

"Have you ever seen anything like it before?"

"My experience is not as wide ranging as this. I mentioned you were my first client, didn't I?" She chuckled. "The things I've seen before were from another realm. I didn't see any actual hauntings at Ravenmeols, just the shadowmen."

"That wasn't a shadowman?"

"Trust me, you'd know one when you saw one."

Lisa's phone rang. Her dance-tone ringtone blasted into the car, surprising Judy. "Sorry," Lisa said.

"Hi Mum... wait, slow down. Let me put you on speakerphone. Judy's with me now but she's driving."

Lisa pressed the screen and Faith's voice sounded breathlessly through the handset. "I don't know what's got into him."

"Hi Faith, got into who? Is everything all right? Is Jemma all right?"

A pause. "We're not meant to be leaving for two hours, and now he's got me going straight to voicemail."

"You're not making any sense, Mum."

"Adrian got a call. We were loading the car, ready to go to the lakes. He went all quiet, then went off to his office to speak to whoever it was. I don't know who he was talking to, but he never goes off to take private calls."

"What's happened? Is Jemma with you?" Judy asked.

"She's in the car. She was sat in the back playing on her phone whilst we were loading up. Adrian came back out from the office and got straight into the driver's seat. He pulled away without checking. He was very upset."

"What do you mean? Where's Jemma?"

"She's with him, in the car."

"Mum, calm down. Where was he going?"

"I don't know. The luggage is still here. I don't know what's got into him. It's to do with the phonecall. It's all to do with the phonecall."

"We're coming over, Mum. Don't worry, we'll be there in ten minutes."

Lisa ended the call and was ready to say something to Judy but she was already accelerating, her face frowning in concentration.

36

Judy screeched the car to a halt outside Faith's house and was out of the vehicle before Lisa unclipped her seatbelt. Faith was waiting for them by the open door.

"I've tried calling him but it's going through to voicemail. I don't know what else to do."

"What did he say?" Judy asked, struggling to keep from shouting at the woman. Faith looked as shaken up as Judy felt inside. What could have happened for him to abduct Jemma like that?

Lisa was out of the car, shouting for Judy's attention. Judy glanced, irritated by the interruption, then she realised Lisa was holding her phone. "She's calling you," Lisa said, then to make sure it didn't go to voicemail, Lisa answered before passing it to Judy.

The voice on the end barely sounded like Jemma. There was a nervousness to it that set Judy's teeth on edge.

"Mum, I'm not sure what's happening." Her daughter was fighting back the tears, trying to put on a brave face but her voice was betraying her vulnerability.

"Where are you?" Judy responded firmly, determined not to show how close to the brink of panic she was.

"Granddad's taking us somewhere. He won't talk to me. He's in a strange mood."

"Put me on speakerphone. Let me talk to him."

There was a fumbling then the telltale expansion of the soundscape, and Judy knew Adrian could hear.

"Adrian, it's Judy. What's going on? Where are you taking Jemma?"

Adrian wasn't in the mood for talking. She tried again though. What else could she do? "Adrian. You need to stop and bring Jemma back home. Whatever you've done, we can work this out. You don't need to run."

When Adrian's voice came on the line, it sounded different, less confident than the hard businessman she'd known all these years. He sounded younger. Scared.

What do you have to be scared about, she thought? Who called you?

"I didn't mean to bring Jemma. She was in the car. I didn't notice. I've got to meet someone. I won't be long. We'll still be back in time for the holiday."

"I can't let you take Jemma somewhere I don't know. You need to either come home or tell me where you are, and I'll come to you. Look at her Adrian, she's frightened."

There was a pause on the phone, then the phone line went dead.

Judy felt like she'd been kicked in the gut. What had she just done? Made it worse by the sound of it. The fogginess at the edge of her thinking was threatening to consume her rational decision making. Adrian hadn't meant to take Jemma, that meant that Jemma wasn't in any danger. But Adrian also said he was going to meet with someone, and it was clear from his voice that he was scared. Why was he scared? If he feared the person he was going to meet, then Jemma was still in danger, despite Adrian's reassurances.

"We have to call the police," she told Faith.

But Faith snatched the phone from Judy's grip. "No. You can't. He's done nothing wrong."

"He's kidnapped my daughter!"

Faith shook her head. "I heard him too. He said he didn't know she was in the car. He won't hurt his own granddaughter."

"Right now, Faith, I don't know what he's capable of. And I don't think you do either or you wouldn't have called us in a panic."

"She's right, Mum. We've got to do something." Lisa urged her mother inside the house and passed the phone back to

Judy. "Wait a minute," she told her, and they all went inside. "Perhaps there's something else we can do."

Judy held her phone in a deathly grip, glancing at the screen, waiting to see whether Jemma would call. The sudden cut off suggested that Adrian had taken the phone from her. If that is what happened, then Jemma had no way of keeping in touch. "Wait, I can try something." Judy opened Google Maps and chose the location sharing option, selecting her daughter's profile picture and waiting for it to refresh. The map redrew and focused in on a section of road leading on the edge of Southport. The legend beneath the map informed that the refresh of Jemma's location had happened three minutes ago. Judy tried to force a manual refresh, but the app frustratingly kept informing her that it couldn't refresh Jemma's location.

"They're on the coastal road, past Marshside." That suggested they were heading out of town, heading north towards Preston. But without an updated location, the information wasn't much help.

Judy tried ringing Jemma again, but this time the call went straight through to voicemail. The map refresh had told her that Jemma's phone was on 90% battery, which could only mean one thing. "He's turned her phone off." Judy banged a fist against the wall. "Faith, think back to the phone call, what did he say? Who was he talking to?"

But Faith was already shaking her head. "I can't remember."

"Were you in the same room?"

"No. He'd left his phone on the side table in the hallway. When it started ringing, I brought it to him."

"Then you saw who was calling." Judy kept her voice calm, but commanding. She wanted to get as much information from Faith as she could before she called the police. She couldn't afford to let Faith forget anything.

Faith was shaking her head. "I don't know if I did."

"Think, Mum," Lisa said. "You must have seen the display. It would have been in large letters."

"I don't think..."

"Did it say unknown number?"

Again, a shake of the head.

"Then, did it have a number displayed at all?"

A spark of energy flashed in Faith's eyes. She stopped shaking her head. The pressure lightened on Judy's temples as she considered the possibility of getting some useful information from the woman.

"No number. There was a name."

"Can you remember whose name? Who was he going to meet?"

Lisa had her hands on her mum's shoulders and Judy was struck by how much love there was between the two women. As much as Lisa felt she needed to know who her biological mother was, it was clear that Lisa had always been honest as to her reasons. Faith would always be her true mother.

"Matt! The name was Matt Hodgson."

The delight on her face was countered by the sinking feeling in Judy.

"Who is he?" Faith said. "I don't know that name."

Lisa looked across at Judy. "That name means something to you. I can see it in your face."

"He works at Hosforth House as a maintenance guy."

"Hosforth House, where Adrian had his first office?" Faith asked.

Judy nodded. "It's also where you met with the agency who arranged Lisa and Phil's adoption."

"You went there?" Lisa asked.

"I wanted to see if I could find anyone from the adoption agency. Find out where they were now. Maybe someone could help us work out what the paperwork meant, see if there were more details we'd missed. There was no one who remembered the adoption agency, but I spoke to Matt. And I met him on another occasion. He was talking to your father at his new office. I caught the two of them talking."

"Caught them?" Faith frowned.

"It looked like they didn't want to be seen together. There was something off about their body language. I don't know what. I didn't ask Adrian at the time. Something about it just felt wrong."

"And you didn't think to tell me about it?" Lisa asked, her tone suggested she was offended by this omission.

"You had enough going on, and it wasn't as if I had much to tell you. I'd seen your dad talking to a man he used to know from his old office building. So what? Nothing that can't be explained away."

"But it's harder to explain away his actions now," Lisa said. "He's going to meet this Matt again, and it's got him angry and worked up."

"And he's still got my daughter in the car."

Judy clenched her fists. The powerlessness was something she'd vowed never to experience again. It had been there throughout her marriage to Phil. Whenever there was an argument and things threatened to get ugly, she'd be stuck, scared to leave the house with her daughter still inside, scared to take Jemma with her because she had nowhere else to go.

But that all changed when he got his diagnosis. The power shifted then. That was the first time she'd seen him scared, the day he'd come back from the consultant with the news that he had cancer. And it was hard for Judy to hear the news as well. In that moment she had a rush of emotions. Yes, she was terribly sorry for him, sorry that he was about to go through a world of discomfort and uncertainty. But was she ever sorry that he had cancer? Hadn't she at some point in her time with him secretly wished something terrible would happen to him to get him out of their lives?

You caused this. Your wishful thinking brought this terrible thing to him and you know it.

"We have to go after them. They were heading out of Southport. Maybe he'll turn the phone on, if we head that way now, when it gets turned on, we'll be so much closer to intercepting them."

Faith had scurried into the lounge and was pulling open the drawers in the sideboard.

"What are you doing Mum?"

"Looking."

"For what?"

Faith pulled and dropped a letter from the drawer. Then another. Then an entire notebook. Pens followed.

"Mum?"

Faith turned, in her hand a piece of paper. "It's information about the tracker he had fitted to the Mercedes. He was paranoid that someone would take it."

Judy's chest lifted. Did this mean what she thought it meant? "He's got a GPS tracker in the car?"

Faith shrugged. "I don't know about that. It's a little box that fits in the glovebox. You can use an app to tell you where the car is and can report it to the police."

Lisa took the piece of paper from her mum's hand and poured over it. "Bloody hell. We just need to log into the app." Her face dropped. "Tell me you've got the app on your phone as well, Mum."

Faith nodded. "Oh yes, he was adamant, in case he left his phone in the car and it got stolen." She crossed to the mantelpiece and took her phone, switching it on and logging into the app. "Here you go, looks like he is on his way up to Preston."

Lisa put her hand out and her mum placed the phone in it.

"I don't understand what's going on. This isn't like him." Tears started rolling and her back arched as she burst into tears. "Please, find him. Make sure he's OK."

"Yes, we'll do that," Judy said.

But if he harms one hair on the head of my daughter, I will make him pay.

37

They'd been driving for almost two hours, heading north up the M6 towards the Lake District. Half an hour ago, they'd turned off and Judy was driving faster than Lisa's nerves could take along country roads.

"How far ahead is he?" Judy asked, her face grim and determined and never leaving the road in front of her. Lisa didn't think she'd ever seen her so worried.

"I'm not sure. Maybe half an hour." Lisa didn't want to mention that it looked like he was getting farther ahead. That would only encourage Judy to drive faster. Lisa wasn't sure her nerves could take it.

"I think it's time to call the police." Judy said.

"What? No. Why would we do that?"

"He's kidnapped my daughter."

"He was taking her on holiday."

"Yes, and this isn't what he's doing now. He doesn't have my permission to take her to random places without first telling me what he's doing."

Lisa knew that Judy was right, but calling the police was crossing a line they wouldn't be able to cross back over so easily. Having outsiders inspect their family was a level of scrutiny she didn't want to deal with.

"Any idea where he's going?" Judy asked.

"No. Wait a second, he's come off the main road."

"Do I need to turn?"

"Not now. Keep going. He's stopped. Wait, I know where we are. We're close to the caravan site."

"What?"

"He's down the road from the old caravan site we had a static caravan on."

"You don't still have the caravan, do you?"

"No. Dad got rid of it years ago when we started moaning about having to travel. That would have been in our teens."

"Coincidence?"

"Yeah, probably." Except Lisa's skin was tingling and she couldn't fathom why. It was like there was something in the air, pressing her senses. Memories of events yet to happen.

She was jolted out of her thoughts by her phone ringing. "It's Mum. Hi, wha—"

"Jemma's home," her mum said, her voice excited and relieved. "He dropped her off in town by the station with some money for the train, but he kept her phone."

When Lisa told Judy, the car veered alarmingly into the right-hand lane of the bypass. "Let me speak to her," Judy said.

"Hang on," Lisa said, then put the phone on speaker. "Mum, can you put Jemma on?"

A moment later the young girl's voice came through the phone. She was talking quickly, almost excited by what had happened.

"Mum?"

"Hi sweetheart." Judy glanced down at the phone. Lisa was holding it between them. "Are you OK?"

"I'm fine. He dropped me off at the station. Told me to get a train home. Gave me twenty quid. Told me to get some lunch as well. He didn't seem mad at me. Just in a rush."

"Why didn't you call?"

"He kept my phone. Said he was sorry, but he didn't want me telling you where he was going. He'd put it in his satnav. I guess he thought I might have seen it, but I was too worried to be looking at his satnav."

"Don't worry about it. Just stay with your gran and I'll be home soon."

"OK, Mum. Love you."

"Love you too."

Lisa hung up. Judy indicated to turn off at the next junction, then flicked the indicator back off.

"What are you doing?" Lisa asked.

"We're not going back yet. I want to know what he's doing."

"Why's it important? Let's leave him to it. He'll come back when he's ready. He probably just needed to get out for a drive." But even as she said those words, she knew she didn't mean them. Dad might have been many things, but he wasn't someone who ever took himself away from a situation. He didn't need timeouts. He was heading into something. And he was worried.

38

"Dad used to own all of this. He got rid of it when we were kids. I wonder what's made him come back after all these years."

Judy had parked the car in front of a low bungalow just inside the entrance to Sunrise Holiday Park, a caravan site boosting such amenities as an onsite swimming pool, play area, and free wi-fi in the club bar.

"Adrian used to own a caravan site?" Judy said, locking the car doors and pocketing the fob.

"He used to caravan here a lot as a boy himself. When he got older, he was able to buy the place to stop it shutting. The tracker shows that his car is somewhere on site," Lisa said. "Should I call him?"

Judy shook her head. "I don't think that would be a good idea. I want to see where he is first."

"He's not a bad person. I don't know what got into him today."

"He's behaved erratically. I'd like to see what we're walking into before announcing our presence."

Lisa nodded, but it was a reluctant agreement.

"I'll ask at reception. See if anyone's seen him." Judy went into the converted bungalow leaving Lisa to her thoughts.

The car park fed into the rest of the caravan park via a single track lane, in much better condition than she remembered as a child, with newly installed speed bumps and passing bays. The site itself had about thirty caravans amidst broken woodland. What had always set this apart from other sites had been the woods. The caravans were set amongst the trees in the wood rather than having the trees cleared to make space. You could walk through the site and still feel part of the surrounding nature.

She looked around at the woods on either side and shivered, pulling her jacket closer around her. It might be very appealing to the older types looking for a peaceful retreat, but there was something unwelcoming about the encroaching woods on either side. The caravan they'd owned had been towards the back of the site, in the most private of pitches with plenty of room around them. Dad didn't like any of the neighbours being able to see his kids playing, nor did he want to have any visual line of sight from sitting in the lounge of the caravan to any other caravan around them.

This was all fine in the middle of summer when the light was high and gave them warm blankets of summer to play in, but when the nights grew short and they still came to stay, it was a different story.

Back when they were children, the site had yet to install any kind of street lighting on the access road. if they wanted to head up to the bar, they always walked up the track with their own torches and kept huddled together. Or dad would drive them up the path, throwing drink driving laws into the wind.

And the woods in the winter were the worst. What were natural places of wonder during the day, became places to avoid once the light waned. Lisa never wanted to play out once the shadows stretched, despite Phil's protestations. He was always the fearless one, always pushing her to get over her fears. But she never caved in. She never went into the woods after dark.

Except that one time.

Judy returned from the reception. "They say he arrived about thirty minutes ago. And there's something else weird."

"What?"

"You said Adrian sold this when you were children."

"Before we went to high school."

"They told me he's still the owner." Judy grimaced. "I'm afraid, I don't know why he'd lie to you about that."

"Surely, they've made a mistake." Lisa's mind was racing, trying to recall conversations they'd had about this as a family. But that had all been so long ago.

You're not going mad. He sold it. Mum was angry because she loved coming up here. They didn't speak for a whole week.

Was that why he'd changed his mind then? Because Mum hadn't approved?

"It doesn't make sense," Lisa continued, racking her brain. "Mum didn't want him to sell it. They'd rowed about it. If he'd changed his mind why would she never have come up here again?"

"I don't know. I'm just passing on what they told me. They also said it's unusual to see him up here at all. He normally sends someone else from the agency to inspect the site, but he comes up twice a year and supervises the inspection himself. Only it's a little early for that they said."

Judy looked uncomfortable. There was more she wanted to say but was holding back.

"What else? I think we're past the point of trying to save each other's feelings."

Judy nodded. "The woman in the office said that he normally rings ahead and books in when anyone from the agency comes to do a site visit, but he hasn't. I asked her when he'd last been up and she said he'd already visited twice this last week. He dropped in the first time to say hello but on the second time when he didn't come into the office, she tried to find him. Eventually, she did. There are some old holiday lets on the edge of the site. She found him up at one of these. It's one they never let out because it's never been refurbished. She saw him at the house talking to someone. She had to get back to the reception because a resident had just called her mobile, but she said he was talking to a woman."

She broke off, caught Lisa's eyes, then looked away, not wanting to make this hurt any more than it already did.

"He's been coming up here to see a woman. Are you saying he's having an affair?"

"I don't know what it means, but I suppose it's possible." She realised she was raising her voice, but she didn't care. If she didn't do what she could to release that frustration burning her up inside, she thought she would explode. How could Dad do this? How long had he been coming up here for his little affairs? How long had this one been going on?

"We don't know if it's true. It's just what she told me in the office."

Lisa paused. She bit her lip and glanced back at Judy's car. It was tempting to just go back home and forget all this. But that wouldn't solve anything, not really.

"Let's find him. He's got some serious questions to answer."

Judy nodded. She came and took Lisa's hand in hers and looked her straight in the eye. "We'll do this together. There's nothing to be worried about."

But she's wrong, isn't she? She knows nothing.

It took them five minutes walking through the caravan site to reach the pitch which used to house Lisa's caravan as a girl. The caravan had long been replaced, probably half a dozen times, and it seemed alien to her. If she looked through half-closed eyes, and allowed her gaze to follow the tree line, she glimpsed how things were when she was a girl, and turning back to face the way they'd come, the edges of the woods hadn't changed much, everything was taller, but still as unwelcoming. A clear warning to not veer off the beaten track.

They'd passed a few residents on their way, exchanged a couple of hellos, but nothing more. None of these people were familiar to her from her time here.

"It's like someone's been inside my head and redrawn my memories. None of this feels right, yet it's the place we used to come most weekends."

"Must be strange, coming back to your childhood haunts. It's been such a long time since I've been back home. Whenever I do attempt to see my parents, I sneak a look around the old estate we used to live on. But two minutes is all I need to remind myself of why I left."

"Do you not miss them, being so far away?"

Judy shrugged. "Nothing much to miss. They weren't exactly the parenting kind. Not sure why they ever had me. I think I must have been a mistake."

"I wonder if that's what I was to my parents."

Judy's face reddened. "Oh, I didn't mean it to sound so dismissive. Just I've never got on with them."

"I know that. But it doesn't make it any less true for me. It must have been a mistake for my parents. Something mustn't have been right when they had me and Phil. Timing, or circumstances or whatever. If we were planned, they would never have given us up for adoption, would they? That's not what you do?"

"People don't always know what they're getting into with a pregnancy. Their circumstances may have changed during the pregnancy. Money troubles, family putting too much pressure on them. Life was different forty years ago, they were living a life we can't imagine, and to be fair, it's not our place to imagine it. They were adults. We know that from the adoption papers. Don't read into it what we don't know. If you do, you will drive yourself mad with it all."

A dog barked as they passed in front of a caravan sited close to the road. They both jumped.

"So, what now?" Judy asked. "Should we check out those holiday houses?"

Lisa shivered, then drew her arms in close. The dog had unsettled her, and she placed a hand to the side of her temple, rubbing gently. The headache that had been threatening her ever since they'd arrived at the site was steadily getting worse, and the nausea she'd felt since that morning was stronger than ever. She'd hoped to never have to step foot in this caravan park again, and yet here she was, heading deeper into the unknown.

39

Thirty years ago

On the face of it, there was nothing unusual about the building. A rather squat compact house, with a ground floor and one level above. The windows were dark and unwelcoming, wooden frames, once painted brown to match the dark panelling under the windows, were peeling, flakes falling off like dead skin. There were a handful of tiles missing from the roof and Lisa knew that that would cause a problem. Two windows had missing glass and had been boarded up with hardboard panels.

The house was terminally sick and desperately unloved.

"It's watching us," she murmured, more to herself than to her brother. Phil's demeanour had changed upon the approach and he came to stand beside her now, placing an arm around her shoulders.

"Don't be silly, it's a house."

But she felt the tremble in his body. He felt the same way. She knew him and he knew her. The gift of being a twin.

It was quiet in the house's clearing. The whispering breeze that had eased them along the track had muted, and although the branches of the surrounding trees were still moving, Lisa couldn't hear them. She pressed her fingers to the back of her neck, certain that she'd felt something there. The hint of a breath. A murmur by her side.

"I don't like this place. Why did Dad never refurbish it? Why leave it to die like this?"

"I don't know. Money, I guess. It costs a lot to keep houses maintained."

"But these places don't rent for cheap. The caravans are usually pretty full all year round. And the other four houses are rarely empty."

"How would you know that," Phil asked, surprised.

"I read a lot. When I'm in the site office, I see what's in the booking ledger. And I hear him talking to Mr Melbourne."

Mr Melbourne was the site manager. He ran the place so Dad didn't have to. A short fat man with spectacles, he had a slow ponderous manner about him that reminded Lisa of an ageing hippo. When he was standing in the site office behind reception, sweat would be dripping in rivulets down the sides of his forehead and he constantly seemed to have a handkerchief in his hand wiping them away.

"Melbourne knows nothing. He's an idiot," Phil announced.

"What was he doing here last night? What did you see?"

Phil looked down at his feet, then began walking back up to the house like he'd had to psych himself up to approach. "I hung back. I didn't want him to see me, but it was cold last night. For a while, must have been at least five minutes, he just stood in front of the house, looking up at the windows. He put out the cigarette he'd been smoking, then immediately lit up another. He really isn't on the verge of quitting despite what he tells Mum.

"After his second cigarette, I heard him mumbling to himself. I was too far back in the bushes to catch what he was saying, but I figured he was bothered by something. It was almost like he was laying out what he was going to do, like he was readying himself for something. Then he went in through the front door."

Phil stopped. He was looking up at the top window in the house, the one that had a sharp crack in the glass. It needed replacing, but this one hadn't even had a board placed in front of it yet. Lisa hurried to stand beside him, curious as to what had caught his attention. Curious and scared as to what she might see. Coming down to this house was like stepping off the pier into the dark waters of the unknown. Once again, she felt the pressure building around her, not sure what part of her would crack first. Every fibre of her being was screaming at her to leave this place, to take Phil and run back to the caravan, taking her brother back to safety. He was too full of bravado to think straight about most things and his mind was clouded in this instance.

But Phil was walking once again to the front door, and like an obedient puppy, she couldn't help but follow him.

He'd taken his eyes away from the upstairs window and was now focusing straight ahead. And he'd speeded up, eager perhaps to get this over and done with.

"Phil, wait. Tell me what else you saw? You didn't go into the house last night, did you?"

"Nah, I moved closer though, found a better place to stay hidden where I could see more of the house." He pointed to a place about twenty metres away from the front door where the shrubbery was every bit as dense as the side of the track. He'd have got a good view from back there, with coverage over all the windows on the front of the house.

He continued to the front door; Lisa came beside him.

And they waited.

"What are you doing? You're not going to go in there are you?" She was whispering. Why on earth was she whispering? There was no one inside, the place was empty.

But if it was empty, why was Dad here in the middle of the night?

"You said you thought he was meeting someone. Did you see anyone else?"

Phil shrugged.

"What's that supposed to mean?"

"It means," he hissed, "I don't know. But if we don't go inside, how are we going to know for sure?"

"We can't go in there. That's trespassing."

"Dad owns this house, just like all these other houses. It's not trespassing if you own it, stupid."

And there was that little sliver of malice in his eyes that almost made her wince. Belittling her was his defence whenever he got threatened. She'd wound him up sufficiently on occasion that he'd raised a fist, ready to hit her, but then thought better of it and calmed himself. It made her brother look ugly, and it made her feel stupid and ashamed.

"I'm not stupid," she whispered. "I just don't see how we'll explain this to Dad if we get caught."

"We won't get caught. No one knows we're here. There's no one around."

"The other houses," she pointed out.

"Are too far away to see us. Look, can you see the other houses?"

She did as he bade and had to concede that no, there was no chance of anyone from the other houses seeing what they were doing. The trees were too dense, the branches too full of leaves.

So, anything could happen to you inside and no one would ever know. How long will it take them to realise we've come here?

Nice, cheery thoughts. Way to go, Lisa. She swallowed, then nodded, indicating to her brother that they should proceed.

Phil pushed his hand on the door, and they stood silently as the door opened into a black rectangle of corridor.

40

"I remember it now, or part of it at least." Lisa had stopped moving and Judy worried that she was going to turn around and run back out of the park.

"What do you remember? Tell me."

"It was one of the holiday houses. Phil and I broke in and I got trapped."

Judy tried to take Lisa's hand, but she snatched it back, the eyes seeing something that wasn't there anymore, hadn't been in front of her thirty years. When she realised she'd overreacted, her shoulders relaxed, and she looked at her and nodded. "Sorry," Lisa said. "It was coming back to me."

"Are you good to go on?"

"Yes, I think so. It's been there for so long, this memory, but until now, I've never been able to get past the first part, the part where we got beyond the front door."

"Maybe it's because we're so close, the memories are freeing up."

Lisa continued walking up the track and Judy stepped in alongside her, her senses attuned to the surrounding woods. If Adrian was close by, she wanted to know, she wanted to see where he was before he saw them. Her skin was itching with the bad feelings she was getting about this place. She paused at a road sign, partially hidden by overgrown bushes.

Hampton Street

The place Phil had mentioned in his journal. The street that his dad had shouted at him about.

"Did Matt Hodgson ever have anything to do with this place?"

Lisa shook her head. "Not that I can remember."

"But you know who I'm talking about?" Judy had slipped Matt's name into the conversation, hoping with Lisa's memories being a little looser, she might recall some people that had worked here when she was little. If Matt had had anything to do with the caravan site when she was younger, it might explain why hearing from him might have affected Adrian.

"I don't know. I think I know him."

As they rounded the bend in the track, the house came into view and Lisa stalled once again. There were no signs of life in the house, but it was not what Judy was expecting. The building looked like a cheap seventies build, a combination of brick and wooden structures. None of the windows were unscathed, most had been boarded up and even those boards looked like they should be refreshed. The trees were trying to reclaim this plot of land and Judy figured if no one took care of the land then it would succeed in another fifty years. What grass there was was knee high and clumps of nettles were taking over around the edges of the plot, narrowing in on the house.

But it wasn't just the house that had caused the women to pause. There were two vehicles parked in front of the house. The first was Adrian's Mercedes, the second was a white van that Judy had seen once before this week.

"That's Matt Hodgson's van. The man who was calling your dad. I saw him drive off in it from your dad's office."

"Why is he here?"

Judy had no answer for her. Whatever the phone call had been about, it had stirred Adrian into meeting the maintenance guy, but why would he be meeting him all the way up here? Why not somewhere local?

"This is the house you went inside?" Judy asked, but she didn't need to. Lisa's reaction said more than words could. "I've seen this before," Judy continued, then it came to her. "This is the house we saw on the television at your house." Her instinct was to turn and run back along the track until they reached their car, but she ignored the tingling along her arms and the dryness in her throat. What had the ghost wanted them to see this house for? Why was it so important?

"What aren't you telling me?" Judy asked.

"I... I know this place."

"You've been here before and so has our ghost friend."

Lisa was staring at the building, unable to tear her gaze from it. Judy saw the trembling build in her body and grabbed hold of Lisa's arms before she fell.

But as she looked back up to the house, she saw something that made her blood go cold. "There's someone up there."

41

Thirty years ago

Phil's nose wrinkled in disgust at the smell that slunk from the dark hallway. Lisa put her hand over her mouth and tried not to gag. He stepped over the threshold, reaching a hand behind for his sister to take. Lisa accepted it and stepped inside beside her brother.

The smell seemed to dissipate, or she'd got used to it very quickly, because once standing on the worn red carpet in the hallway, she no longer felt the need to vomit or even hold her nose.

"I don't like this," she said.

"U-huh."

"No, I really don't like this. I think we should go now. There's nothing here."

"We haven't even been in any rooms yet. Give us a chance. Dad was here for a reason. What if he's got something hidden here that he doesn't want anyone to know about?"

"Like what?"

"Money?"

"Don't be daft. Dad's rich enough that he doesn't have to hide money."

"But what about taxes? Maybe he's hiding it so the tax man can't get it."

"What have you been listening to?"

Phil shrugged. "Stuff. I've heard him on the phone. I can eavesdrop as well as you."

"You listen to some weird conversations."

A staircase to the right led upstairs, a turn in the stair made it impossible to see what was on the first floor, but Lisa didn't care, she had no interest in going upstairs. As far as she was concerned, she'd done more than enough by crossing the threshold.

The hallway door creaked open ahead of them. They looked at each other, Phil's eyes had widened, and that self-assuredness was gone.

"It's the breeze, that's all. Some windows are damaged, and it's affecting the air flow in the house," he said, then swallowed.

She didn't believe that he believed that for a second. There was something wrong in this building and it was nothing to do with airflow. She took a step forward, then another, her hand reaching for the internal door.

Phil's hand touched the small of her back but she didn't look, just moved forward, her feet heavy like they were working their way through mud, each lift another weary effort.

When the front door slammed shut, she jumped and shrieked. Spinning around, she realised she'd been mistaken. Phil wasn't behind her. A banging on the other side of the front door confirmed he was back outside.

So, who touched you?

"Lisa! Stop messing around. Come out." Phil's voice was panicked. He banged again on the door.

Lisa ran and tried the latch, but the mechanism didn't shift. "The lock's broken. Why did you do that?"

"I didn't do anything."

"Help me, this isn't funny."

She felt the weight of his body slam into the door. He tried again to knock it open, but the door was far stronger than it looked.

"It's jammed."

"I know," she cried. Oh God, what was happening? Why had she let herself get stuck in here? "This is not funny. Let me out. You've had your fun."

"It's not me. I swear."

But he would swear it wasn't anything to do with him. This was a typical Phil prank, and she'd fallen for it hook line and sinker. The story of following Dad, the destination a forbidden building. How could she have refused?

He must have come here earlier when I was reading. Broken in maybe, or more likely lifted the key from reception when Mr Melbourne wasn't looking. And once inside, he didn't waste any time in letting you go forwards so he could sneak out behind you and lock the door.

But the door didn't have a second lock on it. There was just the familiar Yale style lock they had at home. There was no way to lock that from the outside in such a way that would prevent her getting out.

"Why did you go outside if you weren't trying to lock me in?"

"I heard a noise. Someone talking. I thought it might have been Dad. I just came to the door to look but someone shoved me outside and then the door closed."

"Bullshit. You are in such deep shit. I'm telling Dad."

"Lisa. You need to get out." His voice had changed. The bravado kid who thought he knew everything had been replaced with the scared kid who woke up in the middle of the night terrified about the voice at the end of his bed. The one that would tell him to go back to sleep. The same one that had been with him since they were little.

She tried the door latch again, but it refused to budge.

There are other doors, she thought. I'll go out through one of those. No problem. And when I do get out, I'm going straight to Dad to tell him what a jerk you are.

No. Even better. She'd merely have to threaten telling Dad. That threat would keep her brother in her pocket for a few days at least. Maybe give her enough time to finish her book without him picking on her until they got back home.

"Lisa," Phil's voice came from the other side of the door. He must have his face pushed up against the wood. "Lisa, are you there?"

"Of course I am, idiot."

"I saw the curtains move in the upstairs window. There's someone in there with you."

Her blood ran cold, a shiver ripped across her shoulders and down her back. "Don't mess with me," she hissed.

"I'm serious."

And then she heard the creak of floorboards above her head. She stared at the ceiling, tracking the noise. It came from above and to her left. She twisted her neck and dared the noise to come again. It did soon enough, and she could follow its progress as weight shifted on the floorboards, moving from her left to directly overhead. She glanced at the staircase.

They're coming downstairs.

Her heart thundered in her small chest, impossibly fast, making her head dizzy with the increased oxygen flow. She needed to move. Move or hide.

The door banged behind her again, and she forgave her brother for thinking ill of him. He was as scared as she was.

Move, she told herself. Move now and move quickly. Move before whoever it is upstairs comes downstairs and finds you.

What if there wasn't just the one person in the house? What if there were others downstairs? They'd not been quiet when they came into the house. Anyone would have heard them. And what kind of people hang around in old run-down houses, anyway? Lisa understood that some people liked to use drugs, or sniff glue, and they needed privacy to do that. A nice house out here in the woods gave them all the privacy they could want.

She forced her legs into action and with the lightest movements, she crept along the hallway, her back to the internal door, keeping her eyes on the staircase, her ears attuned to the slightest noise from above, her eyes expecting to see a shape appear around the turn in the stairs.

The noise continued overhead. Not air currents. Footsteps.

Lisa pushed open the internal door and entered a lounge dining room. There was still furniture in here. Old and covered in dust, but besides that, it looked nothing like she'd imagined. Someone could come in and tidy this place up and it would be almost habitable. Wallpaper was peeling and she could see dark patches of mould and damp. That would explain the musty smell that was so rich in her throat.

The light was dim. This window had been boarded up outside and the curtains had been drawn inside, filling the room with shadows and irregular shapes she didn't have time to process. Lisa darted to the only other door in the room and found herself in the kitchen. Breathing a sigh of relief, she saw the kitchen had its own door to the outside, and she ran for it.

The door was locked.

Shit. Shit. Shit.

She ran her hands around the lock, hoping to find something obvious that she'd missed. No, she'd missed nothing. The door took a key and there was no key in the lock. Without it, she'd have to break it down to get out.

Hide.

That was the only option she had left. From the kitchen, she couldn't hear any movement from upstairs.

That's because they're on their way down to meet you.

She glanced at the door back to the living space. Where could she hide in there? And how long for? Was Phil still trying to make his way inside? Or had he run to get Dad? Dad would be angry, but he'd be more angry at whoever was in the house threatening his kids.

You're the intruder, remember that. You've broken into their space and you expect them to be nice to you.

A creak on the floorboards. That was close. That came from the hallway.

No time to find another hiding place.

She flung herself under the kitchen table. Her heart fluttered in another surge of panic and she almost lost it then, figuring it might be best to plead forgiveness from the stranger. What was the worst they would do? Shout at them? Take them by the hand and deliver her back to her dad who would then shout at her? That wouldn't be so bad. She'd had plenty of dad shouting.

But you know this won't end like that. Whoever was in this house heard you and Phil approach the house, then they heard you enter and talk in the hallway. Only then did they come and see what was happening. And why haven't they said a word? Not even a shout out to scare you away. That isn't normal. That's damn creepy.

Lisa thought she might cry, but she bit her lip and closed her eyes and tried to still her heart from pounding so stupidly loudly in her chest. If she could last a few minutes without being found, dad would turn up and get her out, or maybe the person hunting her—

Oh, that's dark even for you. Is that what this person is doing? Hunting you?

—would just give up and go back upstairs thinking the intruder had already left.

She held her breath as best as she could and tried to block out the sounds of the approaching footsteps shuffling across the lino like a monster.

The sound stopped.

Lisa thought she felt a trickle of air disturb her hair. Almost a breath. She opened her eyes. The tablecloth had been lifted and she could see a pair of legs, the hem of a black skirt, and two pale fingers holding the tablecloth tight against the underneath of the table.

She was frozen. Her blood had turned to ice and all thoughts of escape had left her. Dad would not get here in time to save her from this. Phil wouldn't get the door open. This thing had hunted her and had her trapped.

Her mouth opened in a silent scream as the body shifted, legs bending as the figure lowered itself awkwardly, a movement that seemed to take an ungodly age and looked uncomfortable and unnatural.

And the lower features of a face appeared, a thin grey chin, too thin, too pale. Then the rest of the face appeared all at once, and it stuck itself under the table so it appeared directly in front of Lisa's own.

Lisa screamed.

42

Judy pulled Lisa aside, back into the undergrowth where they couldn't be seen from the house, or at least, she didn't think they could be seen from the house. The figure, she hadn't been able to determine whether it was a man or a woman, had been standing in one of the upstairs rooms. The cracked window was partially boarded, but she'd definitely seen a pale face staring out through the gaps.

"What did you see?" Lisa asked.

Judy's heart was thundering as she told her.

"Are you sure? Was it Dad?"

"I don't know. It might have been." Judy realised she was keeping her voice low. In the quiet of these woods, their voices would easily travel and be heard through broken windows.

"Why are we hiding?"

Judy looked at Lisa, the thought catching up with her. It had seemed the right thing to do, an instinctual response to the face she'd seen, the fear, yes that's what had driven her to hide, a fear of the stranger in the house.

Whatever Matt and Adrian were up to, it was something they wanted to keep hidden. How bad could it be?

Judy brushed aside a small branch and checked the first-floor window again. There was no sign of a face this time.

She stood and Lisa followed her to the front door. Lisa hesitated and Judy let her linger behind. She was prepared to do this on her own if she had to. All she had to do was tap into that anger she felt towards Adrian. It was there now, a little dagger of rage nestling in her chest.

"Hello?" she called out as she pushed the front door open. The door was unlocked, the paint flaking off in huge strips like a giant had scratched at the surface in an attempt to break in. A smell like ancient sewers struck her in the face and she staggered back, caught by Lisa. But as quickly as the gross smell hit her nostrils, it was gone again, leaving only the damp musty smell she'd accustomed to old property.

Brushing a strand of hair away from her face, she stepped further into the hallway, keeping a wary eye on the staircase leading to the upstairs.

Lisa was behind her now and she reached for Judy's hand, taking it and gripping tightly. "Keep an eye behind us," Judy said. "I don't want anyone surprising us."

Lisa nodded and together the women entered the lounge. A huge brown sofa, its heavy-duty fabric long-since threadbare and destroyed by mice, took up the far wall, opposite the windows. Dirty slats of grey light broke through the gaps in the boarded window, catching the dancing motes of dust they'd disturbed by their entrance. Angels and demons circling each other.

A small gas fire was still attached to the wall, and Judy hoped they had cut the gas supply off as the pipework looked bent and unsafe. The place stunk of mouse droppings and urine and she wondered whether anyone else had been in this building recently. Could it be home to local homeless people? Somehow she doubted it. Whilst it afforded some shelter from the elements, it was too rundown for anyone to seriously consider living here. And besides, there was no sign of any belongings, no bags of clothes or food.

She turned to look in the kitchen and saw that Lisa had frozen in the doorway, looking back to the front door.

"What's wrong?" Judy hissed and came to stand beside her.

The front door was closed. And Lisa was shaking.

"She was there. I saw her. She closed it."

"Who?"

"The ghost from my house. The woman from my dreams."

"What do you mean, from your dreams?"

Judy walked past Lisa and tried the front door. It refused to budge. She noted the broken Yale lock, the metal latch flopping in its housing. It had been a long time since that had worked, and there were no other locks on the door. Yet it was refusing to open.

Lisa needed some encouragement to come back into the hallway. "There's nothing here. Whatever you saw has gone." For now, she wanted to add, but didn't. Judy didn't doubt that Lisa had seen the ghost again, and it bothered her that it wanted them both here.

But what was the connection with this house? Why had she seen it here? Was it just following them?

"What aren't you telling me, Lisa? Why did you say the woman from your dreams?"

A floorboard creaked overhead. Judy's head snapped back as she sought the location of the disturbance. Someone was up there. She knew she'd seen someone. She took a step towards the staircase, realised that Lisa wasn't moving, then went to take her by the hand to lead her upstairs.

As they rounded the turn on the staircase, Judy could see her way up to the first-floor landing. There were four doors, all open, and the signs of decay were just as clear up here. She wrinkled her nose at the smell of more unpleasantness. Mice again. Or worse.

She thought the creak must have come from the room above the lounge. The one where you saw the face from the window.

Yes, there had been no mistake. She'd seen someone.

As she pushed open the door and stepped inside the room she saw Adrian, leaning against a wall like he'd been waiting for them. And by his feet, the dead body of Matt Hodgson, the blood from an ugly wound on his neck pooling around him, seeping into the carpet.

Judy froze. Her body refused to move despite her mind commanding her to get out of there immediately. She quickly took in the bed with no bedding, the peeling wallpaper and the black mould perimeter around the ceiling, but her eyes fixed on the wooden cot beside the bed. There was something inside the cot, two somethings, and Judy swallowed as she forced her legs to move closer.

Adrian approached Lisa, taking her hands in his. He was shaking his head in admonishment.

"Why did you have to come here? You shouldn't have come."

"Dad, I don't—" Lisa was glancing down at the body, then up into her dad's face, looking for an explanation that she could be happy with. It wasn't forthcoming. Judy didn't think either of them would be able to look at Adrian in the same way again. His face was that of a stranger. Somebody else walking around in a second-hand body.

Adrian glanced at the body. "I didn't do that, oh my god, surely you don't think I could have done that."

"Then how? You're the only one here."

Except, Judy didn't think that was true. There were more than the three of them here. The others just hadn't shown themselves yet.

Judy reached the cot and looked down inside. A thin cot mattress lined the bottom. There were no sheets and the mattress had been nibbled away over the years by mice. Inside, were two teddy bears, brown bodies and striped limbs; one with pink stripes, one with blue. Without ever seeing the bear that Lisa had described from her house, she knew that she was looking at it now.

"What happened, Adrian?"

Adrian noted her for the first time. "I have you to thank for bringing my daughter into this. Ever since that night at the restaurant you've been interfering. What's wrong with you? Is your life so empty now that my son's gone that you keep feeling the need to poke your nose where it's not wanted?"

"Lisa asked for my help. I couldn't turn her down."

"She asked for your help in finding her birth mother. It wasn't a shopping trip, for Christ's sake. You didn't think that people wouldn't get hurt."

"I certainly didn't think anyone would get murdered." Judy had seen dead bodies before, and recently too. She didn't think it was a thing that she would ever get used to.

"How did he die?" Lisa asked.

"His throat has been slit," Judy replied, then to Adrian, "Why did you do it? I don't understand."

Adrian held his hands up. There was blood on them. As he moved around the room, the broken light caught the shadows on his trousers and revealed the dark patches with just that tinge of red. "I didn't kill him."

"You're the one standing there with blood all over you."

"I tried to save him. He was trying to blackmail me, but I never wanted him dead."

Blackmail? What did he possibly have to blackmail him about?

Judy had her suspicions, and like Adrian had alluded to, it all came down to the night at the restaurant, and Lisa's determination to find her birth mother.

"We should go. The police need to be involved."

Mention of the police set Adrian's eyes ablaze. "No! You can't involve the police."

"But you've killed a man."

"I didn't kill him," he spat. "I didn't do it." And he strode towards Judy, his bloodied hands reaching out for her. She turned and was ready to run from the house. But as she turned, she saw that there was a likelihood that Adrian had been telling the truth.

There was another figure blocking the doorway. The ghost she'd seen in Lisa's house, the same ghost she'd seen in her own house.

Judy froze, Adrian stood behind her, his hands gripping her arms. And she could feel his panic coursing through her.

"She did it," he said. "Sarah killed him."

"Sarah?" Lisa said, her voice wavering, "how do you know that's her name? That's the same woman I've been seeing in my dreams, in my house. She's following me."

"Sarah likes to keep an eye on us, on her... family."

Judy stared at the ghost. Even in this light, now that the ghost wasn't moving, it was possible to get a much better look at her face, and there was something familiar about her. Something turned over in her stomach, like that first terrible dip of the roller coaster as all you can see is the track below you and the wind tearing at your hair and you know that you are headed for certain doom.

And she knew what Adrian was going to say before he said it.

"I'm so sorry, Lisa, but Sarah was your mother."

43

"What are you are talking about, Dad?"

No one had taken their eyes from the ghost blocking the doorway. Judy wondered if they would be able to get out of the room without interference, but judging by how hostile it had been at Lisa's house, she guessed they were here to stay. There was no escaping this entity.

This entity's name is Sarah. And she's Lisa's birth mother.

Things were falling into place. Ever since the night at the restaurant, hadn't Sarah been there, watching, helping them uncover the truth?

No, it didn't feel like she was helping them at all. There was anger emanating from this entity, clouding the room.

"Lisa, you said there were two people who attacked your cat and locked you out of the house."

"Yes."

"There's more than one of them. This is more than just Sarah."

Judy spun around, sensing another presence in the room, and there he was.

Phil looked just as she remembered him. His oversized frame was even more intimidating in his death. He had been capable of so much when he was alive, what was he capable of now that he was dead? He was wearing the ill-fitting jeans and polo shirt that he'd wear whenever he wasn't working. The face was a pallid white, with skin stretched over sunken cheekbones. This was the Phil she remembered during his illness, when treatment had started for his cancer. His eyes locked on her, the intention clear.

You're not going anywhere. Not until we're done with you.

They were in the most terrible danger. Sarah had shown how powerful she was when she attacked them at Lisa's house.

Two of them together was an entirely different proposition. As if reading her mind, the bedroom door swung shut behind Sarah. Their only escape route had been cut off.

"Dad, what the hell's going on? How can this be my mum?"

"It's to do with the adoption, isn't it?" Judy said, directing her question at Adrian. "It wasn't a coincidence that the adoption agency you used was in the same office as your letting agency. It was stupid of him really, to let you have the paperwork at all. I imagine he trusted that upon hearing that your parents were dead, you'd give up on any hope of tracking them down. And it worked, didn't it? You passed the paperwork to me and you'd given up. But, I was curious. It seemed such a turnaround from your dad who only a few days before had been vehemently opposed to you finding out the details of the adoption." She addressed Adrian, trying to ignore her tightening chest. "You should have taken more care over the paperwork. Leaving a trail would only encourage me to follow it."

Adrian turned his attention to Judy. "You should never have got involved. It was supposed to be over with. Lisa didn't need to know."

"Know what, Dad?"

But Judy interjected. "Know that he'd faked the whole thing. There was no adoption agency. That paperwork was a fake, the adoption agency never existed. Matt Hodgson knew the truth though, didn't he?" Judy racked her brain, trying to piece together how this ruse had played out. Had Faith known that the adoption wasn't genuine? No, she couldn't have. This was done for her benefit, no one else's.

"I don't understand. How can the adoption agency have been fake? Where did Phil and I come from? How did we get adopted?"

Adrian was still throwing daggers at Judy, but he swallowed and straightened.

"Your mother and I had wanted children for years, but it wasn't happening. It was difficult to get much help from the

NHS in those days. There was no such thing as IVF and fertility treatments were in their infancy. Besides, your mother was only blaming herself for not being able to have children. She'd resolved herself to it and had given up.

"The letting agency was doing all right, better than all right—it was thriving. But it was taking all the spare time I had to build it up. I was looking at other opportunities and happened upon this caravan site. We used to come to the area when I was a boy and I suppose I was thinking of the good times we'd had, and how it might be a good project for your mum to be involved with, take her mind off the pregnancy thing. But then I met Sarah."

He glanced at the sentinel blocking the doorway. Neither Sarah nor Phil were showing any signs of movement against them, perhaps they were as keen for the story to be told as Judy and Lisa were.

Adrian cleared his throat, then glanced up at the ceiling, anything to avoid looking his daughter in the eye. "We fell in love."

Lisa stepped back, her face displaying the hurt for all to see. Her eyes were wide, her lips curled down. It looked like she was on the verge of tears. "You cheated on Mum?"

"I'm not proud of it, but understand that it was difficult for us. The pressure of starting a family was showing. Your mum was blaming herself and I just did what I'd always done, throw myself into my work. So, when Sarah showed me some interest, I couldn't help myself.

"She worked on the site, lived at Castlerigg, and was happy to show me around. She knew I was married, and at first, she kept her distance, but the more I came up here to check on the progress of the site, the more I realised I wanted to spend time with her. I didn't realise how unstable she was."

Judy felt a chill down her back, and she noticed that Sarah had shifted position. She'd lifted her head higher, and she was regarding Adrian as a hungry animal might regard its prey. Adrian didn't seem concerned, his focus was very much on telling his story, getting the truth out. He was relieving himself of the burden, the lies that had been binding him to this place.

"I suppose now, you'd call her a bunny boiler, but in the sixties, we didn't have a term for it. Needy, perhaps? But obsessively so. She argued with me when my visits were due to end, when I had to go back home. She threatened to reveal our relationship to your mother or embarrass me in front of my employees at work. The only way to appease her was to spend even more time here, to make promises I didn't intend to keep. You've got to understand... this affair was over from my point of view almost as soon as it started. Two months if that, and then she became obsessed. But I needed time to work out how to deal with the situation. I didn't want to hurt Sarah. But it had to end.

"Then Sarah became pregnant. She told me on the night I gave her my latest ultimatum. I'd warned her about keeping her distance, how I didn't want her working here anymore. We argued. There was shouting. She threw things. Then she told me."

"She was pregnant with Phil and Lisa?"

Adrian nodded. "We didn't know it was twins, but yes. She was pregnant. She threatened to terminate them. And if the doctors wouldn't help her, she was threatening to take matters into her own hands. The pregnancy changed her. She became more unstable, more desperate for me to leave Faith and raise our family together. But even then, I knew that I couldn't do it. I couldn't spend my life with a woman who'd threatened to kill our children."

"What did you do?" Judy asked.

Adrian looked downcast as if every sentence he uttered was taking him further back in time.

"It just wasn't fair. Me and Faith had been desperate for kids and had been trying for years. And here Sarah was, threatening to kill the very things we were dreaming about. I knew then that I couldn't let that happen. I would not let her take them from me." He threw a look at Sarah and the ghost's expression seemed to change. The corners of her mouth curled ever so slightly. Judy realised with horror that Sarah was smiling.

"Is that when you came up with the idea of faking an adoption?"

He nodded. "I didn't know whether Sarah would ever be happy with letting me and Faith adopt. I offered her money."

"You tried to buy her children? Tried to buy me?" Lisa sounded aghast at the idea.

"You are my daughter. I'd have paid any amount of money to keep you safe and that meant getting you away from your mother. She was using you as a bargaining chip, trying to blackmail me to leave Faith. If I'd have said yes to her blackmail, how long would it be until she came up with a new set of demands? There was never any chance of me leaving your mother. I love her too much. Sarah was a mistake."

The floor rumbled. A vibration building, rising through Judy's legs. She looked at the others to see whether they'd noticed it, but they were too lost in the past.

Adrian continued. "It was the best for everyone. She would never have the stress of raising children on her own, and I'd make sure she was comfortably enough off that she would be able to start again with a new life, meet someone else. That did it. She wasn't prepared to meet anyone else or call our relationship a day. She wanted me and the kids be damned. She was almost full term by this point and living in this house. I'd set things up nicely for her. She ended up giving birth on the bed in this room.

I was the only other person present."

He looked sullen. There was something else even worse to come. He steeled himself before picking up the story. "But after the birth, something went wrong. She wouldn't stop bleeding. I'd never been at a birth before so didn't know what to expect, but she needed medical attention."

Adrian looked at the ghost of Phil at the far side of the room. Neither Lisa nor Phil was reacting to the news that Adrian was actually their biological father. It was news Judy thought under other circumstances, they'd be happy to hear.

"I took the babies, did what I could for you to make sure you were safe and warm. Then I took you with me."

"And what about Sarah? What did you do for her?"

"I left her to die."

44

Adrian's words hung in the air.

I left her to die.

He had nothing else. He was waiting for some reaction from his daughter. Judy regarded the pair of them, then looked at the two ghosts and wondered what they were thinking. Did they even think? Were they just reacting? She thought the latter was the case.

So, when Sarah spoke it came as a shock to all of them.

"You left me to die."

Whatever predicament Adrian had found himself in, he was guilty of murder, or at the least manslaughter. What must have gone through Sarah's mind as she lay on her bed, dying after giving birth, feeling her life draining away?

Lisa and Adrian were shocked at the sound of Sarah's voice and it helped pull a reaction from Lisa. She turned away from her dad and stood beside Judy. Judy reached for her sister-in-law's hand.

"I'm sorry," Judy said.

"You don't need to be sorry," Lisa replied.

"I did it to save you and your brother," Adrian said. His eyes were pleading for understanding, but it was an understanding that would never come. Judy knew Lisa well enough that this revelation was enough to drive a permanent wedge between them. She would never see her father in the same light again. And neither would Judy.

"You faked the adoption agency. How do you even do that?"

"When we started out, we bought all the cheap housing we could. Homes for the desperate. Some of those were less reputable than others, but I wasn't about to turn away people with criminal records if they could still pay their way. I made contacts that I thought could be useful. One man was an expert in faking identity documents.

"It wasn't difficult to get the birth certificates made. It was even less difficult to fake the necessary paperwork to show that we'd adopted the babies. After what happened, I took the babies to a friend's house. Another desperate soul who owed me several favours. She looked after them until I'd sorted everything out with the adoption and introduced Faith to the idea. She would never say no to the possibility of two beautiful twins."

Faith had never struck Judy as particularly gullible, quite the opposite in fact. So, the idea that she'd totally believed what she was being told about the adoption didn't ring true. If Adrian had struck deals with the shady underbelly of Southport setting up his business and she'd not objected, why would she object when promised two children, the one thing that she desperately wanted? And so what if she didn't look too closely at the forged paperwork, squinted over the details, never questioned her husband on why he kept going up to a caravan site that didn't warrant that much personal attention? Faith was as complicit in this as Adrian. Only, she'd never need to admit to that.

"What about him?" Lisa said, pointing at Matt's dead body. "What's he got to do with this?"

Judy had an idea. "He was the caretaker of the offices where your dad's business was set up."

Adrian nodded, keen to tell the story from his perspective. "Matt helped me set up the adoption agency in one of the vacant offices. Just enough set dressing to make your mother believe that the whole thing was legitimate."

Except, she must have smelt the bullshit from the beginning. Judy kept that thought to herself.

"So, what went wrong? Why is he here?" Lisa pressed.

"It was her fault," Adrian said, pointing at Judy.

Lisa looked quizzically at Judy. A sinking feeling struck Judy. There was that plunging drop of the roller coaster again, tugging at her insides. She realised that she must have been a contributing factor in the man's death. "I was asking around at Hosforth House. Asking for details about the adoption agency. Matt was suspicious. No one should know about that, so he got in touch with Adrian and he understood that there was an opportunity. If Matt said the wrong thing, the whole stack of lies would come tumbling down. I doubt he knew about Sarah. If he did, he would have been stupid to agree to visit Adrian at the scene of the crime. I think he was just promised a little extra hush money. A nice bonus after forty years." She looked up at Adrian. "How close am I?"

"The bastard was trying to hold me to account for faking the adoption. He didn't know about Sarah. Only that I needed some help in setting up a fake adoption agency. He even acted as the administrator. Fair play to him, he did a good job of it as well. Faith didn't suspect a thing."

She suspected, you naïve fool. She just didn't want to risk bursting the bubble in case she lost what you were offering.

"But you killed him," Lisa said, her head shaking all the time like she was on the verge of a total breakdown. "You didn't have to kill him."

Adrian continued. "He came to the new offices and hinted that he was a little broke and asked for some cash to help tide him over. I knew then that something had happened, but I didn't want to rock the boat so gave him two hundred quid and told him he could keep it as long as I never saw him again. That was a mistake. He just saw the open wallet and imagined what else he could have. He rang me this morning, told me that Judy had been asking questions about the adoption and he knew that he was onto a nice pay cheque. This time he wouldn't settle for a couple of hundred quid, he wanted much more than that." Adrian rubbed the back of his neck. "I wasn't about to be blackmailed. I wasn't stupid enough to think that would end well."

"So, you invited him up to the caravan site? Why?" Lisa asked.

"I wanted to implicate him in what happened. I'd buried Sarah's body in the woods, but there's enough evidence in this house to implicate anyone if the right piece of evidence is found. I thought I'd turn the tables on him."

"By bringing him into your murder scene?"

"Yes. What good would it do to bring up Sarah's death now?"

"What good? She's been missing for over forty years. What about her family? What must they think has happened to her?"

"I had a few trips to France. I used her letters to me as the basis for some faked postcards. She only had her dad, and he was an alcoholic. He wouldn't miss her, but a few postcards suggesting she'd started a new life in the south of France was all it took for him to stop asking questions. She's not missed. No one is looking for her."

Judy got a sense that Sarah had shifted position again. And if it were possible, her face had deepened into a scowl. She was not happy with the story that Adrian was telling. Not happy at all. After seeing what she was capable of in Lisa's house, Judy didn't want to see what she'd do to them when she was furious.

"Matt agreed to meet me here. I told him he could have his money, but that I kept it safe in this house where the tax man couldn't get to it. The greedy idiot believed me. He met me here, and I told him to come upstairs. He was nervous. He told me he thought he'd seen someone else in the house and wanted to leave. But then Sarah showed herself. Matt didn't stand a chance. She slit his throat."

Judy swallowed. She wanted to cough, but all she could think about were the two ghosts in the room. Neither of which had shown their intention towards them yet.

"What do you want Phil? Why are you here?"

Phil looked at Judy, surprised that he'd been addressed so directly. She wasn't expecting him to speak, so when he eventually did, her knees buckled, and she almost reached out to Lisa for support.

"Isn't it obvious?" His voice was just as she remembered.

The undercurrent of malice is still there, she thought. Be careful, very careful with what you say next.

"No," she replied. "I don't get it. You didn't die here. You didn't know Sarah."

"Phil," Lisa said. "Was that you back at my house? The night I was locked outside."

"You needed to listen. You weren't listening to our mother."

"Listening? What was I meant to be hearing?"

"The truth. The truth about how we came to be stolen from our birth mother and ended up with the man who murdered her," Phil said, spitting the words across at them.

"Don't be ridiculous, Son. I never meant anyone to die. Your mother on the other hand…"

Sarah moved so quickly that she became just another shifting shadow across the room. She reappeared behind Adrian, the knife in her hand catching a shard of sunlight as she drew it across Adrian's neck.

Blood spilled from the gaping wound. A thick scarf of dark crimson flowed down his skin.

Lisa screamed and ran to her dad.

Sarah disappeared; the knife she'd been holding dropped to the floor. Adrian's dying body slumped backwards. He placed his hands behind him as he staggered back into the wall. Lisa tried to ease him to the floor, but he was too heavy for her and he fell, his head knocking against the wall as he went.

Judy spun and saw Sarah at the top of the stairs. When she looked back into the room, she saw that Phil too had vanished.

She went to help Lisa, but it was too late to do anything for Adrian. Lisa's hands were pressing down into the opening in his neck, but no matter what pressure she applied, it would not make any difference; the cut was too long, the knife had dug in too deep. Adrian was dying in his daughter's arms.

"Don't try to talk, Dad. We'll get help." Then to Judy she snapped. "Call an ambulance."

Judy tried her phone but it wouldn't turn on. "It's not working. Where's your phone?"

"In the car."

"Then we've got to go."

"I'll stay and keep him safe."

But Judy could see Adrian wouldn't make it. You couldn't lose that much blood and survive; it just wasn't possible. Already his breathing had slowed, his chest rising and falling only intermittently, and no longer smooth, but jagged and unexpected, as if every breath was a surprise to him.

"He's dead, Lisa. Look at him. He's dead and I'm sorry, but we can't stay here. We have to go."

"He's not dead." She was panicking, but when she lifted her bloodied hands to move him into a more comfortable position, the blood from his neck had slowed to a trickle, the pressure diminished so much. His chest wasn't moving. His eyes were grey and lifeless.

"I'm not leaving him."

"You've got to. We'll fetch help. I promise we won't leave him here for long. But it's not safe. I don't know what Sarah will do, but after the way she's just reacted, I think anything's possible."

"She won't let you leave." Phil's voice from behind Judy made her jump. He looked so solid; not like how she imagined a ghost should look.

"Phil, why are you doing this?" Lisa was pleading.

"I'm just here to observe, to keep an eye on you. I want you to be safe, both of you," he looked at Judy and something crossed his eyes that she didn't care for. "But she's been angry for a long time. She blames us for what happened. She's angry that you're still alive, and she's not. Angry that she had us taken away from her. She's always been around us. Ever since we were kids."

Judy thought back to Phil's journal. He'd mentioned seeing the woman from his dreams, the woman from his childhood. And Lisa had seen her too. How far back had she been haunting them? Edging into their lives, growing angrier as they grew up.

"I used to have nightmares—you remember?"

Lisa nodded, her hand going in front of her mouth. "I remember."

"I'm not sure they were ever nightmares. I think it was always her, always trying to get into our lives."

"Go back to sleep..." Judy muttered.

A hint of a smile flashed on Phil's face. "She used to say that a lot whenever we'd wake or be scared. Her way of acting maternal, I guess."

"Oh my God, all those years."

Judy thought of all the doctors Adrian had put Lisa in front of. Surely just his way of denying anything weird was happening to his children. A way of absolving himself of any guilt.

"I'm sorry, Phil," Judy started. "How do we stop her?"

His frown deepened. "What makes you think you can stop her?"

"She can't keep tormenting us like this."

"But you are part of this. You were helping Lisa get rid of her. You were looking into an exorcism with your vicar friend." He spat these last words out. "She's got every right to be pissed at you."

"She wants to hurt me, Phil," Lisa interjected. "This isn't about Judy."

"I'm pretty sure she wants you dead. She's realised that that's the best way for her to have her children back around her. All three of us, together."

Lisa was shaking her head. "No. That's not going to happen."

"You must find a way to stop her first."

"Help us, Phil. You don't want to see us hurt." Judy wasn't sure whether this was exactly true.

"How did you react when I got ill?"

The attention was back on her and Judy squirmed at the question. How could she answer this without riling him? Perhaps truth was the safest option.

"I was glad," Judy said plainly.

Lisa flinched. "What? What did you say?"

Judy glanced at her sister-in-law and repeated herself. "I was glad."

The smile had returned to Phil's face. He was enjoying himself. "Glad? Is this the true Judy now?"

"I was glad because it meant you would finally stop dominating our lives. I was never happy that you would need months of painful treatment, I'm not such a bitch. But the man I lost was not the man I married. You'd changed so much, I barely recognised you." Speaking the words out loud for the first time, was lifting Judy. Perhaps she wasn't as damned as she thought.

"We all change. Throughout our lives we change. You changed. Look at you now, different, more confident, more outgoing. You even had a boyfriend. You didn't grieve for me for very long."

"I grieved for you plenty. Did you never think that what you were doing to me was wrong? Did it never occur to you that I might want my own life? That I could have my own thoughts and feelings? How many of my dreams did I give up because of you? I left my job when we had Jemma. You told me I never had to work again. I wanted to. You forbade it. My friends, I had so many when we met, but slowly and methodically, so perhaps you'd think I wouldn't notice, you cut them from my life. I depended on you for everything. And that's exactly how you wanted it. Me, trapped at home. Your personal slave. Jemma wouldn't stand a chance. Already, you'd limited her friendship circle. You only let one of her friends into our house. You were on her all the time about her schoolwork. Never giving her any chance to breathe or develop as a person. You were smothering her.

"And she knew what kind of person you'd become. She'd seen the bruises. Not just the ones I hid with the long sleeves, but the ones that took far longer to heal. The ones I'm still dealing with now. I would not let her live a life with you in it."

Lisa was still staring at her. This was the first time she'd ever said this out loud to anyone.

"No. This isn't what he was like. Phil was never as you described him. He was a good man." Lisa was doing her best to defend her brother, but Judy knew that there was a part of her that believed in Judy's story. The part of her that had experienced the same controlling behaviour from her brother.

"I'm sorry, but you didn't know him the way I knew him."

"Lies."

"It's not. Why would I lie?"

"You want to justify your own behaviour. Your boyfriend."

Richard was dead. She glared at Phil, trying to reduce the shaking she felt, trying not to let the red mist descend. "You killed Richard, didn't you? I sensed a presence in his shop, I thought it was Sarah, but it wasn't. It was you, watching me. You couldn't let me be happy, could you? Not for a moment."

Phil took a step towards her and Judy instinctively took another one back, keeping the distance. "He was an idiot. He was married. Didn't that bother you?"

"I didn't know. If I'd have known, do you think I'd have been seeing him?"

"It didn't take long before you invited him into our bed. Less than a month. That's some hard-core whoring right there."

The words hit her like a slap and she reeled. The mood had darkened. This wouldn't end well. Sarah was close, she could feel that, but Phil was right in front of her getting angrier by the second. "I'm not a whore."

"You slept with him. You didn't even ask whether he was married."

"You murdered him."

"Dicky heart. He had it coming. Justice for cheating on his wife."

Judy glanced at Lisa who was looking confused. Had she never seen this side of her brother before? Lisa stepped beside Judy, the pair of them backing slowly out of the room. Lisa's fingers brushed against Judy's, then a gentle tug and Judy knew that she was prepared to run.

"No one deserved to die. Not even you," Judy said.

"I didn't understand you all that well when I was alive. I always sought to see the best in people, but you would always undermine me. Always putting putting me down in front of our friends."

"Your friends, Phil. I had none. You wouldn't let me have any."

"All those times. And even now, trying to make me look bad in front of my sister." Phil eyes widened as if he'd just come to a big conclusion. "You can't ever leave. We won't let you."

But even as he said those words, Judy had turned and was running for the door, Lisa a split second behind. She recognised the tone in his words, the certainty that came with his arrogance. He meant every word of it. If they were ever going to get out, it would have to be now.

45

The vibrations Judy had felt earlier were back in force, the storm was building up to hit and they would get caught inside the house when it did. There was no way they'd survive against two angry spirits. That look in Phil's eyes told her she was more in danger now than she'd ever been when he'd been alive. She should have been more careful not to rile him.

But hadn't it been worth it, to see Lisa's view of him change before her eyes?

She followed Lisa down the stairs but in her rush, her foot caught on the top step and she tripped, her momentum too fast to stop herself from falling. She thudded down the stairs, her back hitting step after step. Lisa grabbed her, and stopped her as she came to rest at the turn in the stairs.

"Where is he?" Judy asked, as she let Lisa help her down the stairs. There were aches in her body, but fear and adrenaline were keeping her too high to feel much of the pain.

The front door wouldn't open.

"There's a door out the back."

Judy groaned. The fall had twisted a muscle in her back. She didn't know how severe an injury it was, but there was a sharp pain at the base of her spine that flashed in anger when she moved. She couldn't allow herself to be trapped in here. The ghosts were out for blood and she was a sitting target.

Why is Sarah targeting Lisa? Judy thought. The ghost of Sarah was angry, she understood that, and it wasn't hard to see why she would have wanted vengeance on Adrian. But her own daughter?

They crashed into the lounge and Lisa paused.

"What's wrong?" Judy asked.

"I was in this house once before. Phil and I broke in when we were young. It was like this even then."

Judy sensed there was more. Lisa's hand was trembling, her skin was cool.

"Something happened?"

Lisa nodded. "Come on, the back door is in the kitchen." Lisa led the way, speaking as she went. "I got trapped in here on my own. Phil had managed to get out. But then I heard someone moving around upstairs. I got scared and hid under there." She pointed at the kitchen table, the chairs knocked aside. "I didn't know what else to do. Damn."

The kitchen door was locked and there was no sign of a key. Judy pushed her aside, and tried putting pressure against it, testing the door against its jamb, seeing how weak it was but the movement caused her back to flare again. "How did you get out?"

Lisa stepped back and slammed the sole of her foot into the door where the lock was, but the door was too solid to break open like that. They would have to try the windows. Most had been boarded up, but there were still cracks of light breaking through. And with any luck, the boards would have been untouched in the years since they'd been put up. They would be the weak points.

Judy led the way back into the lounge. It was troubling her how Sarah and Phil were not down here. What was their agenda? They'd trapped them in here. What next?

"Help me with this," she said to Lisa and headed for the back window, behind the dining room table.

"What are we going to do?"

"It's our way out."

Quickly, they moved the furniture to one side, tossing the chairs aside. Then Judy picked up a chair by its back and wielded it like a weapon. "Stand back, cover your eyes." Closing her own eyes, she swung the chair in a wide arc, smashing it into the window. The glass shattered, heavy pieces tumbled to the floor, a fine rain of smaller fragments blew back into the room. Judy opened her eyes. They were just a few boards away from freedom.

A cry behind her made her spin around.

Lisa was stretched out against the wall, her arms out by her sides. "I can't move."

Sarah stood in the centre of the room. The ghost had a devilish glint in her eyes, her mouth slightly open revealing a line of decaying teeth and blackened gums. A line of saliva coursed its way along deep lines in her pallid skin.

"Let her go, Sarah. You don't want to do this. That's your daughter you're hurting."

A gasp from Lisa, then Judy's belief was tested to the limit as she watched Lisa lift from the ground. Flat against the wall, with nothing to support her underneath, an unseen force held her there.

"I can't breathe," Lisa choked, coughing. Judy ran across the room, aiming to pull Lisa down from the wall, but something knocked her aside. A blinding light hit her eyes, and she screamed in agony as her head smashed against the opposite wall. When she could bring herself to look up, she saw Sarah staring at her.

She's too powerful. If she can throw you across a room without so much as breaking a sweat, what chance do you have? What can you hope to achieve?

Even escape was not the long-term answer. Sarah was haunting them, not this place. And she was madder than ever.

Judy picked up one of the fallen chairs and swung it at Sarah, aiming to knock her head from her shoulders, but the chair passed straight through her. It seemed that Sarah was only a real physical manifestation when she chose to be.

She can't be harmed. What kind of defence is there against an entity that can't be harmed?

She wished she had Seth by her side. He'd know what to do.

"Sarah, you've got to let her go. You'll kill her."

"Then she won't have to leave." Sarah's voice was flat and emotionless. If there had been anger there, it had been replaced with acceptance that this was the only way it would end.

"You don't want to kill her."

"Don't presume to know what I want." Sarah threw a look as sharp as the broken glass on the floor, and for a second time a terrific force hit Judy in the stomach. She flew back across the room, landing on the floor of the kitchen. The door in front of her, separating her from Sarah and Lisa, slammed closed.

Judy was trapped.

She scrambled to her feet and hurled herself at the door, wincing at the pain in her back, the adrenaline keeping her going for now. She grabbed the handle and pulled down, but the door refused to open.

Judy slammed her fist against the wood. "Let me in, you're not thinking straight. This isn't the way you want to be with your daughter."

A tickle of wind against her neck and Judy spun around to see Phil standing there. A curious look in his eyes. "She wants Lisa to join us. I guess inevitably, it would come to this."

Judy no longer felt afraid of her husband. There didn't seem any point. He was either going to kill her or he wasn't. She'd run out of places to run to, what followed next was inevitable.

But she owed it to Lisa to at least try.

"Lisa will die unless you help me get out of here. She can't hold on for much longer, and despite what you say, I can't believe for one minute you want your sister to die in this way, surrounded by all this decay, her head full of fear. What does that say about you that you'd be prepared to let that happen?"

"Don't put this on me. This was never my fault. This was Dad's doing. It was him who had the affair, left our mother to die."

"Yes, you're right, it was Adrian's fault. I'm not suggesting for one minute that he didn't deserve what happened to him. But we're not talking about what your dad deserved, we're talking about what you're letting happen to your sister. She doesn't deserve to be punished for what your dad did."

For a moment, Judy thought they had reached an impasse, and that Phil would never help, preferring to let his sister die than do anything to impede his mother.

"She is strong, but she's not thinking straight. She's had too long to brood on what happened to her."

"So, help me."

"You were going to get rid of me."

A breath caught in her throat. "What do you mean?"

"You had your vicar friend round to the house. You wanted him to perform an exorcism." He smirked. "I'm not a demon. I'm pretty sure I'm not the intended target for one of those."

"I didn't know what you were. I just wanted to keep Jemma safe."

"Don't you think I want the same?"

Judy doubted it. Phil had shown no such concern for her when he was alive. She wanted to say that but bit her tongue. "I'm sure you do."

"I've been keeping you safe for days."

"Was that you in Jemma's bedroom?"

He shook his head. "That was Sarah. She's angry and confused and lashing out."

"Phil, your sister is dying. You don't want her to die and join you in the darkness. I've seen what the other side is like. I know some of your pain."

"How can you?"

"I can see things. I guess I've always been able to see things, but over the last few months, I've been able to sense more, so much more. And it scares the crap out of me. That's why I had Malc come around to the house and try to remove you. That's why I want nothing to happen to your sister, because I know that where she's heading for isn't the bliss Sarah thinks it will be. Help me, please, I'm begging you."

For an agonising few seconds, all Phil did was stare at her, daring her to challenge his authority again. But finally, the kitchen door creaked open.

"Go quickly," he said. "They're in the crib."

Judy nodded. Her mind flashed back to when they'd first entered the bedroom and she'd looked inside the crib. She thought she understood, and without another word, she flung open the kitchen door.

Lisa was still against the wall, her hands to her throat. Sarah was no longer around. Perhaps the pain of watching her daughter transition to the other side was too much for her to bear and she'd retreated into the dark places until it was over.

The stairs cracked alarmingly as Judy thundered up the staircase, twisting herself around the turn in the stairs and keeping her momentum going.

It won't take long for Sarah to work out what I'm doing. I've got to be fast.

There won't be a second chance, not for Lisa at any rate, and the moment Sarah realised what she was about to do, Judy had no doubt that she would put a stop to it.

In the bedroom, the two bodies were as they'd left them. It was difficult to look at Adrian. The skin was ghastly and pale and contrasted with the rich dark red from the wound on his neck. As she approached him, she tried not to think of the smell from the butcher's counter at Tesco after new trays of meat had been brought on display.

She found what she was looking for in Adrian's trouser pocket. The silver lighter, a gift from his father. She wondered if the lighter was the reason he'd never tried to give up smoking. Giving up smoking would give him precious little opportunity to use the one gift his father had given him. It was a connection to his past that he wasn't ready to let go. Now that she had it in her hand, she saw on the flip side to the initials, a message had been engraved.

Endurance

The shadows moved and Sarah was standing at the far end of the room. Judy darted for the cot and snatched up both the teddy bears. They were dry to the touch, and lumpy in her hands as the remaining stuffing shifted. The mice had done a grand old job on these.

Sarah's reaction was instantaneous. She strode from the shadows; her face twisted in rage.

Judy flicked open the lighter and spun the flint wheel. Sparks came but no light. She tried again, her heart sinking as she remembered the trouble Adrian had had with it that night at the restaurant. But she wasn't about to give up now. On her third attempt, a flame appeared. Sarah froze. Judy positioned the flame under the teddy bears, her intention clear.

"I'll do it. Don't think I won't."

Sarah didn't speak, her twisted features revealed all that needed saying.

"Let Lisa go," Judy demanded.

A noise from below, falling, closely followed by a cry for help.

You can do this, Judy told herself. You've got the power. Don't screw up.

Judy backed slowly from the room. "Don't follow me or these go up in flames. I know you don't want that to happen."

No, because that would end your fantasy about having your children back with you, wouldn't it?

It was like slipping on ice. Judy fell to the floor, her feet dragging behind her. Sarah would not let her go without making her pay for her interference.

But Judy still had her trump card in her hands, and she flicked the flint wheel on the lighter again, delighted when an inch-high flame ignited. Without warning this time, she brought the bears to the flames and watched as the flame quickly caught.

"You could have let me go," she said, then tossed the flaming bears back into the cot where the flames accelerated.

"NO!" Sarah raced to the cot where she uselessly tried to put the flames out.

Judy turned to run and almost collided with Lisa entering the room. Lisa's expression was determined. Whatever feelings she'd had for her mother upon finding out what had happened to her, had surely changed.

The vibrations started again through the floor, riding up through Judy's legs. Something was happening. A crack appeared in the wall to Judy's right. She flinched as pieces of plasterboard fell from the ceiling. A larger chunk fell on Lisa's head, fragmenting into dust.

"We've got to go," Judy said, griping Lisa's arm.

The bedroom door slammed shut. Sarah looked up from the burning cot. Her face thunderous. She was shaking her head. "I'm not losing you again."

Judy tried the door. The heat from the fire was raising the room's temperature uncomfortably. If they couldn't get out of the room, they would have to put out the fire before it got out of control. The flames were already higher than the sides of the cot. It had grown faster than Judy would have thought possible. The crackling as it bit into the wooden slats of the cot made Judy wince and amid the flames, she could barely distinguish the remnants of the children's bears.

"Stop it, Mum. Let us go."

Suddenly, with the same invisible force that Sarah had utilised before, Lisa was flung sideways into the wall. She cried in pain. Judy noticed Lisa's hands reaching for her stomach, then before she could rush to help, pressure grew around Judy's throat. Invisible fingers squeezed the life from her.

"Stop, Sarah," Judy gasped. "What about my daughter? Your granddaughter needs me." It was a desperate plea from one mother to another, but there was nothing on Sarah's face other than plain acceptance that this was how things would be. It was getting difficult to breathe. Each gasp of air became a struggle, and the light faded from the edge of her vision, creeping in like the shadows. She wondered whether an Almost Door would appear for her, but she wasn't about to pass over to the other side without a fight.

Lisa was sitting on the floor, one hand on her neck, the other touching her stomach. Judy thought she was trying to say something.

Smoke from the fire was rising and spreading across the room making Judy's eyes water. Lisa pushed herself up from the floor.

The hand was back to her stomach and Judy realised there was more going on there than indigestion.

"Mum, I'm pregnant. Don't do this. You don't want to kill us both."

Sarah paused.

The pressure around Judy's throat vanished and Judy hurried to stand beside Lisa.

"What do you mean?"

"It's true. I went for a scan last week. I'm thirteen weeks pregnant," she said, looking at Judy, glancing across at her dead mother to see her reaction. "It's Ellis's."

"Ellis's?"

"We got drunk and stupid. Swore we wouldn't mention it again. I haven't told him about this yet." She patted her stomach.

Judy embraced Lisa, her heart beating so fast, she could feel it as their bodies pressed together. When they separated, Sarah seemed different. Her face had softened, the rage subsided.

"I won't stay, Mum. I need to be here for my baby. You know what it's like to lose your children. Mine isn't even born yet. You've got to give me a chance to give it a good life. A life you'd want it to have. I know you just want me to be with you, as if that will somehow make up for the life together we never had, but despite what Dad did, I had a good life. It's not something to be ashamed of. But taking my life now, just so we can be together, means sacrificing the life of your grandchild. You don't want to do that."

In her head, Judy commended the speech, but she didn't know whether there was enough left of Sarah's mind to rationalise Lisa's argument.

"You don't have to be alone," Lisa said. "You have Phil with you. I promise I won't try to shut you out of my life. I've spent all my life wondering who you were and I hate that I will never get to know you, but perhaps it's enough that I can now find out about you."

The cold expression on Sarah's face evaporated and whilst a smile didn't materialise, there was a look of calm that hadn't been there before. Perhaps after what they'd been through, that would be enough.

Like rainwater fading after the sun comes out, Sarah melted away, leaving nothing behind.

For a moment, Lisa and Judy stood there, watching the space where the ghost had been, not quite believing she had gone.

Judy coughed at the smoke. The whole cot was ablaze now, the flames were licking the ceiling.

"We need to get out of here," Judy said and ran for the bedroom door. It clicked and swung open on her approach and she thought she glimpsed Phil across the landing before his image too vanished.

Was that the end of it? Judy dared to hope that it would be.

Outside, Judy took one last look back at the house, the flames now visible through the windows, and thought she saw two figures standing in the bedroom window, surrounded by the fire that was quickly taking hold of the house.

She turned to Lisa. "We will need help. There are two dead bodies inside. I don't think the police will believe that a ghost did that. I need to make a phone call."

46

Judy's phone call had been to the Vigilance group. The paranormal investigation society that had existed for over a century, keeping the world safe from those that would seek to use the paranormal against humanity.

But the fire engines arrived first. By the time they did, the house was in the final throes of its descent into a burnt-out shell. Judy had watched alongside Lisa as the fire fighters contained the fire, making sure the flames didn't spread into the surrounding woodland.

It took the fire fighters less than an hour to dampen the flames and that was enough time for the first of the Vigilance vans to arrive. Judy had hoped that Seth would show his face, but the figure that stepped from the lead vehicle was unexpected.

Olivia Gwinn approached as two of her entourage headed to intercept the fire chief that was getting ready to wave the vans back down the dirt track.

"Good to see you again, Mrs Doyle," Olivia said. The woman looked sterner than she'd remembered, if that was even possible, and Judy felt her back twinge as she straightened.

"I wasn't expecting you to turn up."

Olivia frowned. "You asked for our help. Who were you expecting?"

Judy had hoped that Malc would have been able to pass a message onto Seth and get him to meet them here, or failing that, for Malc to show up himself. The last person she expected was the mysterious leader of the Vigilance Society. What did it imply that neither of her friends were here?

"I had hoped that Seth might—"

"He's indisposed. And even if he wasn't, he's not experienced enough to handle this."

"Excuse me, but who the hell are you?" Lisa stood looking exasperated at the newcomer. She and Judy had both been encouraged to move further away from the burning building, but Lisa had only begrudgingly allowed the fire fighters to move her at all, and the moment they were left to their own devices, Lisa had been the first of the pair to lead the way back.

If Olivia was bothered by Lisa's abruptness, she didn't show it, her implacably calm exterior remained cool as she introduced herself. "And what the hell is this?" Lisa continued. "Where are the police? My dad's been killed inside that house."

"The police will be attending shortly, after we're finished here. I take it you are Lisa Doyle, daughter of Adrian."

Lisa nodded. "How do you know that?"

"It was all in Mrs Doyle's report." Olivia regarded her like she was a child needing everything explaining to them slowly and carefully. "And I'm not sure it's a good idea that you remain here." She directed her attention to Judy. "Is the entity handled?"

"I think so. It vanished." Judy brought Olivia up to speed with the events of the last few days, taking care to talk respectfully about Adrian, aware that his daughter still hadn't fallen into full shock.

"I'm sorry for your loss," Olivia said to Lisa. Two men came over from one of the Vigilance vans. They conferred in private with Olivia before hurrying back over to their van, phones in hands.

"What's going on?" Judy asked.

"We need to ensure that the area is secure. We've held back the police, but there are reporters on the way. We're laying down a cover story for what's happened here."

"And that would be?"

"Mr Doyle and Mr Hodgson came to view this house on the premise that it would become Mr Hodgson's retirement property. He'd come to view the house when he noticed a gas leak from a badly installed gas fire. Unfortunately, in attempting to repair the damage himself, he accidentally caused a gas explosion that led to the house going up in flames. Both men were killed instantly in the initial explosion."

"But there hasn't been an explosion, and their throats have been cut," Judy began, then realised how insensitive she'd sounded, she lowered her voice. "How will the police explain that?"

"There hasn't been an explosion yet... and afterwards we'll be removing the bodies, taking them to our facility for the post-mortem. The police won't get the opportunity to view anything that would contradict our story. Trust me, it's better this way."

Lisa looked like she was about to start a fight, but Judy put her hand on her arm and nodded. "She's right. It sucks, but what good will ever come from allowing the truth to come out now? The police can't arrest a ghost."

Lisa shook her head and wandered away from Judy, heading back towards the dirt track. Judy wanted to hurry after her, but she held back. What else could she say to her that would take any of the pain away? The poor woman had just discovered that the ghosts that had been tormenting her had been her brother and the biological mother she'd been so desperate to track down. Add into the mix her father had allowed her mother to die in the hours after giving birth and that was enough to keep her in therapy for decades.

"Thank you for coming," Judy said. "I don't know what I'd have done if the police had showed up."

"This is what we do. You don't need to thank me."

"I feel I do."

"What was it like in there?"

"Intense," Judy resisted the urge to shiver. "I didn't think we would get out alive. Sarah wanted us both dead."

"Well, good work in getting out."

"I had something else to ask. It's about Seth."

Olivia's eyes narrowed. "I'm afraid Seth's been working very hard for us."

"But I've not heard from him since he went to work with you. It's not like him."

"You haven't known him very long have you?"

"I guess not."

"You met him at Ravenmeols. Then after letting you think he was dead, you were together during the Adam Cowl business with the painting."

Judy didn't care for Olivia's tone.

"You know this."

"My point is, it's not a long time is it? You're more acquaintances than friends, aren't you?"

"That's not how I see it."

"But that's how Seth sees it. He's got a lot of important cases to work on and to be honest, I'd prefer it if you didn't continue to press the issue. I'm sure when he becomes free again, he'll reach out."

"The collection?"

"His uncle's collection is being well taken care of. Don't worry about that. Now, if there's nothing else, I'd suggest you run along after your friend. The police will be here soon, and it might be easier for everyone if you give us the time to lay down our story."

Judy looked up the dirt track after Lisa's departing figure, then back again at Olivia. Nothing about this felt right, but the moment she'd brought Vigilance into this, it was out of her hands.

"I'm sure we'll meet again," she said to Olivia, and Olivia smiled.

Yes, this was far from over, Judy thought.

47

Judy was sitting on a bench outside the hospital, watching patients come and go through the main entrance. The sun was out for the first time that week after a stretch of miserable rain and Judy closed her eyes, soaking up every last ray of warmth.

It had been three months since the fire at the caravan park and there hadn't been a sign that Sarah or Phil were haunting her own house. Lisa said that occasionally, she'd glimpse her mother in the mirror at her own home, but the presence was always accompanied by a warm feeling of peace. Sarah had done trying to pull Lisa into her realm and was content to watch Lisa's small family develop naturally.

Olivia had kept to her word and Vigilance had protected Judy and Lisa from the fallout of the fire. Their cover story about the gas explosion had held and there was never any police questioning regarding the fake adoption nor the true manner of the men's deaths. She'd asked Malc about how they could do that, influence the police investigation in such a way. She'd always assumed that the Vigilance Society were truly secret, treading around the outskirts of the establishment. But perhaps that was an erroneous assumption to make. Vigilance were more influential than Olivia Gwinn had suggested and Judy didn't know how she should feel about that. Malc had been little help when she'd questioned him about it. In fact, he'd looked apprehensive and tired, and suggested that it would be better if she tried to keep away from the society and let them do their own thing.

As for Richard, Judy had sent flowers to his funeral but didn't attend, figuring that his widow would be keeping an eye out for any single females in attendance. She'd had to change her mobile number as his wife did not let up with the harassing text messages and phone calls. She didn't blame her for acting that way, and the Judy didn't think the guilt surrounding Richard's death would ever leave her. His death was her fault. She was certain of it. If she hadn't been so quick to jump into bed with him, Phil wouldn't have done whatever it was he'd done to scare the man into a heart attack.

After Adrian's funeral, Judy had attended a private interment with Malc and Lisa. Sarah's remains had been found by the Vigilance team buried under the patio behind the holiday house at the caravan site. Adrian must have gone back to the house shortly after taking the twins away to clean up the evidence and sow the seeds for the story of her disappearance. During the service, Lisa had spoken to Sarah, her hands on the growing bump in front of her, telling her mother that she was expecting a baby boy and that she was undecided on the name.

"Hey," Lisa's voice startled Judy. Her sister-in-law sat down beside her on the bench, a smile on her face.

"How did it go?"

"Baby's fine. More than fine. They say he's going to be a big'un. Not sure I'm quite ready for that challenge at this time of life, but I'll take healthy any day of the week."

"That's excellent. I'm so pleased." Judy reached for Lisa's hand and squeezed it. "You will be an awesome mum."

"I'll have to be. I'm not going to lie, it's not panning out how I'd expected it to be. Ellis is still being a dick."

Ellis had moved out of the house and was no longer working at the same marketing firm. He'd taken the news that he would be a dad pretty well considering, but he would not take an active part in the baby's life.

"He'll come round."

"Not so sure he will. But perhaps it doesn't matter any more. Mum wants me to move back in with her. She says the house is too large for her on her own."

"That's good, isn't it?"

"It will give me some more options when it comes time to going back to work."

"You're not taking your mum up on the offer?"

Lisa shrugged. "It wasn't part of my plan to run the letting agency. I guess I always assumed Phil would get to take it over when the time came. But Mum really isn't cut out for it. She's already threatened two of the staff with the sack. If I let that continue there won't be a business to take over. Unless... I don't suppose you fancy a manager's job? It would help me out."

"You know I'll be there to help you with the baby, anytime, just shout. But you don't want me running a business. Besides, I've got some more clients. And Jemma's school got back to me about a possible opening. I think I'm going to explore that first."

Lisa smiled. "I guess Dad's still calling some of the shots for me then." She sighed and put her hand up to shield her face from the sun. "Perhaps I'll be a good landlord. Dad never made it look difficult."

"You'll be excellent. And just think what security it will give you. It's a gift, don't throw it away."

"I think Mum's desperate to be a stay at home grannie."

"Then it's a win-win." Judy stood, and held out a hand to Lisa. "Should we get going?"

*

The letter was waiting for her on the doormat when she got home after dropping Lisa off home. At first, Judy hadn't noticed the handwritten envelope, mixed up amongst the junk mail and local newspaper, and it was only after she'd switched the kettle on and started to sort the mail that she found it.

She paused, holding the envelope in her hand like it was a sacred object. It was unusual to get any letter with a handwritten address at this time of year. Christmas and Birthday cards were the only time she'd see something like this.

But this was something different. The paper of the envelope was thick and high quality. She could feel the texture rubbing beneath her fingers and let her fingers outline the embossed 'V' in the top-left corner. She realised she was holding her breath as she carefully tore it open, lifting the flap and removing a single sheet of paper, the quality as high as the envelope that had contained it.

Gingerly, she unfolded the letter and read.

Judy,

It's gone too far. I need your help. They're coming for me.

Seth

And there was an address.

Her heart racing, she put the letter down in front of her on the kitchen counter and considered what she'd just read. It had been five months since she'd had any contact from Seth, and now he had the audacity to ask for help.

Judy picked up the letter again and reread it, making sure there was nothing she'd missed, no more clues to what was troubling Seth. But there was just the envelope and the letter and the words.

I need your help.

Judy picked up her phone and made a call. She wasn't about to let her friend down. He'd saved her life twice now and it seemed like now was her chance to repay the favour.

Also by Robert Scott-Norton

Tombs
The Face Stealer
The Faceless Stratagem

Tombs Rising
The Remnant Keeper
The Remnant Vault
The Infinity Mainframe

Dark Corners
The Correction Floor
All the Darkness is Alive
Go Back to Sleep
The Haunting of Classroom 6
Midnight Guests

Printed in Poland
by Amazon Fulfillment
Poland Sp. z o.o., Wrocław